GUILT & REDEMPTION

DENISE CARBO

For my youngest son, Ethan. Your intelligence and kindness make me so proud. I'm amazed by you every day and can't wait to see what the future holds for you.

CHAPTER

ONE

"Do you have any idea what time it is?" Allison planted her hands on her hips and glared at the man leaning over the noisy contraption. She'd finally drifted off to sleep as dawn streaked across the sky, only to be jarred awake by the horrendous noise next door.

He straightened and flicked a switch. The saw stopped its incessant squeal and trailed off to silence, leaving a slight ringing in her ears.

"It's not even eight o'clock in the morning, and some people are trying to sleep. This is the third morning in a row that you've woken me. I'd appreciate it if you would wait till a more reasonable time to make such a god-awful racket!"

Sleep was a precious commodity these days, and she couldn't afford to have it interrupted by inconsiderate construction workers.

He lifted the safety goggles covering his eyes and rested them on top of his head. His gaze flicked over her, and he grinned. "Good morning, ma'am. I apologize about the noise and if I woke you."

His eyes were brown, milk chocolate brown. Flecks of wood chips dotted his dark hair and black T-shirt, the material stretching taut over an impressively well-defined chest and shoulders.

Allison blinked and raised her chin. *Snap out of it! Who cares how attractive he is? He woke you up. He called you ma'am, damn it!*

Heat burned her cheeks. She stared at a spot about two inches to the left of his right ear. "Thank you. I realize you have a job to do, but I would appreciate it if you would please pass on my request to your employer. Good day."

She nodded and turned to go.

"Don't have one."

Allison stopped and glanced over her shoulder. "I beg your pardon?"

His smile dimmed but remained in place. "An employer. I don't have one. I'm Jim McGregor, your new neighbor."

He wiped his hand on his faded blue jeans and extended it towards her. Allison automatically stepped forward and accepted his handshake.

"You bought this house? You're going to live here?" She glanced at the brown Victorian behind him. The house had been vacant for years and was quite the eyesore with peeling paint, broken or sagging pieces, and an overgrown yard. Alan used to complain about it lowering the value of the neighborhood. A pang spread across her chest.

He chuckled and replied, "Afraid so."

"I...um...see. Welcome to the neighborhood. Excuse me."

Great, she could now add screeching like a shrew at her neighbor to her list of sins.

"You didn't tell me your name."

The rich timbre of his voice sent a tingle down her spine. Her sleep-deprived brain must be going haywire. It's the only logical assumption for her reaction.

"It's Allison. Allison Delaney."

"Nice to meet you, Allison Delaney."

Silence stretched behind her as she strode back to her house. The saw didn't resume. Was his gaze pinned on her? Her steps quickened. The cold, damp spring grass slapped at her ankles and bare feet. It was way overdue for a mow.

How ridiculous would she look if she broke into a run? Only a few hundred feet separated the two houses, but it felt like a mile before she reached the back porch.

The screen door snapped shut behind her. Allison winced and wiped her wet feet on the blue rug inside the screened porch and walked to the back door.

Once in her kitchen, she closed the door and leaned back against it, taking a deep breath. She stared down at her ten-year-old white, worn nightgown and groaned. Gripping the thin material in her fists, Allison dropped her head back against the door and closed her eyes.

Quite the impression she must have made on her new neighbor. He probably thinks he moved into next to a crazy person.

Another tidbit for the town gossips to add to her notorious rap sheet.

When had she become a person who berated her neighbors in her nightgown? She opened her eyes and stared at the empty kitchen. "I've finally gone and lost my mind!"

Only silence echoed back.

"And now I'm talking to myself too."

Her lips twitched as she trudged down the hall to the stairs. Maybe she should embrace the crazy and become an eccentric shut-in who mutters to herself. It might be better than the stories circulating about her now.

CHAPTER

TWO

A siren shrieked.

Allison dropped the garden spade and jumped up to stand next to the flower bed. She shifted her weight from foot to foot. The repetitive wail continued, and she ran to the front of the house, scanning her neighborhood for smoke. A large red firetruck sped into view.

She wrapped her arms around her waist and gripped her elbows. The rough gardening gloves abraded her skin as her fingers dug in. A tremor quaked through her. The lights flashed as the truck passed her house and disappeared around the corner. She stared at the empty road, listening to the fading whine of the siren.

What lives would be ruined today?

"Ma'am? Excuse me, ma'am?"

The soft voice jolted her. A boy stood a few feet behind her. He was at that awkward age where his legs and arms seemed to outgrow the rest of his body. The white T-shirt he wore, though clean, was as well-worn as the jeans and sneakers that completed his outfit. His straight dark blond hair brushed the tops of his glasses when he pushed them back up his narrow, freckled nose.

Allison smiled slightly and tried not to wince. Ma'am, again. When had she become a ma'am? Granted, she was on the wrong side of thirty, but did that really warrant a ma'am? Probably to this kid, but surely not her new neighbor. She tried to remember if she'd seen the boy in the neighborhood before, but she drew a blank. "Can I help you?"

The boy swallowed audibly. "Um…I'm looking for my cat. She's white with some black patches and is kind of chubby."

"Charlie?" A woman wearing white shorts and an eggplant-colored top accentuating her tall, hourglass shape and long, thick red hair waltzed up the sidewalk. Her face resembled a flawless porcelain doll with big blue eyes and perfectly proportioned features.

She looked like a movie star. Although the likelihood of a movie star showing up in Arlington, Connecticut, was slim. The town had its own charm but nothing to draw in any celebrities.

Allison glanced down at her beige cotton pants with the pale stain from a blueberry pie she'd made a few summers ago splattered on her thigh and controlled the urge to run for the house. She hadn't expected to encounter anyone in her gardening clothes. Least of all someone who looked like they were ready for a photoshoot or something.

The woman walked up the brick steps and across the lawn. "Hi, I'm Karen. In case this scamp failed to introduce himself, he's my son, Charlie. We live in the brown ranch on the corner." Her smile was wide and welcoming, and her voice low and laced with amusement. She wrapped her arm around Charlie's shoulders and gave him a quick squeeze before extending her hand to Allison.

Allison quickly removed her gloves and wiped her hand on her pant leg before shaking Karen's hand. A hint of flowery perfume emanated from her.

Karen ruffled her son's hair. "Mouser, that's the cat, didn't come home last night and Charlie's worried about her. She never misses a meal, and she's been acting a little odd lately. I was going to take her to the vet today. I swear that cat understood me and took off to avoid it."

More new neighbors. She really needed to get out more. Apparently, the neighborhood was changing all around her, and she'd been oblivious. "I'm sorry, but I haven't seen a cat."

"You're Allison, right? Mrs. Pannelli, across the street, mentioned your name when we stopped there looking for Mouser."

Allison simply smiled and nodded, hoping that would be the end of it and she could escape back into the house. She was out of practice making small talk.

"We moved here over the winter. It's such a lovely town, but you know that. It's been a bit of a change for us coming from the city, but it's for the best. You know, clean air, safe streets, good schools, the whole small-town package."

Her ring-adorned hands waved about as she talked, and her smile never dimmed. "Did you grow up here like most people seem to have, or are you a transplant like us?"

"No, I moved here when I got married. My husband grew up here."

Something flickered in Karen's eyes, and her smile dimmed just for a moment. Allison suspected Mrs. Pannelli had imparted more than just Allison's name.

Karen gestured to the house. "You have a beautiful home here. I've admired it many times during my evening walks."

Allison glanced up at the white cape. "Thank you."

"Walking is the extent of my exercise regime. I can never drum up enough enthusiasm to join a gym and sweat alongside a bunch of other people. Honestly, sweating just isn't something I like to do, period. Which is why I constantly battle with an extra ten pounds— that and my obsession with dessert."

Should she protest Karen's need to lose weight, commiserate with the struggle, or offer some kind of encouragement?

Before she could decide, Karen continued the mostly one-sided conversation. "You're not one of those health nuts, are you?"

"Uh, no." Exercise hadn't been on her list of things to do in years.

"You know the type, watches every bite that goes into their mouth to make sure it's free of everything, including taste. Gets on the scale every morning and exercises with religious zeal?" Karen shrugged and waved off any response Allison might have attempted.

"Don't mind me. I honestly believe to each their own, but life is just too short, you know? Anyway, I own a salon in town. It's called Guilty Pleasures, just off Main Street in the plaza. We do hair, makeup, nails, waxing, the works. You should stop by. I'll give you a discount."

"Uh...thank you."

"Mom!"

Charlie had wandered down the side of the house during their conversation and was peering into the latticework underneath the porch. "Mom, come look. Oh wow!"

Allison followed Karen to investigate. What on Earth could he have found under her porch?

Charlie was on his knees in the flower bed, which extended along the sides and front of her house. Karen gingerly stepped onto the mulch and bent over next to him. "Oh my!"

Allison stepped around a clump of purple tulips and ducked under the lilacs perfuming the air. "What is it?"

She squatted next to a holly bush and looked under the porch. The sharp leaves scratched her skin. A piece of lattice had broken off. That would have to be fixed. She'd add it to the never-ending list. She doubted that held their captive attention, however. A black and white cat sprawled out with four little balls of fur draped around her.

"Well, it looks like Mouser wasn't getting chubby after all." Karen chuckled and hugged Charlie.

He grinned and stared down at his cat and the little kittens. "Look, Mom, there's four of them!"

Allison couldn't help but smile in delight. "Aren't they the most precious things?"

Mouser softly meowed when Charlie moved the loose lattice aside and climbed underneath the porch with her.

"Allison, do you have a box we could transport them home in?"

"Oh, of course. I'll be right back."

She dashed into the house to the basement and grabbed an empty box. The cardboard was smooth and clean, nothing for the cats to harm themselves on, but not exactly comfy. An old towel might make it more comfortable for the temporary residents, so she went upstairs to find one.

Charlie and Karen carefully placed Mouser and her kittens in the container when she returned.

Allison couldn't help looking over Charlie's shoulder one more time. "They are so adorable." She touched the top of one kitten's head with the tip of her finger. Silky fur caressed her skin. The mama cat raised her head a little and peeked up at her before closing her eyes and laying her head back down.

Karen glanced over her shoulder. "Do you want one? I mean, when they're old enough. After all, Mouser chose your porch to deliver her kittens under. It's almost like she wants you to have one."

"Oh, I don't think... I mean, I've never had a pet."

"Never? Wow, that sucks," Charlie pronounced.

Karen rolled her eyes. "Charlie, not everyone is an animal lover."

"You don't like cats?" Charlie's mouth was agape.

Allison smiled at him. "I like cats very much, but my mother, and then my husband, was allergic, so we never had pets."

"Well, what about now?"

"Charlie, it will be about eight weeks before we can wean the kittens from their mother. That gives Allison plenty of time to decide if she'd like a pet and plenty of time for us to convince her it's a great idea."

Karen laughed as Allison struggled with a response that wasn't rude or encouraging.

Why not? Maybe a kitten was a good idea after all. There was no one else to consider but her. It all came down to whether or not she wanted a pet. Instead of talking to herself, she could talk to a cat. Would that make her more or less crazy?

"Actually, I think I would like to have a kitten—when they're ready, of course."

"Fantastic! You'll have to come visit them a few times to decide which one you want."

Karen lifted the box and smiled down at her cargo. "In fact, why don't you come to dinner Friday night? The kittens will be almost a week old then, and you can get another look at them. It'll give Charlie and I a chance to thank you too."

Allison wrapped her arms around her waist and shook her head. "Oh, you don't have to do that. I didn't do anything."

"Knowingly or not, you provided a safe place for Mouser and her kittens. Besides, it'll be nice to get to know our neighbors."

A refusal sprang to her lips, but she hesitated. Scrounging around in her cabinets or freezer for another uninspired meal for one changed her mind. "I...well...thank you."

"Great, Friday it is then. Is 6:30 okay?"

Allison followed in their wake around to the front of the house in a bit of a daze. "Sure, sounds great. What can I bring?"

"How about something for dessert?"

"I can do that." Maybe. She'd have to rummage through the cabinets. It had been a while since she baked anything.

They walked down the sidewalk with the makeshift cat carrier. Charlie struggled under the weight of the box and shifted his hold. Karen glanced back and waved.

Good Lord, she'd just agreed to dinner. How on earth had that happened?

THREE

Jim stared at the pink envelope in his hands. *She couldn't have found me already.*

He sniffed the envelope. No perfume.

All her previous deliveries had been heavily scented.

He tore the top off and shook out the contents onto the table, not wanting to touch anything inside. A thick piece of paper floated down to the wooden surface.

Jim snorted and shook his head. It was just a welcome-to-town note from a local store with a ten percent off coupon attached.

The rest of the mail contained junk mail. He tossed it into the garbage bin in the kitchen.

He rubbed the back of his neck and surveyed the room. The structural work on the house was finished. There had been some rot in the sill, and he'd also had to replace the ancient roof. Now he was ready to renovate the kitchen.

It was a decent size, taking up half the back of the house. He picked up his sketchbook and flipped through the pages until he came to his design for the kitchen. The cabinets were solid. He was keeping those, which meant the layout needed to remain the same basic U-shape.

Jim unhooked his measuring tape from his tool belt to double-check some measurements he'd already jotted down. He would refinish the cabinets, but replace the laminate countertop and vinyl flooring.

He usually spent around a year flipping one house before he moved on to the next, but this reno job was moving along nicely. He might complete the work and get it sold in six to nine months instead.

Shrugging, Jim clipped the tape measure back on his belt and went out the back door to make a list of materials he needed to buy at the store. He wasn't in a hurry. If he finished early, he might stick around and enjoy the place for a while. On the other hand, if he located another house that interested him, he would move on. A perk of his lifestyle, he could stay or go based on his whims.

Money didn't drive him. He could turn a decent profit, but rushing through a reno to flip houses as quickly as possible wasn't his operation. He tilted his head back and gazed at the side of the old Victorian. The sad old house had tugged at him when he'd been scanning homes for sale online. He'd driven by it a few times before finally following his gut and calling his realtor. There had been two other houses available which would have earned him a greater profit, but the brown Victorian had called to him almost as if it was asking for his help.

He snorted. He was starting to sound like his buddy, Brian. A master craftsman who insisted every piece of wood had a personality, and it was his job to show it in its best light.

The rumble of a large engine brought his head around. A brown delivery truck pulled into his neighbor's driveway.

Jim smirked. That was quite the introduction to his new neighbor the other day. Her blonde hair had been in wild disarray around her pale face. Big, blue eyes dominated her features. The dark circles underneath gave him a pang of guilt for his part in placing them there, but the picture she made standing in her nightgown, reaming him out, made him smile.

He doubted she knew how see-through her nightgown had been with the morning sunlight shining behind her. She had a desirable shape, the kind he'd like to get his hands on. But she wasn't his type; she fell into the stick around, relationship, and marrying category.

No, not his type at all.

~

THE KNOCK at the front door froze Allison in place. Who could it be? She certainly wasn't expecting anyone. Drying her hands on the hand towel, she paused at the archway separating the kitchen and hallway.

It was too early in the week for Mrs. Pannelli to stop by and try to convince her to attend church on Sunday. She had apparently decided Allison needed to be saved and made it her personal mission to be the one to save her.

A shape moved in front of the door. No, not Mrs. Pannelli. Whoever was on her front porch was much too tall to be the petite elderly woman from across the street.

Allison walked down the hallway and peered through the frosted glass before opening the door. "Oh, hi Bruce. I wasn't expecting you today."

Bruce paused halfway down the front steps and turned around to face her. "Hi Allison, wasn't sure if you were home." He jerked his chin to the cardboard package on her porch next to the door. "You have a delivery."

She glanced down at the package. What had she ordered? It was too early for her monthly subscription of household goods to be delivered. Had she pre-ordered some books and forgotten?

"Hmm...I guess I must have ordered something and forgot."

"Happens to the best of us. How did that new birdfeeder you got last week work out?"

"Great! I hung it on the corner over there." Allison pointed to the green tube decorated with metal flowers and leaves.

Bruce smiled. "Looks good. I had a blue jay sitting on my railing the other day. Was thinking about hanging a bird feeder myself."

"I might get one for the other side of the porch too."

"Then I guess I'll be seeing you soon. I better get going. I have a bunch of deliveries left today. Take care."

"Bye, Bruce."

Allison leaned against the railing while he walked to his truck and backed down her driveway. She returned his wave as he drove down the street.

It was a good thing she had accepted Karen's invitation to dinner at the end of the week. She needed to get out more and have conversations with someone besides the delivery man. It was a sad sign when most of her interactions were with Bruce. He was here at least once a week since she ordered everything online and rarely went to an actual store to shop. If she wasn't careful, she would become borderline agoraphobic.

Her new neighbor came out of his house and strode to his truck; his long, jean-encased legs made short work of the distance. He opened the door of the red truck and looked over his shoulder at her.

Allison lurched away from the railing. Did he see her?

Of course, he did. If she could see him clearly, he could see her too.

He smiled and lifted his hand in a wave before he climbed into the truck and closed the door.

She waved and dropped her hand. Heat surged over her face. She really needed to apologize to him for her tirade the other morning.

Her mother would have been appalled by her behavior and would've told her to march back over there. She also would have instructed her to bring something for a welcome gift, too. Her father would've steepled his hands underneath his chin and given her that small smile. Then he would've asked her a series of seemingly unrelated questions until she concluded for herself that she needed to apologize.

Sighing, she picked up the package and went inside. Now she had to apologize *and* bring him something, or the guilt would drive her crazy.

Some might argue it would be a very short trip.

CHAPTER

FOUR

Despite her plans to finish the gardening today and mow the lawn, Allison spent the day hiding inside, finding one project after another that needed her attention. She was avoiding her new neighbor, who was once again outside sawing wood. At least this time, he waited for a civilized hour to begin. She caught herself peeking at him out the window several times and blushed over her antics. "Really, Allison, you're thirty-two years old. He's just a man. An attractive one, but still just a man."

The oven timer beeped as she padded barefoot down the hall. The unmistakable aroma of freshly baked dessert filled the kitchen. She took a deep breath. It'd been a long time since her nose had been treated to the delicious scent of baking. Too long.

She shut off the timer and opened the oven door to check on the chocolate Bundt cake she'd made for her dinner with Karen and Charlie. The slim metal cake tester she slid into the middle came out clean, so she grabbed a pair of oven mitts and set it on a rack on the counter to cool. Steam wafted from the shiny, delicate, crack-free crust.

After shutting off the oven, she loaded the dirty dishes into the dishwasher. Baking had always been a form of therapy for her. When she'd had a bad day at school, her mother would open the cabinets and stack ingredients on the counter, all while listening to her grumble about whatever travesty had befallen her this time. They would mix or knead shoulder to shoulder, and by the time whatever they made was popped into the oven, she would be smiling and laughing.

When had she stopped letting the miracle of sugar, flour, and eggs work their magic?

No, the question wasn't when, but why?

God knows she needed the therapy now more than ever.

Allison removed the cake from the pan to finish cooling and admired the turns and swells fanning the dark chocolate confection. Not bad to look at, and hopefully, it would taste even better. She glanced at the time. It was getting late. She washed her hands and went upstairs to get ready for the visit.

After much deliberation, Allison settled on black pants and a royal blue silk blouse. They were about a size too big, so the material sagged and hung on her frame. She hadn't stepped on a scale in a long time, but clearly, she'd lost weight. Maybe she'd stumbled on a new diet—stress, grief, and sleep deprivation. Not sure anyone would want to sign up, however.

She frowned at her long hair and pulled it back with a silver barrette. Any style it once had was long gone, so maybe she should take Karen up on the offer to visit her salon. She bit her lip and pawed through the only drawer of cosmetics she owned. It had been years since she'd worn any. Everything must be expired. Sighing, she shut the drawer and left the bathroom.

Downstairs, she added a simple sugar glaze to the cooled cake and unearthed a cake container from the cabinet over the fridge to transport the dessert.

She stood at the counter drumming her fingers on either side of the cake container. Why did she agree to dinner?

Oh yeah, because she was sick to death of eating unpalatable meals alone. And she needed to get out of the house before she became a hermit.

It's just dinner.

Balancing the container in one hand, she stuffed her phone and keys in her purse on the foyer table and then slipped the strap over her shoulder. After shutting the front door with her foot, she gripped the cake with both hands and marched down the steps.

She breathed a sigh of relief when no one was outside the Pannelli's colonial or Jim's Victorian. There were four other houses between hers and Karen's, two on each side of the road. A young couple lived in the sunny yellow ranch, a family of four or five lived in the gray cape, an older woman with two adult children lived in the white colonial, and the last house had school-age kids. Were they Charlie's age? There had been a for sale sign in front of the tan colonial last year, but it was gone now. Had someone new moved in, or had they changed their minds?

She was out of touch with her neighbors. Everyone, really.

Karen's house was less than a half-mile down the road, but by the time she reached the driveway, Allison felt like she'd traversed a mountain. Maybe she should add some exercise to her growing to-do list. A daily walk would probably do her some good on many levels—fresh air, cardio, and getting out of the house.

Her gaze flickered over the small, brown ranch. Neatly trimmed bushes flanked a bright orange front door, a breezeway connected the house to a single bay garage, and a child's green bike leaned against the side.

Allison took a deep breath and held it for a count of five before she approached the front door and rang the bell. The door swung open, and Karen stood in the opening wearing a black jumpsuit and heels. Gold hoops swung from her ears, and her hair was piled on top of her head with loose tendrils artfully framing her beautiful face.

Okay, a makeover from this woman was definitely on the top of her to-do list.

"Hi. Don't you look lovely? Come in, come in. I can't wait to see what's in that cake box!" Karen grasped Allison's elbow and ushered her inside during her chatter.

She only got a vague impression of the light blue furniture in the living room as Karen escorted her to the kitchen at the back of the house. Charlie looked up with a shy smile and pushed his glasses back up his nose. He sat on the floor in the corner next to his cat and the kittens. They were all comfortably ensconced on a bright red, plush pet bed. Mouser cleaned one of her kittens while they all dozed, cuddled up to her side.

"Hi, Charlie. How are Mouser and her little additions?"

"Great!"

"Get washed up, kiddo, and set the table. Dinner is almost ready." Karen took the cake from Allison and set it on the white-tiled countertop.

"Can I get you something to drink? Would you like a glass of wine?"

"Thank you, no, I'm fine. Is there something I can do to help?"

"Nope. I've got everything under control. We're having my specialty, chicken parmigiana. It's one of the very few dishes my mother managed to teach me to prepare." Karen glanced over her shoulder as she opened the oven to check on dinner. "My mother is a terrific cook. Unfortunately, I didn't inherit her abilities. But don't worry, this dish is foolproof."

"It smells wonderful." The savory scents of tomato sauce and melting cheese melded together. The kitchen had a homey, country vibe with white painted cabinets, yellow walls, and scattered pictures of farm animals. There were tiles of roosters, cows, and geese over the stove. The dishtowels and potholders depicted little piglets cavorting in mud. A laugh escaped her and caught Karen's attention.

"Cute, aren't they? I couldn't resist when I saw them in the store. They make people smile to look at them, so to my line of thinking, they've fulfilled their purpose."

Karen set the food on the table. "Charlie, grab the salad out of the fridge, please. Have a seat, Allison."

Silence settled as everyone sat and was served. Charlie dug into his meal with gusto. She took a small bite of the dinner and savored the thick, flavorful sauce and moist chicken. It had been a while since her taste buds were treated to a home-cooked meal.

"This is delicious. Thank you very much for inviting me."

"Our pleasure. It's nice to get to know our neighbors. So, have you lived here a long time?"

Allison lifted her napkin over her mouth while she finished chewing. "About ten years. What made you decide to move to Arlington?"

"I wanted a small town, and when I found the retail space for my salon, it seemed like a perfect fit. It's worked out well for us, hasn't it, kiddo?"

Charlie nodded but didn't pause in his chewing. He kept glancing over to the kittens, now awake and climbing all over their mother.

The cloying smell of smoke invaded her nose and throat. She choked.

Oh God, was she hallucinating?

"Mom!"

Charlie jumped up from the table and pointed to the stove.

"Damn it!" Karen sprang up and rushed across the kitchen.

Smoke billowed from the oven.

Karen shut off the oven and jammed her hands into a pair of oven mitts. When she opened the door, thick gray plumes surged out.

The smoke alarm screeched.

She clutched a pan with charred lumps on it as she slammed the oven door closed with the heel of her foot and raced to the sliding glass doors.

Charlie had the door open and ready. She ran out onto the deck and threw the burned mess, pan and all, over the railing.

Karen pulled off the oven mitts as she hurried back inside and grabbed a dishtowel. She waved it underneath the smoke alarm in the hallway, but it continued to shriek.

She tossed the towel on the counter and grabbed a chair from the table to stand on. Karen twisted and yanked the alarm from the ceiling so it dangled by a cord then took out the battery. The screeching ended.

Stepping down from the chair, she wiped the back of her hand across her forehead. "There, that's over. So much for having garlic bread with dinner." She carried the chair back to the table. "Charlie, leave the door open so the rest of the smoke clears out."

Karen smiled and glanced at Allison as Charlie sat.

Her smile faded.

"Oh sweetie, are you okay? It's perfectly safe, I promise. Are you allergic to smoke? Do you have asthma?"

Allison dropped her gaze to the table. She clenched her knife and fork in her fists. One by one, she released her fingers, laid the utensils down, and clasped her hands in her lap.

"I'm fine."

"Are you sure? Do you want to go on the deck? We could finish eating out there?"

"No, really, I'm fine."

Karen sat. "Sorry about that. I wish I could say it's never happened before, but..." She shrugged and resumed eating.

"It's pretty routine around here. We call the smoke alarm the steak alarm, but Mom can pretty much burn anything."

"Watch it, kiddo, or you'll be taking over the cooking."

Charlie laughed. "You'll have to increase my allowance."

"That actually could be discussed." Karen pointed her fork full of chicken in his direction.

Allison shifted in her seat and concentrated on breathing slowly. Perspiration caused her blouse to stick to her back, and her hands ached from clutching the utensils too tight.

Once she was certain her hands wouldn't tremble, Allison picked up her fork and pushed the chicken around on her plate. If she tried to swallow a bite, she would surely choke.

Charlie and Karen continued their mother and son banter.

The smoke cleared from the room, but the suffocating smell lingered.

Allison took a healthy swallow of water. She needed to say something, anything to divert attention from her reaction to the smoke.

"Tell me about your salon. You said it's called Guilty Pleasures?"

Karen grinned. "My favorite subject, other than Charlie."

Charlie rolled his eyes.

"It's in this fabulous old building in town. I do hair, nails, and makeup on the first floor. The second floor is for the spa and massage offerings."

"I'll have to stop by. I could use a makeover."

Karen's eyes lit up. "Just put yourself in my hands. I'll be gentle, I promise."

Allison smiled and took a bite of chicken. It went down without a hitch.

Her eyes only glazed a little when Karen described possible cuts and styles before moving on to colors.

They finished eating, and Allison insisted on helping Charlie fill the dishwasher as Karen set out the dessert. "Oh Allison, this looks scrumptious!"

"Awesome! Chocolate!" Charlie hopped in a chair and reached for the piece his mother cut.

Karen laughed and served Allison and herself. "As you can see, Charlie inherited my love for dessert. I'm afraid he's a chocoholic." She took a bite and closed her eyes. "Mmm...this is so good."

Allison shrugged. "It's a simple recipe. I'll give it to you if you like."

"Oh, yes, please."

Charlie finished and returned to his cats.

"Time to hit the books, kiddo."

"Mom, it's Friday."

"Yes, but you have that project due on Monday, and you are nowhere near done. Get to it." Karen nodded to the hall. Allison assumed it led to the bedrooms.

Charlie trudged down the hall as Karen cleared the table.

"Would you like some coffee? We can take it in the living room to chat."

While the coffee brewed, Allison wandered over to the kittens. The black and white balls of fur with tiny pink noses and big gold eyes surrounded their mother. A crackly meow whispered out of one as it climbed in between its siblings.

"Cream, sugar?" Karen held out a blue mug.

Allison shook her head and stepped forward to take the coffee.

She followed Karen into the living room and looked around at the eclectic selection of furniture and knickknacks. A large assortment of photos decorated the room. "Do you come from a large family?"

Karen followed Allison's gaze and chuckled. "Four brothers, all older."

"Wow, that must be interesting. Are you close?"

"Very. It's been a little difficult moving farther away from them, but we still see each other as often as we can. Of course, there are family dinners when we can all manage it. How about you? Any siblings?"

"Um, no. I was an only child." Allison perched on the sofa and sipped her hot coffee while Karen leaned back and tucked her feet beneath her.

The last thing she needed was caffeine at night. She wasn't a coffee drinker, but she'd accepted the offer while her mind had still been fixated on the stale smell of smoke. It would have been rude to refuse it once Karen had already made it and probably just as rude to waste it. She sighed and tried not to grimace over the bitter taste.

"There were times I wished I was an only child, but never for long. My brothers tormented me, but they also doted on me." She gestured towards Allison with her cup. "Do your parents live nearby?"

Allison swallowed hard and shook her head. "They both passed several years ago."

"Oh, I'm so sorry."

Forcing a slight smile to her lips, Allison cast her gaze around the room, searching for a way to change the subject. A picture of Charlie standing next to a man holding a fishing rod sat on the shelf.

"Is that one of your brothers with Charlie?"

Karen glanced over at the picture. "No, that's Charlie's father, my ex-husband."

Way to go, Allison. Bring up the ex-husband, always a comfortable topic between practical strangers—not.

"I'm sorry."

"Don't be. I'm not." Karen waved her hand. "He's not going to win any awards for father of the year, but he is still a presence in Charlie's life. We divorced a couple of years ago, but it was never a good fit."

"It must be hard being a single parent, especially if he doesn't help much."

"It is, and it isn't. Being a parent is hard work, but honestly, Charlie is a dream kid, and I have a very involved family to help. Being a single parent is all I've ever really known since his father was never around all that much even when we were married."

"I used to wonder what it would be like being part of a large family."

Karen grinned. "Loud." She tilted her from side to side. "But wonderful, too. I can't imagine anything else. My brothers are all married with kids. I have more nieces and nephews than I can keep track of. Holidays are chaotic, but I wouldn't change a thing."

Allison stared at the dark liquid in the cup cradled in her hands. Holidays were just another day on the calendar for her. She took a healthy swallow of the coffee until the mug was half empty. It burned her throat all the way down.

"I really should be going." She stood. "Thank you for a wonderful meal."

"Even with the minor emergency?"

"Yes." Allison over her shoulder at the dangling smoke alarm. "I think you can reconnect that now. All the smoke has cleared."

"With the number of times I've had to disconnect it, I should probably leave it that way."

"Oh no, don't do that. It could save your life someday. In fact, you should get a fire extinguisher to keep in the kitchen."

Karen placed a hand on Allison's arm. "I was kidding. The fire extinguisher is a good idea, though."

"Oh, sorry."

"No apology necessary." Karen walked Allison to the door. "Listen, I'm going to be waiting for you to make an appointment at the salon. Don't disappoint me."

"I won't. Tell Charlie goodbye for me."

Dusk had fallen and darkness was fast on its heels. Allison increased her pace as she walked home. She wasn't a fan of the dark.

Bad things always happened at night.

CHAPTER

FIVE

"**S**tupid machine!" Allison kicked the lawnmower. Pain shot through her toes. She grimaced and hopped on one foot. *Stupid! Stupid! Stupid.*

"Need some help?"

Allison froze in the process of rubbing her aching foot through her canvas sneakers while standing on one leg and lost her balance. She grabbed for the handle of the lawnmower, but the machine continued to defy her by rolling forward instead of stopping her momentum. Her humiliation complete, Allison cringed and waited for the crash to the ground.

Instead, warm arms wrapped around her and steadied her. A deep chuckle preceded her release.

Allison closed her eyes and resisted the urge to groan in defeat. Embarrassing herself in front of her handsome neighbor better not be the new trend in her life. Since she wasn't five years old, making a run for the house and hiding wasn't an option.

Heaving a deep sigh, she straightened her shoulders, plastered a smile on her face, and turned to face him.

Jim stood with his hands on his jean-clad hips and a grin on his tanned face. Her breath caught, and a part of her she thought had shriveled up and petrified a long time ago fluttered back to life.

"Thank you. I, ah...seem to be having a difference of opinion with my lawnmower."

"Why don't I take a look at it?" Jim moved past her and bent down to look at the treacherous machine.

Her gaze strayed from the mower to the way his jeans molded to his strong thighs and his white T-shirt clung to sculpted arms.

Allison fanned her burning cheeks with her hands. Now was not the time for her libido to rise from the dead.

Jim fiddled with the machine and then yanked on the cord. Of course, the infernal machine jumped to life with a rumble.

"It seems to be running all right now." He showed her how to set the choke and throttle. "One good pull is all you needed."

"Thank you. I appreciate your help."

"No problem. Enjoy." Jim nodded and walked back to his own yard.

Allison mowed the grass with a desperate concentration. She focused on making even rows, but she was intensely aware of Jim just a few yards away. Why had she filled the darn thing with gas before she started? If the machine ran out of gas, she would have an excuse to go inside.

Why did she constantly make a fool of herself in front of him? The man was too good-looking for her peace of mind. She couldn't help it if her eyes occasionally strayed over to where he was working.

When he bent over a pile of wood, she absently steered the mower right towards her flower bed. Sheer luck had her catching her error before she mowed over the clump of tulips. She glanced over her shoulder at the path behind her, so much for straight lines. This one veered sharply to the right and then curved back to the left.

Maybe she should finish the lawn in a zigzag pattern. Let her neighbors think she was drunk or crazy. It would give them something else to talk about besides the tragic widow who rarely leaves her house.

Smirking, she did the front patch of lawn in concentric circles.

It was the little things these days that gave her something to smile about.

Jim disappeared inside his house. She still needed to come up with a goodwill gesture as a welcome to the neighborhood, a thank you for his help, and an apology for the unladylike outbursts. Avoidance obviously wasn't working, and the guilt was getting heavier. She needed nothing else to feel guilty about.

Allison stored the lawnmower back in the garage and went up the back steps into the kitchen. After she washed up, she decided brownies should do the trick. Who didn't like brownies? Although with her luck, he was probably allergic. Well, he could throw them out if he didn't want them. At least her conscience would be clear.

She mixed the ingredients while the oven warmed. This and the cake she had made for Karen and Charlie were the first things she'd baked in well over a year. Baking used to be one of her favorite pastimes. She'd lost interest in a lot of activities.

Maybe it was time for something new. She had the time and the means. The problem was she didn't have a clue what interested her anymore.

After putting the pan in the oven and setting the timer, she went upstairs to shower and change.

Less than half an hour later, she was back downstairs dressed in baggy tan capris and a peach-colored blouse. She twisted her hair up into a bun as the timer for the brownies went off.

Allison set the brownies on a rack to cool and stepped out onto her screened-in back porch. A quick sideways peek into her neighbor's yard revealed he was still inside or had maybe left. No matter, she could leave the brownies on his steps with a brief note. That way, she could avoid any more awkward encounters.

She sat in one of the white wicker rocking chairs and set the chair in motion. This was her favorite spot in the entire house. The screened porch stretched the entire length of the back of the house and joined the wraparound porch at the corner on the left side. The right side ended before the cement breezeway between the house and the garage. There used to be a door to the breezeway from the house, but Alan turned part of the kitchen and mudroom into his office after they were married. She had to walk around to the front or back of the house from the garage.

The sun had already begun its descent, and a light breeze carried the scent of freshly cut grass. She took a deep breath in.

May was ending. Spring flowers were giving way to the summer blooms. Her backyard was an open green lawn with a few trees dotting the landscape. The old oak tree dominated the center, and a white flowering dogwood and two tulip trees flanked the sides. There was room and plenty of sun for a vegetable and herb garden. She'd always wanted one, but Alan hadn't seen the need, and she hadn't pushed.

She'd never pushed.

It was too late this year, but next year she'd add one. It was her decision now, hers alone. But the never-ending mantle of guilt squashed the tiny seed of anticipation.

Allison dropped her head and stared at the wooden planks of the porch floor. Guilt shadowed her every move. Choices and consequences had brought her here. She needed to make better ones in the future.

She couldn't survive any more mistakes.

The timer went off for the second time and brought her out of her reverie. She went in, cut and arranged the brownies on a plate, covered them with plastic wrap, and walked out the back door with them tightly held in her grip.

If she set them back on the counter, she would come up with one excuse after another to avoid bringing them to her neighbor.

The short walk to his back door passed too quickly, and she soon stood staring at the sturdy wood door with brown peeling paint while chewing on her lip. What should she say if he answered the door? It was a little late to say welcome to the neighborhood. How about short and sweet? Thank you, sorry, and welcome might be too abrupt.

Oh, the hell with it, she would have to wing it.

Of course, first she needed to knock on the door.

Before she could, the door swung open, and Jim stepped out on the porch, wiping his hands on a towel. "Are those for me?"

"Uh..." Allison glanced down at the plate she clutched in her hands and back up. "Yes, yes they are." She handed him the plate.

Jim took the plate with a smile and a brush of hands. "Wow, the plate's still warm. Homemade brownies? I can't remember the last time I had some."

He lifted the plastic wrap, slipped one off the plate, and took a huge bite. He closed his eyes, and a sound that could only be described as a hum emanated from him. He finished the piece in another bite and licked his thumb and finger free of crumbs.

Allison tried to swallow, but her mouth had gone completely dry, and she ended up coughing instead. She blinked several times and licked her dry lips while looking everywhere but at Jim.

"These are incredible. Thanks, do you want one?"

Jim dipped the plate towards her after he grabbed another one and took a bite.

"Um...no. No, thank you. I just wanted to do something to...um... welcome you to the neighborhood, and well, say thank you for helping me with the lawnmower." Allison left off any mention of the morning they met.

One side of his mouth hitched up in a smile, showing an adorable dimple Allison had failed to notice on their previous meetings. She had a tough time pulling her gaze away from the sight.

"You make me some more of these, and I'll fix anything you want." Jim half turned away and pointed to the inside of his house with his thumb. "Come on inside. I need to get some milk to go with these."

"Oh well...I...." Jim walked inside, holding the door open for her to follow him. "Okay."

Allison walked inside the house and looked around. The last time she'd seen the kitchen was when she'd peeked in the window a few years ago. The house had remained empty for at least five years since Mr. Rizzio, the elderly man who lived here, had passed away. It had been in disrepair even then, but she could see the hard work Jim put into it already.

The hardwood floors gleamed and freshly painted walls shined. There was a faint scent in the air from the wood she'd seen him staining earlier in the day.

"It still needs a lot of work. Are you sure you don't want one of your brownies?"

Jim poured himself a glass of milk and ate another brownie. "You're going to make yourself sick eating so many at once." She blushed. He didn't need her to chastise him.

He just smiled and polished off his third piece.

She looked around the room again and gestured to the floor and walls. "You've really done a lot of work. It looks nice. Do you do everything yourself?"

"Pretty much. There might be some plumbing or electrical I'll come across that will be beyond my capabilities, but for the most part, I can handle it."

Allison walked over to the cabinets lined up on the floor and ran her hand along the surface. "These are beautiful. Where did you get them?"

Jim nodded towards the wall. "From right here."

Allison looked back down at the cabinets and back at Jim. "You're kidding. I remember what the cabinets looked like in here. They were painted a dark brown with wooden knobs of the same color."

Jim chuckled as he leaned back against the table. "Yes, and beneath that brown they were red if you can believe it. I sanded them down, and I'm staining them."

Allison examined the cabinets again, hardly believing her eyes. "That's really amazing. I can't believe they're the same cabinets. It's hard to believe this is the same kitchen. What are you going to do about the countertop?"

She glanced at Jim before returning her gaze to the cabinets.

He picked something up by the door and then walked over to stand next to her. "I have this granite countertop on order."

Allison took the sample he held out. It was a deep, rich brown with flecks of gold scattered throughout. She ran her palm over the smooth surface. "It's beautiful."

She looked up to find him staring at her. Why was it that men were always the ones blessed with thick, black eyelashes?

She handed the piece back to him and walked over to the window facing her house while he put the sample back. "Is the kitchen the first room you've started?" His steps approached. Was he coming to stand next to her? Her breath stuttered in her chest, and she closed her eyes. What was the matter with her?

He stopped about a foot behind her. There was a pale reflection of him in the window. "Yeah, I always start with the kitchen once any serious structural problems are handled. A decent kitchen always makes a place easier to live in."

"I don't think my kitchen has been touched in a couple of decades. Seeing what you've accomplished here makes me wonder what I can do to mine."

"I could take a look at it sometime if you'd like and maybe give you some ideas."

Allison stiffened. Did he think she was angling for him to offer his help? "That's kind of you, but I can see how busy you are. I wouldn't want to encroach on your time."

His reflection shrugged.

"Looking doesn't take much time."

She turned around and tried to look him in the eye but blushed again. She sidestepped toward the door while looking everywhere but at him. "Um...thank you, again. I'll keep it in mind. I better get going. It's going to be dark soon."

He glanced out the window and raised his eyebrows but didn't comment. Allison winced over how silly it probably sounded that she needed to get home before dark. But then he probably already thought her a bit strange anyway.

"Thanks again. Bye." She briefly raised her hand in a wave and turned to the door. The silence stretched. Why wasn't he saying anything? He probably thought she was a complete lunatic.

"Thanks for the brownies." When his voice came from directly behind her, she realized he'd followed her to the door. She stumbled and grabbed for the handle, but he was already reaching around her to open it.

The warmth of his body brushed against her. For a moment, she wanted to lean into it, but she caught herself in time. How long had it been since she felt the warmth of a man? Too long—much too long.

Jim rubbed his hand over his mouth and cracked his neck. Allison swung her arms as she charged across her backyard. Either she was in a hurry or doing some kind of speed walking exercise. Why was she concerned about night approaching? Was she really scared of the dark, or did she have some sort of appointment, or was it just an excuse to leave?

He shook his head and wandered back into his kitchen. Whatever her reasons were, it was none of his business.

Her antics with the mower this afternoon drifted into his mind. He'd stared at the lawn mower and tried not to laugh. He'd been behind his house staining some trim for the kitchen when he'd heard the whir of the machine trying to turn over. After several attempts went by and the engine still hadn't caught, he'd given in to his curiosity and followed the sound to the back of her house.

The sight that greeted him had stopped him in his tracks. His neighbor had been bent over the machine, yanking on the cord with all of her might. Her nicely rounded behind topped an impressive pair of legs he hadn't noticed on their previous encounter.

When she'd hauled off and kicked the lawnmower, he'd clamped his hand over his mouth to stop from laughing out loud. He didn't think she'd appreciate the humor of the situation.

He'd reset the choke and tried to concentrate on the lawnmower and not on how good it felt to put his hands on her trim waist. It had obviously been too long since he'd been with a woman.

She'd stood with her arms folded across her waist. He doubted she was aware of how the stance accentuated her breasts. She didn't seem to be the kind of woman to flaunt what God had given her.

He'd looked up to check her progress every now and again—it was the neighborly thing to do to make sure she wasn't having any problems. She'd finished the lawn with a determined scowl on her face and an occasional grin. What thoughts had gone through her head?

Jim snagged another brownie from the plate. *Damn, these are good.* He wasn't kidding when he said he'd fix things in exchange for more of these. He inhaled before taking a bite. Smelled like heaven. She could sure bake.

She was the nervous type. Always balanced on her toes, ready to take flight. Was it him? He wasn't getting the seductive vibe from her, but then she didn't strike him as the type to make the first move —or any move.

Didn't matter. He wasn't looking to get involved, and certainly not with his neighbor. Too much of a sticky situation if things didn't end well.

He rubbed a hand over his abs. She did stir him up, though.

CHAPTER

SIX

Pressure squeezed her chest—her lungs starved for fresh air. Thick, cloying smoke invaded her nose and mouth, and her eyes burned and watered. Darkness surrounded her. Her limbs wouldn't obey her commands to move. A roaring sound filled her ears.

Allison struggled for breath and freedom.

Her throat and lungs burned.

There was no air.

Help! Someone help me!

Allison sprang up in bed, trembling and drenched in sweat. The bedding tangled around her legs. She yanked and shoved her way free. She panted while her gaze darted around the room.

A sob tore through her.

She pressed her fist against her lips, hoping to stem the scream building inside her.

Allison stumbled from the bed and stood in the middle of the room, shaking.

She needed to get out. Now.

Allison yanked open her bedroom door and ran down the stairs, straight through the kitchen to the back door. She scrabbled at the lock, wrenching the door open when it finally turned in her hands.

Her bare feet slapped against the porch floor.

The smack of wood hitting wood echoed through the night when the screen door slammed shut behind her.

Rain poured down as she ran across the lawn to the large oak tree in the middle of her backyard. She bent over at the waist, clasping her knees in her palms, sobbing.

The rain drenched her hair and body, and terror raked over her skin, down deep into her bones.

A nightmare. It was just a nightmare. She repeated it over and over in her mind as sobs racked her body.

"WHAT THE HELL?" Jim heard a door slam and saw a white blur streak across his neighbor's backyard. He leaned closer to the kitchen window, squinting through the rain.

He dropped the handle he was getting ready to attach to the kitchen cabinet and ran out his back door.

"Allison!"

She showed no signs of hearing him.

His bare feet splashed through puddles, and mud squished between his toes as he ran through the construction zone of his backyard. The brief vision of a sharp nail embedding in his foot made him glance down, but he snapped his gaze back to Allison.

He stopped in front of her and searched for an injury but found nothing. Squatting down low, he looked at her face. She stared at the ground with wide eyes. Her face was sheet white, and her breaths were coming fast and furious.

"Allison, what is it? Are you hurt?" There was still no response from her.

He looked beyond her to the house. Lights shone from downstairs and upstairs. Could someone have been in her house?

He grasped her shoulders. "Allison, was someone in your house?"

She stared right through him, her pupils dilated.

"Allison, what happened?" What had sent her running out into the rain-soaked night? He didn't want to leave her to search the house.

She gave a slight shake to her head, but still, no words left her lips.

Her big, blue eyes were like pools of sorrow.

Shivers racked her slender form as she stood in her nightgown, drenched to the skin. He tried not to notice how it clung to her high breasts and narrow waist. He swallowed hard and looked back at her face.

She looked on the edge of hysteria.

He kneeled on the grass, cupped her face in his hands, and stared into her eyes. "Allison, listen to me. I want to help you, but you've got to help me out here. What are you afraid of? Did someone hurt you?"

She gave a definite shake of her head this time. She opened her mouth as if to speak, but no words came out. Her eyes clung to his, pleading for something. What did she need from him?

Was she in shock? How did you treat someone in shock? In movies, they would smack someone. However, he didn't think Allison would appreciate it, nor could he bring himself to smack a woman, to help her or not.

His gaze fell to her parted lips.

A kiss might work. He bent his head and brushed his lips across hers once, twice, and then he settled in. Her lips were cold and wet from the rain but soft and full.

Jim pulled back and stared into her eyes. He resisted the urge to kiss her again. One kiss to shock her back to reality. Any more, and he'd be a perv taking advantage of a vulnerable woman.

The panic seemed to leave her eyes. She blinked rapidly at him as if she was unsure what to do with him.

"Sorry, you looked on the verge of hysteria. It was either a kiss or a slap." He shrugged and gave her a lopsided grin.

Her breaths slowed to hiccups. "That's it, slow it down. Take deeper breaths." He kept his eyes trained on hers and breathed deeply in a slow rhythm for her to follow.

He waited while her breaths slowed and mimicked his. "Are you okay?"

She gave him a short nod. A blush stole over her cheeks. She looked away from his face.

He dropped his hands from her cheeks to her shivering arms and rubbed them to give her warmth. "What happened?" He looked up at the house. "Did someone break in? Should I call the police?"

She shook her head and pressed her lips tight together.

"Let's get you inside and dry."

She straightened, and he followed suit. Jim wrapped his arm around her shoulders and led her back to her house.

Jim's arm around her was like the eye of a hurricane—the storm of memories raged around her in a frenzy, but his warmth and strength anchored her. A large part of her wanted to turn, bury her face against his chest, and weep. The rest of her just wanted to run and hide from the past and the need to make explanations.

He led her into the house. She needed to say something, but what? He'd witnessed her panic attack. They were coming more often. How could she explain she'd run out into the night in the rain because of a stupid nightmare? An achingly real nightmare.

Jim looked around the kitchen and then walked down the hallway. He ducked into the bathroom and came back with a blue hand towel. He dried her face like she was a child.

"I'm going to take a quick look around the house and make sure everything is okay. Then we'll get you into something dry and warm, okay?"

Tears filled her eyes as she forced herself to meet his concerned gaze. "I...that's not necessary." Humiliation burned her cheeks and the back of her throat. How was she going to explain this? If he hadn't believed her crazy before, he most definitely did now.

He smiled at her. "It'll just take a minute."

Jim walked back down the hall, checking the living room and dining room before disappearing up the stairs. She should've called him back and explained, but she wanted another moment to gather her courage. No one was in the house, but the fear lessened as the sounds of his steps upstairs moved from room to room.

Allison stood where he left her, dripping on the floor, trying to figure out what to say to him when he came back. *I'm so sorry to have bothered you. You see, I have these nightmares, and tonight they were a little stronger than usual.*

He would recommend she seek professional help and quickly.

Jim jogged back down the stairs with a couple of towels in his hands. He handed one to her and used the other to dry himself.

Taking the towel, she dried her arms and tried not to stare as he removed his soaked shirt and dried his chest with the towel. She swallowed hard and wrapped the towel around her shoulders.

He watched her a moment before looking over his shoulder. "I didn't check that room." He turned towards Alan's office.

"It's locked. No one could get in there without a key."

"Okay."

She bit her lip and pulled the towel tighter around her. "It was my husband's office. There's no one in there." She took a deep breath and forced herself to meet his patient gaze. "There was no one in the house. I just...I um...had a nightmare."

She waited for his incredulity, hoping he wouldn't laugh.

"Must've been a whopper."

She couldn't help the smile or the tears that briefly came to her eyes. "Yes, yes it was."

"Well, you can tell me about it after you get into some dry clothes and get warmed up."

Tell him about it? He wanted to know about her nightmares?

Why was he still here? Why wasn't he making excuses and exiting this melodrama as fast as possible?

Rain drummed on the roof of the screened porch, and the icy shiver down her spine snapped her attention back to the situation. His soaked jeans were plastered to his legs. He was as drenched as she was.

"I'm sorry. I didn't thank you or offer you anything. I can make some tea. There might still be some of my husband's clothes that fit you." She scanned his body. Actually, it would be difficult to find something that would fit. "I'll get them now so you can change."

He didn't say a word as she practically flew up the stairs to her room. She went straight to her closet and pulled out the box of clothes she'd yet to donate. If she remembered right, there were a pair of athletic pants her husband had never worn. They were the only options that might fit Jim. He was several inches taller and significantly more muscled than Alan. She located the pants and a T-shirt that might stretch before going back downstairs.

Jim waited in the kitchen, leaning against the counter.

"I hope they fit." She held out the clothes.

He smiled and took them. "They're dry; that's all that matters. Thanks."

"Uh, you can change in the downstairs bathroom." She turned away but swung back. "Unless you prefer to use the guest bathroom upstairs. There are towels if you want to warm up in the shower."

"Sounds like a good idea. You should do the same. You're going to catch a cold if you don't get out of those wet clothes."

Allison looked down at her nightgown, which was glued to her in a big wet soggy mess, and almost groaned. She also needed to get some new nightclothes since apparently, she was getting into the bad habit of parading herself around in them in front of him. She went upstairs without a word, extremely aware with every step she took that he was right behind her.

CHAPTER

SEVEN

"Was the nightmare about your husband?"

Allison leaned back into the gray couch and cradled the warm mug of tea in her hands. After she'd showered and changed into dry clothes, she'd come downstairs to find Jim in her kitchen already making tea. He seemed perfectly at home rummaging through her cabinets. He'd glanced over his shoulder at her and told her to go sit in the living room, that he had everything under control.

Rather than answer questions or make explanations she wasn't sure how to give, she'd taken the reprieve he'd given her and sat waiting for him. He'd walked in and sat down but had said nothing for several minutes. She'd begun to think he'd remain silent. Not everyone pried into a stranger's private affairs—even when the crazy kept seeping out everywhere.

But then he'd broken the silence. He thought her nightmares were about Alan. Should she say yes? Would the questions end there? It might be easier.

Then again, probably not.

One lie had a way of snowballing into another.

Jim sat across from her in one of the blue plaid wing-back chairs. The borrowed white T-shirt stretched tightly across his chest and shoulders. His elbows rested on his thighs. The gray sweatpants ended at his calves instead of his ankles. He took a sip from his mug and watched her, patiently waiting for her response.

"No, they're not about Alan." Not tonight's anyway.

"They? So this isn't a one-time thing?"

So much for giving a quick and easy answer to laugh off the nightmare as not a big deal. Allison sighed and closed her eyes for a moment. There were no quick and easy answers. At least if there were, she didn't know them. She didn't know why the nightmares still plagued her or why they came more often lately. Maybe talking about it would provide some enlightenment. The worst that could happen was he would think her nuts. But after tonight, she was sure that opinion was already firmly embedded in his brain.

"I have them several times a week."

"The old lady across the street mentioned something about a tragedy. I guess I assumed it had something to do with your husband."

Allison grimaced. Gossip was a sin, wasn't it? Maybe she should bring that up the next time Mrs. Pannelli stopped by to convince her to go to church.

Ugh. Mrs. Pannelli didn't talk about her maliciously. She probably saw it as neighborly. Allison shifted into the corner of the couch with her legs tucked up next to her. She took a sip of the hot tea, and mint tingled her tongue. He'd chosen the peppermint tea.

"No, you were right. Mrs. Pannelli was referring to my husband. He died over a year ago after being sick with cancer for several years."

"I'm sorry."

A simple statement. There was sympathy and understanding but no questions or platitudes. He wasn't going to ask for details or tell her everything would be all right in time.

She looked into his eyes and smiled slightly. "Thank you."

Her gaze dropped and sidled over to the brick fireplace behind him. There were no doors needed to keep smoke out of the room, just a metal rack holding a few pristine logs of wood. There had never been a fire lit in there the entire time she lived in the house. One of the few demands she'd made of Alan. No fires in the fireplace. No candles. No open flames of any kind.

Jim continued to watch her. He wasn't going to let this drop, obviously. Why did he care what the nightmares were about?

"Does it really matter what they're about?"

He leaned back in the chair and seemed to contemplate her question for a moment. "Well, in the normal scope of things, having a nightmare is a pretty common occurrence. But having them repeatedly and terrifying you so much you go running out into the pouring rain in the middle of the night? That says something serious is going on. I always thought talking about nightmares was supposed to help, but it's your business. If you don't want to tell me about it, that's fine."

Was she being a bitch? He'd been nothing but nice and understanding to her despite her crazy moments. Maybe he was right and talking about it would help. Keeping everything locked up inside certainly hadn't helped.

"I'm sorry. I really don't mean to be rude. You've been exceedingly kind. I'm embarrassed about having nightmares and not being able to deal with them."

"You're not being rude." His mouth quirked up on one side, and that dimple appeared. "I don't think it's in your makeup to be rude. And there's nothing to be embarrassed about."

"I can be rude. You forget the day we met."

Jim chuckled. "You weren't rude. You were very proper about your displeasure."

Allison rolled her eyes. "Alan used to say the queen had come to call when I got mad. He thought it was funny, but it usually made me madder and probably more imperious."

"Most people get a little cranky if their sleep is interrupted. And if you've been having nightmares, I imagine losing any more sleep is difficult."

"Yeah, I come by these dark circles under my eyes naturally."

She set her mug down on the coffee table, sat back, and sighed. "The nightmares are about the night my parents died."

Allison massaged her forehead with the tips of her fingers. Pain drummed a fierce tempo inside her head. She stared at the swirling blue and gray patterns in the ivory rug.

"They died in a house fire. I was the only one who survived."

Rain still beat against the house. The grandfather clock in the corner ticked.

"I think that would give anyone nightmares for a long time."

She pulled her knees into her chest and rested her chin on the top. "I don't remember anything from that night past going to bed. My next memory is waking up in the hospital the next day to be told my parents were gone."

"How old were you?"

"Twenty-one. I was a senior in college. I had come home for the weekend for a surprise visit because I hadn't seen them for a while."

"You went to school far away from them?"

"No, well, it was only a couple of hours. I was just wrapped up in school and Alan. We'd just met and started dating that year."

"Alan, being your late husband?"

Allison nodded.

"Did you ever see anyone about the nightmares?"

"You mean a psychiatrist?"

"Yes."

"No. The nightmares started after the fire, but Alan and I thought they would go away in time. And they did, mostly. Months would go by before I would have one. It wasn't until after Alan passed away that they came back and became more frequent."

"Do you have something against going to a therapist?"

Allison smiled and shook her head. "No, not exactly. My father was a psychiatrist. I guess it seems rather silly that I haven't gone to someone considering, but I hoped they would go away. I thought the stress of losing Alan brought them back, and once I dealt with that, they'd go away again."

"I've never been to one myself, but both my mother and sister have their therapist's numbers memorized."

Allison smiled. "My father had clients who would call him at all hours. It used to drive my mother crazy."

Jim rubbed the back of his neck. "I bet."

"Are you close to your family?"

He shrugged and looked around the room. "Depends on what you call close. We talk now and then. Usually when one of their relationships has gone south, and they need something."

"I'm sorry. I shouldn't pry."

Jim simply raised his eyebrow. "Isn't that what we're doing here?"

She smiled. "I guess so."

She leaned forward and pulled the mugs together. "Do you want more tea or anything?"

"No thanks, I'm good."

Allison bit her lip and leaned back against the couch. She pulled her knees back into her chest and wrapped her arms around her legs. The soft fleece material of her pants warmed her chilled skin.

Jim stood and stretched. The borrowed T-shirt rode up to reveal an expanse of tight, tanned skin. "Well, it's really late. Are you going to be okay? If you want, I could crash here."

Allison held her breath for a second. She was tempted to say yes, but that wasn't a solution. There would still be tomorrow night and the night after.

Besides, she doubted she would get much sleep with him just down the hall.

She stood and smiled. "Thank you, but I'll be fine now. You've been a tremendous help to me, again. I can't thank you enough or apologize enough for causing such a fuss."

"Don't worry about it."

Jim walked down the hall to the kitchen as Allison trailed behind. He stopped at the counter by the phone, picked up a pen, and wrote something on the pad lying there. "Here's my number. Call if you need anything, okay?"

"Thank you. That's very nice of you, but I'll be fine, really."

He picked up the pile of his wet clothes by the back door and scanned her from head to toe. He looked like he was about to say something but glanced at the office door and back.

"Goodnight, Allison."

"Good night." She shut and locked the door behind him and flipped on the outside lights to guide his way. The rain was no longer pouring down, but he would still be wet by the time he reached his house. She should have found a bag for his clothes and offered him an umbrella. The white of his bare feet glowed. She winced. She didn't have any shoes to offer him. Had she isolated herself for so long that she no longer had the most basic manners? He jogged up his stairs and disappeared into his house.

She switched off the lights, closed her eyes, and leaned against the door. She hadn't told him the entire truth. The omission lodged in her throat.

It's not like she owed him a full explanation or anything.

They'd had a moment or two of sharing, but they weren't confidants confessing their deepest, darkest secrets.

He never needed to know.

Opening her eyes, she bit her lip. But what if he got curious and looked it up on the Internet?

He didn't know her maiden name or where she grew up, but he might have enough facts to find something if he tried hard enough.

What would he think of her then? Would he say anything? Look at her differently?

Allison banged the back of her head against the door. She should have told him.

But how did you tell someone that you killed your parents?

CHAPTER

EIGHT

Just pick up the phone and dial! Allison stood in front of the phone, chewing on her lip. She'd been rehearsing what to say for the past twenty minutes. It was ridiculous how anxiety took control of rational thought. It's just a phone call. *Pick up the phone!*

Allison finally grabbed the phone and dialed the number before she could change her mind. The phone rang only once before someone answered.

"Dr. Thompson's office. How can I help you?"

Strange, she had expected to hear her father's name still mentioned too. But of course, it wouldn't be. He hadn't been part of the practice for years.

"Is Dr. Thompson available?"

"Who's calling, please?"

Allison frowned. This was a mistake. She shouldn't have called.

"Hello?"

"Allison Delaney." It was unlikely the receptionist would recognize her married name. She was most likely a more recent hire since Molly Danvers, her father's receptionist, had retired after his death.

Unless there had been some sort of initiation gossip about the circumstances of her father's death. Did all new hires hear the tragedy that befell Dr. Thompson's former business partner? That was ridiculous, wasn't it?

"Hold please."

Allison's finger hesitated over the disconnect button. Dr. Thompson might not recognize her name. It had been so many years, and they hadn't kept in touch. If she hung up now, would he call back? And then what? She'd look like even more of a fool.

Why had she called him?

"Allison?"

So much for not recognizing her married name. "Hi, Dr. Thompson."

"This is unexpected. How are you?"

Crazy.

"Fine. You?"

She winced. This was such a mistake. She should have opened a phone book and picked out any psychiatrist, psychologist, or therapist on the list. Instead, she had called her father's former business partner and friend for a referral. Why had she thought it would be easier contacting someone she knew and who knew her past than explaining to someone new?

"Why are you calling, Allison? Is everything all right?"

"I've been having nightmares—about that night. I was hoping you could recommend a therapist near me to talk to."

"I see."

Did he? Because she sure as hell didn't.

"Are you still living in Connecticut with your husband?"

"In Connecticut, yes, but Alan passed away last year."

"I see."

Allison tapped the corner of the phone against her forehead. She'd forgotten how much she hated those two words. He'd always had this way of staring at her like he could see her every thought and found her lacking. Then he would nod his head and say those same words. She'd never been a patient of his, but he'd studied her and questioned her at her parents' parties as if she were. She'd thought it was just his nature, but now she found it creepy.

"Give me your number. I'll make some calls and get back to you."

"Thank you." Allison gave him her number and hung up.

After last night's fiasco with Jim, she'd decided she needed help. Her nightmares were getting worse and affecting every area of her life. They had to stop.

The phone rang.

That was quick. She frowned at it and answered.

"Allison?"

Not the doctor, but the voice sounded familiar. "Yes, Karen?"

Karen chuckled. "Hi. I had a cancellation at Guilty Pleasures this morning and thought of you. Can you come in at eleven?"

This morning?

"Allison?"

"Yes, I'm here. I ah...I'm thinking."

"I'll be gentle. I promise."

Allison closed her eyes and leaned against the kitchen counter. She needed a haircut. She also needed a distraction. "All right, eleven it is."

"Fantastic! I'll see you then. Don't worry, it'll be great. Bye!"

Allison held the phone to her ear and listened to the silence before placing it on the counter. She glanced at the clock. It was almost ten o'clock now. She had less than an hour to pull herself together.

Allison wrinkled her nose as she looked down at her worn sweatpants and T-shirt. The first thing she needed to do was change into something a bit more presentable. And maybe practice some breathing exercises while she did. Rolling her eyes, she climbed the stairs and dug through her closet and drawers. When did she turn into this anxiety-ridden person?

Her parents' deaths probably started the process, but it wasn't instant—more like a slow roll down a hill booby-trapped with emotions like fear, sorrow, and guilt. Always the guilt.

She settled on a pair of leggings that weren't in danger of dropping to her ankles as much of her wardrobe appeared to be and a simple pink shell to complete the outfit. She brushed her hair and pulled it back into a ponytail. There wasn't much point in attempting any sort of style. That was what the appointment was for.

She made it all the way to the garage and into the car.

Allison sat in her sedan, gripping the steering wheel. What if she couldn't bring herself to move it? She didn't want to asphyxiate herself sitting in a running vehicle in an enclosed space. She was borderline agoraphobic and anxious, not suicidal.

Ah, a silver lining.

She tilted her head back against the headrest and chuckled. It must be a good sign that she could still laugh at herself. Then again, it could be the beginnings of hysteria.

All right, Allison. You're simply going to turn the key, put the car in reverse, and back out of the garage.

She twisted the key, and the engine rumbled to life. Step one complete. She shifted into reverse, eased her foot off the brake, and glanced in the side-view mirror.

White filled her view.

The garage door was closed.

Allison slammed on the brake and shifted back into park. She dropped her head onto the steering wheel and winced. *Step one should have been opening the garage door, not turning the key!*

She pressed the button on the remote and sighed as the door rattled up. How many times had she performed these steps on autopilot? Thousands, at least. Now, after a few months of hiding, she forgot everything? Okay, several months, but still. Why was this so hard?

Planting her hands at the ten and two o'clock positions on the steering wheel, she checked all the mirrors and put the car in reverse again. She backed the car out and turned it around to face the road with no incidents.

Okay, next step. Let your foot off the brake, ease on the gas, turn left onto the street, and take a right at the stop sign. Once the car moved, she relaxed. She used to love to drive. She would listen to the radio and enjoy the scenery.

Maybe she would play the radio on the way home. She glanced at the speedometer and chuckled. Twenty miles per hour.

In high school, she and her best friend used to pretend they were little old ladies when they first got their licenses. They would drive well below the speed limit, hunched up to the steering wheel, peering over it.

What had ever happened to Georgie? They'd gone off to different colleges and promised to stay in touch but eventually drifted apart. Then her life had imploded, and she'd buried her past in the depths of her memory and concentrated on Alan.

Two more turns brought her to Main Street. She passed the plaza, turned onto the side street next to it, and found the green, oval sign with gold lettering spelling out "Guilty Pleasures."

She parked her car at the back of the lot, away from any cars. No reason to tempt fate or her rusty skills trying to maneuver between other cars.

The colonial house used to be an insurance office. Once painted a standard white, it now sported fresh, sunny, yellow paint with forest green shutters.

Allison sighed and grabbed her purse. She was a little early, but it was probably best to get inside before she changed her mind.

Not sure what she expected, but it wasn't the warm, inviting décor that greeted her when she opened the dark green door. Wood floors and mint-colored walls were the background for a small waiting area and the wide-open salon. A small counter angled to the right of the entryway with the stairs leading to the second floor behind it. Potted plants separated work areas, and colorful landscape paintings dotted the walls.

Two hairstylists worked with clients on the left, and a manicurist was bent over a customer's nails on the right. Allison debated whether to stop at the counter or take a seat and wait for someone to be free.

A door in the back opened, and Karen stepped out.

She immediately spied Allison and walked towards her with a wide smile. "Allison, you made it." She grasped Allison's hands and gave them a squeeze as she scanned her face.

Allison gave her a smile in return and a slight nod to answer her unasked question. She was all right and ready to do this.

"Let's get started, shall we?" She led Allison to one of the hunter-green chairs. Allison slid onto the chair and balanced her toes on the metal bar beneath it.

Karen chatted about shampoo, conditioning treatments, cuts, colors. Allison's head spun, trying to grasp it all.

"Um...well...I." She looked at Karen's smiling face and relaxed. "I trust your judgment."

Karen's smile widened. "You'll love it!"

"Your place is lovely, Karen. Very welcoming."

"Thank you. I'm pretty proud of it. As you can see, the hair salon takes up most of the lower floor, with the nail section to the right. I'll give you the full tour later."

After draping an ivory-colored protective apron over her, Karen leaned over and smiled. "I don't want you looking until I'm all done, okay?"

Allison nodded. "All right."

Karen turned the chair away from the mirror.

A tiny thrill of excitement unfurled inside her. What did Karen plan to do with her hair? Hopefully, something fresh and stylish that would make her see a different version of herself other than the drab and boring old reflection that stared back at her from the mirror every morning.

Soft music played in the background. An older woman across the room flipped through a magazine while a stylist colored her hair.

Karen reached behind her and dropped a magazine in Allison's lap. "Here, it's going to be a while, and I know it's already driving you crazy."

Allison bit her lip. "I'm sorry."

"Don't be silly. I understand completely. There are some good articles in that one that might distract you for a bit."

"Thanks." Allison glanced at the pages. An article on summer planting might entertain her for a while. She needed some ideas for her flower beds.

The scent of whatever Karen added to her hair caused her to wrinkle her nose. She flipped through the pages of the magazine to a new article. She really hoped Karen wasn't giving her purple hair or something. Drawing attention to herself was not something she was fond of.

Several articles later, and after a few trips back and forth from the sinks to the dryers, Karen led her back to the chair.

Long locks of blonde hair fluttered to the ground around her chair. Allison swallowed.

Don't panic. It's just hair. It will grow back. At least it's not purple.

She peeked up at Karen. "How are Charlie and the kittens doing?"

"Oh, he's in heaven with them. I keep reminding him we can't keep them all, but I think he's going to have a tough time when the kittens are ready for new homes. He already has a place in mind for one of them. Of course, he's letting you have first pick because, as he says, Mouser chose you."

Allison smiled. "The more I think about it, the more I like the idea. I guess I'll need to make a trip to the pet store."

"Charlie will be thrilled to help you. I think he's trying to find homes where he knows he'll be able to visit them."

"Well, it sounds like a good plan to me. I've never had a cat before, so I could use his expertise."

Karen laughed and continued to move around Allison, snipping and shaping as she went. Allison itched to look in the mirror. She held onto the arms of the chair and tried to think of something else.

Karen leaned over her shoulder. "Are you ready for the big reveal?"

Allison gripped the arms of the chair. She closed her eyes and took a deep breath as Karen spun the chair towards the mirror.

"Open your eyes."

Allison blinked and stared. Her hair fell to just below her chin. The cut was angled, and the color was a light, shimmery blonde. It looked like someone else's hair—someone glamorous.

"Say something. You're scaring me. Do you hate it?"

Allison turned her wide-eyed gaze to Karen and shook her head. "No...no...it's ...it's wonderful! I can't believe it's me!"

Karen grinned and hugged her shoulders. "I'm so glad. You look fabulous!"

"I've never had short hair before. Alan liked it long. It feels so light, so free." Allison stared at her reflection, turning right and left to make her hair dance around her face.

"It suits you."

Allison looked up at Karen and grinned. "You're a magician, Karen."

JIM GLANCED out his bedroom window on the way to the hall bathroom. Allison drove into her driveway. The water running in the shower droned from the bathroom. He tossed his clean clothes over his shoulder and moved closer to the window as she reappeared out of the garage and walked to the front porch.

There was an efficiency to the way she moved. She didn't stroll or saunter like some women. She moved quickly with a purpose.

Jim placed his arm along the side of the window and leaned in for a closer look.

She'd cut her hair.

It looked good. She looked good.

As she went inside her house and closed the door, he shook his head and walked away from the window to the bathroom.

He needed to take a step back from his neighbor. He had one ironclad rule when he bought a house and moved to a new neighborhood—don't get involved.

Everything about his life was temporary, and he liked it that way. The houses and people changed like clockwork. Sure, there were a few constants, but they were family members or those close enough to be family.

He stripped and stepped into the shower.

The bathroom wasn't pretty, but it was functional—barely. The water pressure sucked, but at least he had plenty of hot water now that he'd replaced the hot water heater. The chipped pink tiles needed to go. This bathroom was next on his list after he finished the kitchen. Once he combined this bedroom and bath with the bedroom next door, he would have a generously sized primary suite with a walk-in closet.

The current layout of the second floor was four small bedrooms and a single bathroom. When he finished, there would be the primary suite, two other bedrooms, and a bathroom.

The hot water sluiced down his naked back, and steam filled the tiny, enclosed shower.

Allison had been really shaken up last night. He should call and check in on her.

Jim hung his head under the spray. She was fine. He'd just witnessed her walking into her house sporting a new haircut after all.

He still needed to give her his opinion on her kitchen. The brief look last night hadn't given him much more than a snapshot. It was outdated for sure. The layout could be more efficient. Sketching a few ideas out for her wouldn't take much time.

He could find someone to recommend if she wanted work done and let himself off the hook. He shut off the water. Distance was always a good thing, especially with women who needed saving.

Jim stepped out of the shower, dried off, and dressed in a clean pair of jeans and a T-shirt. Walking down the stairs, he avoided the weak railing, another priority on his list.

He walked into the kitchen and opened the fridge. His dinner choices were limited, leftover pizza, a sandwich, or cereal. Not exactly an appealing selection.

When he glanced over at his neighbor's house again, he shut the refrigerator door and rubbed his hand over his face. She wasn't his problem or his type.

Allison was nice to look at, but definitely the happily ever after type, not his kind of woman at all. He only got involved with women who understood the score and felt the same way. Women who understood it was temporary and for their mutual enjoyment.

Jim grabbed his keys off the table. Going out for a few hours suddenly seemed like a good idea.

Somewhere with a different view and where a certain blonde temptation wouldn't occupy his thoughts.

CHAPTER

NINE

Karen walked up Jim's walkway carrying some sort of basket. Allison's hand froze in midair, clutching the duster tight. What was Karen doing at Jim's? Did they know each other?

She inched closer to the living room window and watched as Karen knocked on his door. Her breath hitched in her chest when Jim opened the door and stepped onto the porch with a wide grin.

They looked perfect together. Two gorgeous people smiling at each other and chatting about God knows what. Whatever the topic was, they looked at ease with each other. There were no blushes or awkward movements that peppered her own conversations.

Allison scooted to the side of the window in case one of them glanced her way.

She couldn't tear her eyes away from them.

Karen reached out and touched his arm while they shared a laugh. Allison stiffened as a stab of jealousy pierced through her.

God, what was wrong with her? So what if they were involved? It was none of her business.

Allison turned away from the window and plopped down on the

couch. She rubbed her chilled arms. The silence of an empty house surrounded her.

The doorbell rang.

Had Karen dropped by after visiting Jim? What if they were both at her door?

Allison stood and walked to the front door. Karen's silhouette was easily identifiable through the glass partition.

Opening the door, she pasted on a smile and glanced around the porch, and let out a sigh. It was just Karen.

"Hey there, neighbor. Are you busy? Charlie is with his dad this weekend, so it's just me. The house always feels so empty when he's gone, you know?"

Allison stepped back and opened the door wide. "Yes, I know what you mean. Come on in."

Karen stepped past her and glanced back over her shoulder. "I just met your new neighbor. Why didn't you tell me there was such a hunk living next door to you?"

"Um...well...I guess I didn't think of it." She shut the door and directed Karen into the living room with a wave of her hand.

"Lord, how could you not? I brought him muffins as a welcoming gift—store-bought, of course," she said with a laugh. "When he opened the door, all I could think was yum!"

Allison laughed. "He seems very nice, despite the fact that the first time I met him, I screamed at him."

Karen sat on the couch and crossed her legs. "Tell me all."

"Can I get you anything? Something to drink?"

"No thanks, I'm good. Just the juicy details."

Shrugging, Allison sat on one of the chairs. "I hadn't gotten much sleep the night before, and the loud saw he was using woke me up. I let him know my displeasure. It wasn't until I was back in the house that I realized I was still in my nightgown. It was not one of my prouder moments. Very embarrassing."

Karen laughed. "I just can't picture you yelling at anyone, Allison, let alone in your nightgown. Now, if someone had woken me from my beauty sleep, especially if I had gotten only a little of it...look out! I am not a morning person to begin with. I probably would have used a blunt instrument—until I got a good look at him, anyway!"

"He was very polite about it, even though he must have thought I was crazy."

"I bet he hasn't used that saw early in the morning again, has he?"

"As a matter of fact, you're right; he hasn't."

"Well, I'm sure if you brought him over some of that chocolate cake you make, he'd forgive you anything. He admitted he had a sweet tooth when I met him today."

"Um...actually, I brought him brownies the other day."

There was a loud sigh before Karen replied, "Allison, when I say tell all, I mean all. Leave nothing out. I want to know every detail."

Allison laughed. "Karen, there really isn't anything else to tell you. He helped me with my lawnmower, and I realized I hadn't exactly welcomed him to the neighborhood, so I made him brownies as a thank you and a welcoming gift. That's all."

"Fixed your lawnmower, huh? I think I'd be breaking a few things for him to repair if I were you."

"Considering he witnessed me cursing and kicking the lawnmower and then almost falling on my ass, I don't think I'll go that route, but you go ahead."

Karen's laughter sang through the room for a good, solid minute before she replied. "Oh Allison, that's priceless."

"That's not quite the way I would describe our encounters. More like embarrassment, mortification, and total humiliation."

"Yet you still made him brownies. Good for you, Allison."

"Like I said, I felt like I needed to do something to prevent him from thinking I was the crazy neighbor next door. Although I don't know if the brownies were good enough to completely wipe out that impression."

"After tasting your cake, I can imagine how good those brownies were. The muffins I brought him were from the bakery, but honestly, Allison, they don't compare to your baking. You've got a talent there, and I wouldn't mind a bit if you decide to bake something and have a few extras. Or if you need a taste tester for a recipe..."

"Thanks, I'll keep that in mind. Actually, my groceries were delivered yesterday, so my kitchen is restocked. I'm sure I can whip something up."

"I was less than subtle, wasn't I?" Karen winked at her. "You sure you don't want me to help sabotage your garbage disposal or something so your sexy neighbor can come fix it?"

"No, thank you, but I'll help you sabotage yours if you like."

"Oh no, not me. He's definitely a tasty dish, but there was no chemistry between us, you know what I mean? If it's not there, it's not there. Now I think he would provide an excellent distraction for you, though. A way to get your feet wet before you jump back into the dating game."

Allison's heart rate surged.

Dating? Who said anything about dating?

Karen stared at her for a moment before uncrossing her legs and scooting forward to rest her arms on her knees. "Honey, the ones left behind always feel guilty, but there's nothing wrong with appreciating a handsome man or enjoying a little harmless flirtation either. I'm a firm believer it's good for the soul."

She supposed the guilt must be written all over her face. It was her constant companion.

"Logically, I know that there's nothing morally wrong with moving on. Alan has been gone for more than a year, and the cancer had made him extremely ill a long time before that."

"Finding yourself alone after you've been part of a couple is hard. I know when I got divorced, I needed to redefine myself as an individual, not part of a couple."

Karen placed her hand on her chest and smiled. "Of course, I had

Charlie, and I chose to become single and no longer be part of a unit."

Allison clasped her hands in her lap. "I guess you're right. I've never been on my own before. I married Alan right out of college. It seems like I was always his wife."

"You met in college?"

Allison nodded. "He was a teacher actually, not mine, though," she added hastily.

"What did he teach?"

"Economics. He got tenure the month before they diagnosed him with esophageal cancer."

One day they had been celebrating, and the next, their lives spiraled out of control. They had thought his chronic cough was the onset of allergies and something they could manage. When they heard the word cancer, it was as if the world stopped at that moment and was forever changed.

"How did you meet?" Allison blinked and focused on Karen's question. The memory made her smile.

"At a blood drive, actually. I was volunteering, and he came in to donate blood. He was so squeamish about it; it was endearing. It wasn't until our first date that we discovered he was a teacher and I was a student. I thought he was a student, perhaps a graduate student, and he thought I was older. He was ten years older than me."

Allison shook her head. "At first he was appalled. He didn't want to be seen as one of those lecherous older men who pursued young co-eds. I pointed out that he was only thirty, and just as he had assumed I was older, so would others unless he volunteered my age." She shrugged and took another sip. "We worked it out."

Karen smiled. "It's nice to focus on the happy memories. They help us traverse the pain and make the bad ones seem a little less so, I think."

"How long was it after the divorce before you started dating?"

"Oh well, that's a definite example of heart and head wanting different things. My head wanted to move right on out and find a string of boy toys to erase Steve from my heart, but my heart wouldn't let me. It was about six months before I had my first date, and it was a disaster. It felt strange and awkward, so much so that I didn't try again for another couple of months. Eventually, it became easier."

"I simply can't imagine dating anyone. I never dated much before Alan, so the thought of dating terrifies me."

"It takes time. Eventually, you'll meet someone that makes your heart race a bit, makes your palms sweat. Someone who'll make you want to take that step. Like that sexy neighbor of yours, maybe?"

Allison dropped her head back against the chair. "Considering he suggested I talk to a therapist the last time we talked, I don't think he sees me as anything but a head case."

"For kicking a lawnmower? I guess I misjudged him. Never mind, we'll find you someone else."

"It wasn't for the lawnmower. I had another meltdown, which he witnessed." She covered her eyes with her hand.

"I'm waiting with bated breath over here."

"I have these nightmares. The other night was a particularly bad one, and I ran outside in the pouring rain. Jim saw me and got helped me back inside."

Allison separated her fingers enough to peek through them at Karen. Her mouth was hanging open.

"I know—crazy. Which is why he suggested I speak to a therapist."

"Have you? I mean, it's not crazy, but maybe you should talk to someone. What are the nightmares about? Alan?"

"No, they're about the night my parents died in a fire." Allison dropped her hand. "I could use something to drink. How about you? Can I get you anything?"

She stood and walked down the hall to the kitchen, Karen trailing behind. Allison poured herself a glass of wine. It was past noon, and she was entitled, damn it.

Karen simply held out her hand, and Allison handed her the glass and poured another one. Karen took a healthy swallow and set the glass on the counter with a sigh.

"Full disclosure, I'm a crier. I cry over commercials on a regular basis. Drove Steve nuts."

"Okay."

Allison's eyes widened when Karen's face crumpled, and tears welled in her eyes. She walked around the counter, wrapped Allison in her arms, and sniffled on her shoulder.

"Um...it's okay, Karen. It was a long time ago." She returned her hug and patted her on the back.

Karen lifted her head. "Time doesn't matter with something like that. It breaks my heart what you've been through. No wonder you're having nightmares." She wiped the tears from her cheeks.

Allison's throat dried, and tears filled her eyes.

She was right. The pain never lessened because the guilt could never be erased.

"Oh shit. Oh shit. Did I mention I'm a sympathetic crier too?" Karen's eyes overflowed once again. She squeezed Allison and rocked her back and forth.

Allison choked on a laugh and clasped a hand to her mouth. She pulled out of Karen's arms, grabbed a box of tissues from the nearby shelf, and offered it to Karen after taking one herself.

They both wiped their tears away and noisily blew their noses. Allison took a sip of wine. Here she was again, but she needed to be completely honest this time.

She set the glass down and traced an absent pattern with her fingertip on the counter. "It was my fault—the fire. I forgot and left a candle burning."

"Oh dear Lord." Karen swallowed the rest of her wine and hugged her again. "At this rate, you and I are going to have the crying jag of the century."

Allison laid her head on Karen's shoulder. She'd told the truth, and Karen hadn't stared at her in horror like she was a monster. Instead, she was comforting her again.

Karen rubbed her back. "Well, that explains your reaction to the smoke at dinner. I'm so sorry about that." She looked around the kitchen. "It also explains the number of fire extinguishers and smoke detectors I've seen in your house."

Laughter burst out of Allison in an inelegant snort. There were extinguishers and detectors in every single room of the house.

"There are backups in the closets too."

Karen picked up the bottle of wine. "I hope you have more wine because we're having a girls' night." She glanced out the window. "Or girls' day."

CHAPTER

TEN

Allison finished blow-drying her hair and pondered her reflection. She twisted her head side to side. The blonde tresses swung and brushed her neck. The new hairdo was so light and easy to care for.

The haircut wasn't the only thing making her feel lighter. Talking to Karen and even to Jim had lifted some of the guilty burdens from her shoulders. Sharing dark secrets was evidently therapeutic.

Karen's reaction to the confession had been a relief but having an afternoon chatting and forging a friendship bond was the true therapy. Allison sobered. How long had it been since she'd had a friend to confide in, laugh with, and just talk to while sharing a glass or bottle of wine?

Too long.

Allison leaned into the mirror and studied her face. Except for some faint lines that appeared when she smiled, she was still wrinkle-free. Maybe she should wear a touch of makeup. Not much, just some mascara and a little blush and lipstick.

Rummaging through the vanity drawers, she produced a tube of lipstick. She'd never been much of a makeup wearer, only for special occasions. Over the past few years, she'd stopped wearing it altogether. Oh well, she could order some online. Or maybe she could make a trip to an actual store for a change.

Allison applied the lipstick, smacked her lips together, and studied the result. The color was neutral, but it brought life to her face.

She reached up and lightly touched her lips. Jim had kissed her the other night—if only to shock her out of her episode.

When was the last time someone kissed her? Alan, of course, but when? He'd never been the affectionate type. They'd had sex, of course, but it had always been sporadically. Once he got sick, any intimacy stopped altogether.

Well, that explained why she was thinking about Jim's kiss—it had been over four years since she'd had one. Simple enough to understand. It didn't take a genius to figure that one out.

Her phone rang.

She picked it up and looked at the number. Dr. Thompson. He must have her referral.

"Hello, Dr. Thompson. How are you?"

"Hello, Allison. I'm fine. More importantly, how are you feeling?"

"Surprisingly well, thank you."

"Oh? No more nightmares?"

"Well, yes, but only one that I remember from last night."

"You have them every night?"

"Yes."

"Allison, I have a referral for you, but in the meantime, I'm going to prescribe some sleeping pills for you."

"I don't like taking pills."

"It's a low dose and will help you get uninterrupted rest, which is always a tremendous help to our mental health and physical wellbeing." He asked for her pharmacy and then gave her the doctor's name he was referring her to.

"He's expecting your call. I impressed upon him the urgency of your situation. He will fit you into his schedule."

He made her sound like she was on the verge of a breakdown. "Thank you, but it's not really urgent."

"Until you work through your guilt and grief, the nightmares are likely to escalate. Make the call and fill the prescription, Allison."

She glared at the phone and gave it a mock salute.

"Allison?"

He was only trying to help, exactly what she had called him for. "Yes, Dr. Thompson, thank you."

"Call me if you need anything else." His heavy sigh sounded through the phone. "Your father was more than my business partner. He was a friend. I have been remiss in checking on you over the years."

"That's kind of you, but really, I'm fine. I appreciate the referral. I'll give him a call."

"Good. Don't forget the prescription. Goodbye, Allison."

"Bye."

Allison disconnected the call and leaned her forehead against the wall. Maybe she should have just picked a name off the Internet. Why had she thought a referral would be easier? Nostalgia and the connection to her father? She'd hoped he would explain her past and her part in it. Dr. Thompson already knew the details. At least the ones about her parents and the fire.

Allison stood in the kitchen making cookies to bring over to Charlie and Karen. Charlie wanted her to come and visit the kitten he'd chosen for her. The kittens would be old enough to leave their mother in a couple of weeks. It would be nice to have a pet. The house wouldn't feel so empty, and she could talk to the cat instead of just herself.

She snickered.

Someone knocked on the back door. She jumped and dropped the scoop of dough onto the baking sheet with a loud clatter.

Only one person was likely to use the back door, Jim.

She quickly wiped her hands on the kitchen towel and smoothed the yellow shirt she wore as she rounded the peninsula of cabinets.

Yup, Jim stood on her back porch with his hands on his hips. Was he checking up on her?

She opened the door. "Hi." The heat of a blush climbed her neck and cheeks, and she cursed her fair skin.

"Hey." He leaned forward slightly and sniffed. "Something smells great!"

Allison smiled and stepped back to let him in. He was dressed in his usual T-shirt and jeans. "I'm making cookies. The first batch just came out of the oven. They're cooling but will be ready shortly. You're welcome to have some."

"Yum. Can't wait." He walked over to the stove and sniffed the cookies cooling on the rack. He plucked one up and popped it in his mouth.

"Careful, they're hot."

He just smiled and finished the rest of the cookie. "Perfect."

Allison laughed and walked over to the counter to fill the rest of the baking sheet. "Would you like some milk to go with it?"

"Absolutely. You have to have milk with cookies, but don't stop what you're doing. I'll get it. I don't want to slow down production."

Allison shook her head and pointed to the cabinet to the right of the sink. "The glasses are in there."

"Thanks. You really are a great cook."

The remark brought a warm rush of pleasure. "Thank you, I enjoy it."

Jim snatched two more cookies off the cooling rack after pouring his milk. He leaned against the counter next to her and watched her put the next batch of cookies in the oven.

She turned to him and smiled. "I bet you did the same thing when you were a boy. Eating the cookies before they cooled. You're lucky you didn't burn your mouth."

"They were exactly right. Not too hot, but warm enough that the chocolate is still melted. And my mother was never the type to bake cookies or anything else. It wasn't until I was older that I discovered not all cookies came from a bag."

"Well, everyone has their hobbies. My mom enjoyed baking, and I loved helping her. I guess she was the quintessential homemaker. She did all sorts of crafts and things too."

"To my knowledge, my mother never held a job. And no one would describe her as a housewife, least of all her."

Allison bit her lip. Unless she was mistaken, she detected a sore point with Jim and his mother. "I guess everyone is different for a reason. Everyone has their own niche in life. It's the lucky ones who find it and can do it. Like you with remodeling old houses."

Jim folded his arms across his chest. "Yeah, it took me a while to figure out what I wanted to do. When an injury ended my football career, I was a little lost about what to do with my life."

"You played football?"

She didn't know the first thing about the game. Her school hadn't had a football team, and her father and husband hadn't been interested in watching the sport. Jim certainly had the physique of someone who played sports or worked out a lot.

He chuckled and nodded. "I was only pro for a few seasons before my knee gave out. It wasn't until I ran into an old college buddy that I got the idea to start with the houses. I used to work with him and his dad. His dad owns a construction company. He taught me everything."

"That must have been difficult. Not playing football."

"I eventually dragged myself out of the self-pity spiral I was in. It was all I knew. I didn't have a backup plan. I never thought I could be injured enough not to play. Then there were the perks that went along with playing pro. You get used to things and take them for granted. Like freebies, never waiting for a table, blind adulation, and of course, the money." He shrugged. "It hit me hard, but eventually, I faced reality and realized it was time to move on."

She could relate to the pity party. She'd spent plenty of time on that path herself. Some might say she was still riding on it.

"What led you to remodeling instead of starting from scratch?"

Jim reached for another cookie. "When I worked construction with them, I could always visualize just how the project would look when completed. Then I started redoing houses in my head whenever I went into someone's house. Little or substantial changes I would make if the house were mine. It stemmed from that."

The timer went off, and Allison took the cookies out of the oven. "So, what changes would you make to my house?"

Jim smirked. "You really want to know?"

She looked at the kitchen that hadn't been changed since Alan's parents bought the house in the early nineties—the stainless-steel sink under the window, the almond-colored ancient appliances, the green laminate countertop. "Yes, I really do."

"All right, well, you said you wanted to redo your kitchen. I agree with you there. Your cabinets look solid, so I'd strip them and paint them a soft cream, I think. Maybe put a few glass fronts on some. Then I'd get rid of this countertop and put in a granite one, a neutral tone with some darker flecks. I'd put a bigger window here over the sink. Change the back door to a pair of French doors onto the back porch. You've got nice hardwood floors, but I think I'd darken it up a bit in here. You could even add an archway into the dining room instead of having to go down the hall."

He walked around the room, gesturing to the changes while he talked about them. She could visualize the kitchen through his eyes.

"Yes, I want that, just how you described. It's perfect."

He stopped and looked at her. "Are you serious?"

Allison vigorously nodded. "Yes, very. I know you're busy with your own house, but could you maybe recommend someone?"

Jim rubbed the back of his neck and frowned. "Well, there is a guy I use to help me with some projects that are too big for me, or if I'm on a tight schedule. I could see if he's available."

"Thank you, I'd really appreciate it."

"It's no problem. I'll call him and let you know." He smiled. "Will that earn me some more of those cookies?"

Allison laughed and handed him a couple on a napkin. His hand brushed hers, and she stilled. A fluttering of heat erupted inside her.

She turned away and grabbed a cookie for herself. Okay, her body had obviously decided it was time to wake up and notice the opposite sex. Her mind, however, wasn't exactly on the same page. She had enough on her plate without tossing in an attraction to her sexy neighbor.

Taking a bite of the cookie, she savored the soft, chewy texture. She rarely tooted her own horn, but these were rather good.

She arranged the cooled cookies on a platter for Charlie and Karen. There was a bunch leftover.

"I need these for Karen and Charlie, but you can have the rest of the cookies if you'd like."

"Do you really need to ask?"

Allison clasped her hands in front of her. She looked out the window, not ready to meet his gaze. She hoped he hadn't noticed her reaction to his touch.

"Is Karen the redhead down the road?"

"Uh...yes, yes she is. Charlie is her son. His cat chose under my porch to give birth to kittens, and now Charlie is giving me one when it's old enough."

"She stopped by the other day and introduced herself. Brought me muffins. She confessed they were store-bought, still good though."

Allison laughed. "Yes, she told me. Karen doesn't like to cook much. Her talents lie in other areas, though she made a wonderful chicken parmigiana a few weeks ago."

Was it already a few weeks? It seemed like just the other day when she met Karen and Charlie.

Jim made a noncommittal sound and crossed his ankles as he leaned against the counter again. "Have you had any more nightmares?"

Allison stacked the dishes in the sink and shrugged. "A few."

"Have you considered getting more information about what happened, maybe fill in the gaps of your memory?"

She turned back to him and folded her arms in front of her waist. "Honestly, I'm in the habit of avoiding any thought of that night. I guess it didn't occur to me."

"It might help."

"I suppose so, but I really don't have any idea how to do that. It's been over ten years."

"Where did your parents live?"

"Delton, Pennsylvania. Why?"

"You could check old newspaper articles. Did the town have a newspaper?"

Allison frowned as she searched her memory. "Just a regional weekend edition. It's a small town."

"It's worth a look."

"Maybe. I'll think about it. Thank you."

"No problem. If that doesn't lead to anything, you could always try calling the fire department. You might get lucky and find someone who was there, and there's got to be a report somewhere."

"You've given this some thought."

Jim smiled and shrugged his shoulders. "I like puzzles."

"Oh, I'm a puzzle?"

His face sobered, and he stared at her for a moment. "Yes, you are."

CHAPTER

ELEVEN

"**M**urderer." The whispered voice sounded alien, not human.

The edges of her phone dug into Allison's palm and fingers. Was this a prank call, or did someone know her crimes and was targeting her? For what purpose?

"That's original. What else you got?"

The caller disconnected with a click. Allison gripped the phone against her ear, staring at the honey-colored boards of her bedroom floor. Her hand shook slightly as she lowered the silent phone to her lap. Her bare toe brushed back and forth in a soothing rhythm over the area rug underneath her bed.

If it had been a prankster, then they were remarkably lucky using that approach with her and probably disappointed with her response. If it had been someone intentionally trying to torment her specifically, then again, they probably hadn't expected that reaction from her.

Would it be enough to stop either?

The voice had been distorted too. Was it intentional so she

couldn't recognize the voice? Could it be someone she knew? The number had been blocked. She shouldn't have answered, but she had done so automatically.

Her laptop was on the bureau. It was time to research what she could about the fire and face her past. Maybe it would give her some clue who would call her now after all these years.

No, that made little sense. Too many years had passed. It must have been a random prank call. Karen and Dr. Thompson were the only ones she talked to recently about the fire. Jim knew about the fire, not her role in it. But he might have done his own research and found out. He did say he liked puzzles.

She couldn't picture any of them calling to torment her. The thought was too ridiculous—and depressing.

Allison grabbed her laptop and sat on the bed. She looked out over her backyard while she waited for it to boot up. The first rays of light streaked across the sky as dawn approached. She stared down at the dark shadows of the yard. Her life was full of dark shadows. She wished the sun could chase *her* shadows away.

She'd been lying in bed staring at her ceiling when the phone rang. Another nightmare had come calling and left her wide awake.

Maybe Dr. King would have some wisdom and guidance to impart at her appointment next week. She had followed Dr. Thompson's advice, called his referral, and even picked up the prescription in case he checked.

Of course, the new doctor might believe her paranoid and delusional if she told him about the phone call. When she'd insisted she'd put the candle out, no one had believed her. They told her her mind was protecting her or flat out told her she wasn't telling the truth.

It really was ridiculous to think the call was anything more than a prank.

A spot on one, but still just a gruesome coincidence.

Her computer screen switched to her home screen, a generic

picture of a flower garden, and she clicked on to the Internet. Everything was available online these days. It should at least give her a good idea where to start. Besides, she wanted to know what people would find if they looked.

If they typed in her name, would it say murderer?

She typed her name into the search bar and held her breath.

The screen filled with options. Most were social media accounts. None of them were her, though, because she didn't have one. There were several Allison Delaneys. Who knew?

None of the entries were about her.

She typed in her maiden name and held her breath. Not as many Allison Dunkirks. She scrolled down the entries.

Her parents' obituary. "Survived by their only daughter, Allison Dunkirk."

Tears blurred her vision. She blinked them back. Alan had handled all the details while she recovered from smoke inhalation. The obituary was short and to the point. There was no mention of what wonderful parents and people they had been.

She should have done better.

Another black mark on the scoresheet in her head.

Rubbing the center of her forehead until it hurt, she squeezed her eyes closed. She couldn't change the past. She could only do better moving forward.

A search for newspaper archives provided her with a website to access the articles reporting her parents' deaths. The fire had been reported in the small local paper and the larger circulated town section of the Sunday paper.

Tragic, or some variation of the word, was used repeatedly. She would delete that word from the dictionary if she could so no one could use it ever again.

She gasped when she read the account of how the firefighter saved her. "On the roof? What was I doing on the roof?"

The article speculated that the young woman in question had

crawled out a window before succumbing to smoke. Luckily, she was found before the fire reached her.

Allison saved the articles before putting the laptop aside. Her hands shook.

She didn't remember being on the roof or how she got there. Her bedroom had been upstairs on the opposite side of the house from her father's study, where the fire originated. The garage roof had been just below one of her bedroom windows. Had she climbed out the window and passed out from the smoke like the article said? It didn't trigger any memories. If the fire was already raging in the hall outside her room, the garage roof would have been her only escape. Her other window opened to the backyard and was at least a twenty-foot drop. She would have broken several bones at the very least. If she could have crawled down to the edge of the garage roof, it would have only been ten feet to the ground. She hadn't made it that far, though. If the firefighter hadn't spotted her, she would have died too.

Alan had told her the house was a total loss. There was nothing left of her parents' things, no pictures or other memorabilia. The only things she had were in her dorm room at college—a couple of pictures of her parents and the mosaic table her mother had made for her.

She'd never gone back to the house or what was left of it. Alan had taken care of everything for her. She'd been so grateful for his help.

It had been cowardly hiding from the loss and her responsibilities. Would she still be having these nightmares if she had faced it back then?

Allison frowned. She'd never even thanked the firefighter who rescued her. Was he still associated with the fire department or even still alive? She would make some calls this morning and find out. A belated thank you for her own peace of mind. And maybe he could fill in some gaps in her memory.

Snippets of that day were etched in her memory.

Classes had ended at three-thirty that Friday afternoon. She'd stopped by Alan's office to say goodbye, and he had tried to convince her, once again, to wait and let him accompany her. It had been his idea to visit her parents and talk to them about their relationship, but he wanted to be with her. He worried they would try to influence her to break up with him if he wasn't there.

That was the first argument they'd ever had. She'd felt her parents would be more open to listening to her without Alan's presence. Then they could schedule a visit together later. He'd vehemently disagreed.

She had cried over their argument on the drive home. She'd arrived at her parents' just as they sat down to dinner. Her mother had made her favorite dish, shrimp Alfredo. She hadn't broached the subject of Alan with them because she wanted to wait until she was rested.

They'd talked about her classes and her upcoming finals and graduation. Her father had seemed preoccupied. At the time, she thought it was because of work. Looking back now, it could've been her relationship with Alan.

Her father had gone into his study after dinner while Allison had helped her mother clean up. Her mother had chatted about a project the local garden club she belonged to had started.

After watching her mother's favorite game shows with her, she'd gone into her father's study to read, a practice they'd begun when she was a child. She used to do her homework while he worked. The smell of books and the faintest hint of cigar smoke permeated his office. Mom hated when he smoked, so he would always open the window to hide the smell.

Her mother had come in and said goodnight and kissed her on her cheek. The floral perfume she always wore enveloped her. Her father sat at his desk and glanced up with a smile when she walked in.

She could even describe exactly what they were both wearing that night. Her mother had worn navy blue slacks and a white floral blouse. Her father had on tan slacks and a light blue sweater. She could even recall the scent of the candle she lit before sitting down to read—pumpkin spice.

She'd read less than an hour before the exhausting day caught up with her. Fighting with Alan had taken its toll. She'd blown the candle out, put her book on the table next to it, kissed her father goodnight, and went up to bed.

After that, her memory was blank. The next thing she knew, she woke up in the hospital with Alan at her bedside.

When she'd insisted she had extinguished the candle, he had given her a pitying look and suggested her mind was trying to protect her and not to speak of it anymore.

Maybe she should have pursued it instead of letting the guilt and Alan sway her.

The memory of blowing out the candle was still so clear in her mind.

Allison rubbed the area between her eyes, willing the memories back. She stopped and dropped her hand to her lap. The nightmares stemmed from her memories but were distorted. So if she did remember something, how could she distinguish between nightmare and reality?

JIM USED his hammer to smash the old sheetrock into small enough pieces to fit out the bedroom window and tossed the crumbling sheets into the dumpster waiting below. Clouds of dust hung in the air. The kitchen was finished, and he had moved on to the primary suite upstairs. He tore down the wall between the old bedrooms to open up the space for the suite. It was a dirty, sweaty job, but each board removed was a step closer to his vision.

He stepped back and wiped the sweat from his brow with the back of his arm. White dust coated his skin and jeans. He grabbed his blue T-shirt hanging from his tool belt and wiped his face and chest. He'd removed it when the material had caught on a nail and torn.

The temperature must already be near eighty outside, which meant the bedroom was probably closer to ninety. He guzzled a bottle of water. The condensation made the plastic slick in his hands. The central air system install was scheduled for this week. Once that was in, it would be a lot more pleasant to work upstairs. He finished the water and tossed the empty bottle into a bucket by the door.

He glanced out the window towards Allison's house. It was becoming a habit with him.

Jim frowned and started removing the nails from the next section of wall. He was honest enough with himself to admit he was attracted to his lovely neighbor. There was something alluring about her. His gaze lingered whenever he spotted her. Nothing wrong with looking, but he wasn't about to get romantically involved.

His relationships tended to be short and sweet. In his experience, once the newness wore off, there was a lot less sweet. He didn't want to be around when the whining and demands started.

For some people, marriage seemed to work out fine. It was a personal choice. History had taught him people weren't cut out for the long haul.

His own mother and sister were prime examples. They each had multiple marriages and divorces. He may have lost count, but his sister had just left husband number three, and his mother was up to number five.

The women he met during his football days were no different. It was in people's nature to look out for themselves, whether it was at the expense of someone else or not.

He always made sure whatever woman he got involved with knew the score. It would be a temporary situation for as long as their mutual enjoyment lasted. He'd come close to marriage once, a mistake that didn't bear repeating.

Allison was not the sort of woman who was into casual relationships. Anyone with half a brain could see that. Besides, she was still wrapped up in her husband. She kept his office sealed up like a damn tomb.

No time like the present to put her out of his mind. He pulled off his gloves and stuffed them under his arm. Slipping his phone from his pocket, he scrolled through the contacts until he located Lucas's number and dialed.

"Hey Jim, what's up?"

"Hi, Lucas. How's your schedule look? I've got a job for you. A kitchen reno."

"Since when do you hire out?"

"It's not for me. My new neighbor wants to remodel, and I've got my hands full with my own house, so I said I might know someone. Interested?"

"You talking a total gut job or a refresh?"

"Somewhere in the middle."

"I can look and draw up an estimate. I'm finishing up a basement job this week and have a little time before I start the next project. I can probably schedule her in and have it done in a few months. Think that would work for her?"

"I'm sure it would be fine, but you can work out the details with her."

"I'll get back to you to set up a time to look at the space. Unless you want to give me her number, and I'll call her directly?"

"I'll handle the initial meet, and you can take it from there."

"I appreciate the referral, man."

"Anytime." Jim disconnected the call. He should have just given Allison's number to Lucas and wiped his hands of the project and her, but he felt responsible in a way. She had asked him for the reference, and besides, he needed to be there to explain to Lucas what she wanted done. It was his design.

Once he introduced Lucas and laid out the vision for the kitchen, he'd go back to keeping his distance.

He'd sure miss that baking of hers, though.

He liked the way she blushed too. Her cheeks would go pink, and she would avoid looking at him. He chuckled.

She had a way of looking at him with those big, soulful eyes of hers that made his stomach clench. He was starting to have a thing for those big, white nightgowns of hers too.

Jim stopped and shook his head. Damn, he was fixating on his neighbor again.

CHAPTER

TWELVE

Allison waved goodbye to Bruce and carried the package he delivered to the kitchen. She'd ordered a new cookbook yesterday, but she didn't think it could have arrived already. Besides, the box was too big for one cookbook.

Once she set the box down on the counter, she walked over to the fridge and grabbed the magnetic box opener off the door. A quick slice over the tape released the flaps. She folded them back and moved the paper aside.

Allison gasped and stepped back.

Black candles were nestled inside the box.

She certainly hadn't ordered them. She didn't buy candles—ever. A mistake?

Wrapping her arms around her waist, she took a small step forward and peered into the box. A set of three matching pitch-black candles. No note. No receipt.

Perhaps there was something under the candles or the packaging.

She nibbled on her lip, opened a drawer, and pulled out a spatula. She wasn't touching the damn things if she could avoid it.

81

The spatula fit easily between the paper and box. She used the utensil to push the paper down on all sides and then wedged it under the candles to lift them up.

Nothing.

She tossed the spatula in the sink and frowned.

Okay, someone had sent her black candles. Not threatening by themselves. They're just candles.

Unless someone knew her history.

Allison glared at the box. Could fingerprints be taken from cardboard?

She pulled her phone out of her pocket to search the Internet for the answer but set it on the counter. Literally dozens of people had probably handled the box in transit. Besides, she wasn't calling the police to report someone sending her candles. They would think she was nuts or charge her for a nuisance call.

If she explained why candles were threatening to her, they'd probably think she deserved the treatment. People tended to make harsh judgments. Not that she could entirely blame them. She was responsible for her parents' deaths.

She smacked down the lid of the box and searched the label for a clue of its origin.

Potions and Baubles in New York, New York. A store? For the occult?

Picking up her phone, she looked the store up. Sure enough, it was a store for people interested in witchcraft and other supernatural practices. She found a phone number and dialed. Surely, they kept records of orders and deliveries. If someone called it in or ordered it online, they would need a credit card.

"Potions and Baubles, how can I help you?"

"Hi. I received a delivery, but I didn't order it, and I was wondering if you could tell me who sent it. There's no note or receipt."

"What's your name and address?"

"Allison Delaney. Wigmore Lane, Arlington, Connecticut."

"When and what was delivered?"

"Today. Three black candles."

"Oh, I remember that order. I took it."

"Great, can you tell me who ordered them?"

"'Fraid not. He paid cash."

Damn it!

"You don't keep records of deliveries?"

"Not when they order it in person and pay cash. Is that all? I've got customers."

"How about a description?"

"Don't you have the candles? Look in the box."

Allison grimaced and stared at the ceiling. The voice on the other end of the line sounded young, like a teenager. By the sound of it, she was rapidly losing patience and interest in Allison's dilemma. "Not the candles. A description of the man who bought them."

"Oh, he was tall. But I'm only five feet, so everyone is tall to me."

"How about hair, eye, skin color?"

"Uh...he was wearing a hat and sunglasses. Look, I only remember him at all because he didn't look or act like our usual customers. He came right in, knew what he wanted, and paid cash to have them sent."

Allison sighed. "I appreciate your time. Thank you."

"Sure, no problem—wait, I'm pretty sure he was white."

Pretty sure? "Thanks."

The call ended, and Allison stared at the phone clutched in her hand. The urge to throw it across the room gripped her. Instead, she set it on the counter. She didn't have the time or inclination to go to the store and get a new phone.

Or have to explain how it got damaged in the first place.

She dropped her face into her hands.

When you add in the phone call—well, no one could call her paranoid for thinking someone was terrorizing her.

But who? And why?

CHAPTER

THIRTEEN

When the doorbell rang, Allison froze.

Another delivery? Was she now going to be bombarded with candles or something more terrifying?

No, Bruce wouldn't be returning so soon with another package.

They could've used another delivery service.

Or delivered it themselves?

Allison stalked down the hallway. Well, we'll just see about that. Whoever it was may think they knew what she was capable of, but they had no idea.

She yanked open the door.

Karen stood waiting on the front porch with a smile. "Hi Allison, I brought back your cookie plate. And before you ask, yes, we ate them all already!"

Allison forced a smile to her lips. "You didn't have to do that."

"What's wrong?"

She shook her head. "Nothing."

"Allison, it's written all over your face. What's upset you?"

Sighing, Allison stepped back for Karen to enter. "Come in. Where's Charlie?"

"Oh, he went over to a friend's house to play for a bit, so I thought I'd take a walk to work off some of those delicious cookies of yours and return your plate at the same time."

"Well, I'm glad you liked them. Would you like anything?"

"Just for you to tell me what's bothering you. Unless you'd like me to mind my own business? Though I should warn you, I'm not very good at that where my friends are concerned."

An unbiased opinion on the matter might help her put things into perspective. "Come on back to the kitchen. I made some lemonade earlier. I'll tell you all about it."

"When you say you made, I bet you mean you used actual lemons, don't you? No powder from a can?"

Allison glanced back over her shoulder and smiled. "If I say it's from a powder, will you be completely disillusioned?"

Karen chuckled. "Just a little."

Allison paused at the refrigerator and smiled. "Well then, I'll admit it is fresh-squeezed."

"Hah, I knew it! Allison, you really need to think about selling some of the wonderful food you make."

Allison poured them each a glass and sat down at the kitchen table across from Karen. "I thought about it once a few years ago, but I don't have the faintest idea how to go about it. Alan said it would be too time-consuming and not very profitable."

She shrugged and took a sip of lemonade.

"Mmm...this really is refreshing, thank you." Karen tilted her head at the box on the counter. "What's this?"

"That is the source of my upset."

Karen reached a hand towards the box and hesitated. "Do you mind?"

"Go ahead."

She looked in the box and then back to Allison with raised eyebrows.

"I don't buy candles. Someone sent them to me anonymously. I called the store right before you arrived. All they could tell me was a man wearing a hat and glasses paid cash."

"Well, shit."

Allison laughed. "Yeah, that about sums it up."

"No idea who would do this?"

"Not a clue. I also got a phone call the other day. All they said was 'murderer.'"

Karen's mouth dropped open. She set her lemonade down on the counter and gave Allison a hug.

Allison returned the hug as tears welled in her eyes. She swallowed hard and cleared her throat.

Karen dropped her arms and stepped back. "Did you call the police?"

"No, there's nothing to go on, and if I explain my past or they look it up..." She shrugged and took a drink of her lemonade.

"Honey, you don't deserve this treatment."

Allison leaned her hip against the counter. "What I don't get is why now?"

"Who have you talked to recently about it besides me?"

"I called my father's former partner to get a referral for a local therapist. I have an appointment next week. I researched the fire and found out a firefighter rescued me from the roof of my parents' house. I don't remember that. I only recall waking up in the hospital." Karen rubbed Allison's arm. "So, I called the fire department and found out he still worked there, and I talked to him. Turns out I was his first rescue, and he remembered it well. Anyway, they're the only ones I've talked to about the fire besides Jim. And unless he looked it up himself, he doesn't know I was responsible for the fire."

"How much do you know about your neighbor?"

"Pretty much just what I've told you. You don't think he would do this, do you?"

"I hope not, but I don't know him. But we can change that."

"What do you mean?"

"Look him up on the Internet. Almost everyone has something listed about them. And if he has any social media profiles, all the better."

"He used to play professional football."

Karen glanced up from her phone. "Well, that should make it easier."

"I really don't think Jim would do something like this."

"Good. Let's hope your instincts are right, but it doesn't hurt to do some digging."

Allison sighed. "It feels wrong."

"What's wrong is some psychopath is calling you and sending you things in the mail."

"Thank you."

"For what?"

"For caring and listening."

Karen gave her a one-armed hug and leaned her head against hers. "Anytime, and I genuinely mean that. You're not alone. Don't ever think you have to deal with things by yourself."

"You have no idea how much that means to me." She'd been on her own a long time.

"I can't imagine not having my family around. They're my rock." Karen's nails tapped away on her phone. "I'm not seeing much more than football stats and such. He doesn't have any social media accounts, which is kind of weird."

"Is it? I don't either."

Karen peeked up at her, then raised her head completely. "You're right. I was making assumptions because he was in the public eye and because almost everyone these days has an account somewhere. I can see how it wouldn't suit you, though. You're private."

"I also don't have the friends and family to share posts with."

"This was a cursory look, but he appears normal. Maybe I should stroll over and pay him another visit. See if I get a stalker vibe from him."

Allison snorted. "I really don't think he fits the label."

"You're probably right, but I'll feel better if I check into it." She looked out the window onto the porch. "How about we sit outside on your porch and enjoy the rest of the lemonade?"

"Sure, can we change the subject, though? I've had enough drama for one day."

"Yes, absolutely, but let me fill my glass with more of that delicious lemonade first."

"I'll get it." Allison took the glass and filled it.

Frowning, Karen placed her hands on her hips. "I just had a thought. Bear with me as I mull it over a moment."

Allison smiled. A questioning wrinkle appeared between her brows. "Okay."

Karen took the glass of lemonade and took a sip. "It's completely unrelated to the harassment. Let's go on the porch."

They walked out to the porch and sat. Allison took the wicker chair while Karen sat on the couch.

She tapped her nails against the glass and pursed her lips. "What would you say to making some baked goods to sell at my place? I could set up a display by the entrance. It is called Guilty Pleasures, after all, and if your baking doesn't fit the title, I don't know what does."

Allison gaped for a second before quickly snapping her mouth closed. She bit her lip and stared at Karen's smiling face. "I...I'm not sure. I...wow...I don't know what to say."

"Think about it. The more I do, the more I like the idea. We could start out small, just a few items for variety. You would need to figure out the pricing, of course. I'll check if we'd need a permit to sell food."

Karen tapped her red-polished finger to her matching lip. "I'd take, say, twenty percent. Since it's my place and my people ringing up and boxing up the sales."

She sat back and crossed her legs. "What do you think? If it worked out well, we could make a bigger display area for you. Maybe move it into the small gift area I have upstairs."

Allison was at a loss. She didn't know how to respond. Selling her baked goods? What if no one wanted any? She grimaced. No more negativity. If nobody bought any, she simply wouldn't make anymore. Karen said they would start out small and see how it went. Nothing ventured, nothing gained.

"All right, yes. I like it. If you're sure you want to take the chance, then so am I."

Karen grinned. "What chance? We're just going to put out a few incredibly delicious treats for my customers to indulge in. If they don't fly out of the place, I'll be sincerely shocked."

Allison chuckled. "I wish I had an ounce or two of your confidence."

Karen leaned forward. "Listen, you just need to ask yourself what is the worst that can happen. And then once you've imagined the worst and realized it's not so bad, it's a cakewalk. No pun intended."

"That sounds like a good plan, although I can imagine some pretty harsh scenarios at times. But if we're starting out small, I don't really see what harm it will do. Except if no one buys anything, of course."

"Trust me, Allison, as soon as someone samples what you can do, they'll sell."

"When did you want to start?"

"Well, I'd say that's up to you. You need to figure out what you'd like to start with and how much to charge to make it worth your while. On my end, I just need to drag a shelf I have out of storage and make a little room."

Allison sifted through her favorite recipes in her mind. Things she'd made dozens of times that were full proof. She didn't want to try out new recipes, at least not at first.

"I think maybe some cookies, muffins, maybe a brownie or bar cookie to start. How about some cake slices? Nothing that needs to be refrigerated, of course."

"See, sounds perfect." Karen reached her hand across the low table between the couch and chair. "I'd say we've got ourselves a deal. What do you think?"

Allison smiled and shook Karen's hand. "Yes, we have a deal. Thank you, Karen."

"Thank you. I plan on having your treats bring in some more customers for me!"

"I think this is just what I was looking for. Lately, I've been thinking about what to do with myself. I've considered getting a job to help knock me back into society, but I admit it lacks appeal."

"Who could blame you? Unless you need the money, who wants a job? We all need something to fulfill us, but a job implies doing something out of necessity, not enjoyment."

"Absolutely, that's it exactly. I want to do something, but I want it to be something I enjoy. I'm lucky enough, or unlucky, depending on how you look at it, to not need to work. My parents and husband left me financially comfortable."

Karen reached out and squeezed Allison's hand. "Honey, you've seen plenty of sorrow. It's a good thing to have the financial wherewithal to do what you want with your life. You can certainly begrudge its source, but don't let that stop you from enjoying it."

She patted Allison's hand and sat back in her chair, taking another sip of her lemonade.

"I'll have to ask Jim for that referral for the kitchen remodel we talked about. I'll need an updated kitchen if this business venture goes well."

"What remodel?"

"When I saw what a wonderful job he did with his kitchen, I started thinking about my own, which hasn't been touched in years. I asked him for his opinion."

"And?"

"Oh well, actually, he has a lot of ideas. Changing the cabinets a bit, putting in granite countertops. He talked about opening the kitchen into the dining room. Putting in French doors to the porch and moving the table over to the area by the office."

Karen swiveled her head and peered down the length of the porch towards the office window. "Office? Is that what that window goes to?"

Allison nodded. "Yes, it's Alan's office."

"I've noticed the closed door off the kitchen before. I didn't realize it was his office."

"Um...it's locked actually, has been since Alan died."

Karen stared at Allison for a long moment. "Allison, honey, don't you think if you're going to move forward, you need to unlock that door and clean everything out?"

"It was his sick room the last couple of years." Allison took a deep breath and let it out slowly. "They came and removed the hospital bed and medical equipment shortly after he passed away. All that's left in there is his desk, a file cabinet, and bookshelves full of his books."

The room had reeked of sickness. The antiseptic smell of disinfectant. The citrus-scented bathing wipes. The lotion she had used to moisturize his skin.

Allison swallowed hard and looked back at Karen. "I just couldn't bear to go in there anymore."

Karen's eyes glistened. "Of course, you couldn't then, but what about now? I'll help you."

Could she do it? Was she ready to walk into that room again? It had become such a dismal place. The oppression like a thick blanket on her shoulders every time she'd stepped into the room. So, she'd locked the door and did her best to forget.

"You're right. It's time."

CHAPTER

FOURTEEN

The file slipped off her lap and slapped onto the floor, spilling papers in a fan shape. Allison put the rest of the files from her lap onto the one remaining clear spot on the desk and crouched down to stuff the papers back into the file.

Yesterday, Karen had spent a few hours helping her sort through the major items in Alan's office. There was a stack of boxes by the door full of books she was donating to the college where he worked. Someone was due by tomorrow to pick them up.

She was working her way through the file cabinet. The garbage overflowed with papers. Alan kept receipts and documentation on everything. There were files for instruction manuals, every household account or subject you could think of, and miscellaneous folders filled with an assortment of papers. She never knew Alan was a packrat when it came to files. He hadn't been that way with other things or memorabilia.

The instruction manuals might be useful. She could have used one for the lawnmower or the Wi-Fi router when it stopped working a couple of months ago. Instead, she had called for a service technician who spent five minutes pushing a couple of buttons and left after charging her sixty dollars.

Allison sighed. The likelihood of her searching through manuals to learn how to fix an appliance was slim to none. There were better uses of her time.

The word "arson" on one of the papers on the floor caught her eye. She picked up the paper. It was a report on the fire which killed her parents.

Why did Alan have this? More importantly, why had she never seen this?

She scanned over the document. The point of origin had been her father's study, which she'd known.

The cause of the fire was a candle left burning. Had she really hallucinated blowing the candle out to ease her guilt, or had the candle somehow reignited? Was that even possible?

The high carbon monoxide levels in her parents' blood and their positions in the house led to a cause of death determined to be smoke inhalation. They speculated her father had fallen asleep at his desk. Her mother had been asleep in their bedroom above his study.

Allison leaned back on her heels with the papers clenched in her hands. Should she be thankful the smoke killed them before the fire could? Did it mean they suffered less?

More questions raised.

Maybe it was time to return to her parents' house. At least what was left of it. She still owned the property. She could never bring herself to sell it, or maybe she held onto it as a reminder of her guilt.

Like she needed one.

Someone opened the back porch door and walked in. Allison stood and stuck her head out the open window of the office to see who it was. Jim stood at the back door with his hand raised to knock.

"Hi."

Jim turned his head and spotted her. "Hey there."

"Come on in. The door's open." She pulled her head back into the room as he opened the door.

She glanced down at her navy shorts and pink T-shirt—not exactly a fashion statement, but she hadn't planned on company. Before he appeared in the doorway, she put the papers down on top of the file on the floor to look at later and brushed dust off her shorts.

He stopped in the opening and smiled.

Her hands froze in the act of wiping any dust or dirt off her butt. A tingle spread across her chest and down to her core.

Jim's navy-blue T-shirt hugged the musculature of his arms and chest. A lock of brown hair fell over his forehead. He reached up to push it back, and his bicep flexed. *God, he was attractive!*

She swallowed hard. When had it gotten so warm in here? She should turn on the air conditioning.

His smile turned into a grin.

"What?" He couldn't possibly have noticed her reaction to him. She hadn't even blushed, had she? Of course, heat immediately radiated over her cheeks.

Her hands were still cupping her butt. She dropped them.

"You've been on a cleaning binge, I see." He walked into the room and around the desk.

"Uh, yes."

"There's a cobweb or two stuck in your hair."

Allison went still. Horror raced through her.

Ice cold washed over her skin. She began to shake.

"G...g...get it out."

The smile disappeared off Jim's face and was replaced by concern. "Okay, take it easy." He pulled the translucent strands from her hair while Allison trembled. "There's no spider, just the remnants of its home."

A whoosh of breath rushed from her mouth.

"Not a fan of spiders, huh?"

A shudder shook her body. She dropped her face into her hands.

Jim wrapped his arms around her and rubbed her back.

Allison rested her head against his shoulder and sighed. "I despise them."

He chuckled. "I noticed."

"Sorry." She raised her head.

"No need to apologize. Everyone is afraid of something." He tucked a strand of hair behind her ear. His finger left a trail of heat across her cheekbone.

Her mouth suddenly dry, she licked her lips.

His gaze tracked the movement, and then he lowered his arms and stepped back.

"What are you afraid of?"

"Huh?"

"You said everyone is afraid of something."

"Oh, um, snakes. Can't stand them."

"I'm not a fan of those either, but spiders are worse. They're sneakier. You never know when one will be right there, ready to attack. I read once you're never more than six feet away from a spider. How horrifying is that?"

He smiled. "Well, at least you don't live somewhere like Australia. They've got humongous spiders."

"Don't tell me! I don't want the picture in my head."

Jim laughed. "Okay."

Allison sidestepped him. "Do you want something to drink? I've got some fresh lemonade."

"Love some."

He followed her into the kitchen and leaned against the peninsula with his hands gripping the edge while she got a couple of glasses and poured them both lemonades.

"I got in touch with Lucas, the builder I told you about. He's available to work on your kitchen. He said he could come out tomorrow and look if that works for you."

"Oh, yes, that's fine. What time?" She handed him a glass.

"Thanks. In the morning. Ten okay?"

Allison nodded. "All right, is there anything I need to know before he gets here? Is he going to have specific questions or anything?"

Jim took a sip and looked at the glass. "This is great." He glanced around the kitchen. "Lucas is just going to look and ask what you want done. He'll give you an estimate, and then you can decide if it's something you want to do. If so, he'll let you know when he can start. Simple, not rocket science."

"Okay. Are you going to be here?" Allison frowned. "I mean, the changes I want to make are really the suggestions you made."

"Yeah, I could do that if you want."

"Thank you."

Allison bit her lip and looked up. "I was also wondering if it was possible to add some cabinets to the wall over there."

She pointed to the wall between the kitchen and office. "I've always wanted more storage space, and if I'm going to be changing the kitchen, now seems like the time."

"You could do that. If more cabinet space is what you want, you could forgo the entry into the dining room from here and make the kitchen U-shaped instead of L-shaped. You have enough space for an island too."

He walked over to the back door. "If you're replacing this door and window to the porch with French doors, that space by the wall would be nice for a table. It would also make all your cabinets more accessible if they're closer together and not spread out to the other side of the room."

Allison turned slowly around her kitchen, trying to picture the changes. There was certainly enough space to add cabinets to this side of the kitchen if she moved the table. An entryway into the dining room from the kitchen would be convenient, but she didn't entertain much. The extra cabinet and countertop space would be more useful.

"I like that much better."

"The French doors will allow a lot more light into your kitchen too."

"I can't wait to get started. Now that I might start a little business venture, the expanded kitchen will be an immense help."

"What business venture?"

"Oh, Karen suggested I sell baked goods at her place in town, Guilty Pleasures."

"I'll be a regular customer. I'm sure it will be a hit."

"Thanks. You want to be a taste tester?"

"Sign my taste buds up."

"Good. I'll need to test my recipes before presenting them to the public for sale."

"Happy to sacrifice for the greater good."

Allison laughed. "Sacrifice?"

Jim winked. "I'm a helpful kind of guy."

"Yes, you are."

"Speaking of which, I noticed you have a pile of boxes in the office. You need me to move them somewhere for you?"

"Thanks, but someone from my husband's college is coming to pick them up."

He drank the rest of his lemonade and placed the glass in the sink. "In that case, I better get back to work on my own place."

Allison trailed behind him to the back door. "Thank you for everything. I'll see you tomorrow."

He strode across her lawn to his own. His long jean encased legs ate up the distance. Her gaze strayed to the way the denim cupped his ass.

Lifting the chilled glass, she held it against her warm cheeks.

She followed her instincts and believed Jim couldn't be involved with whoever was terrorizing her. Karen hadn't found anything during her search, and he'd done nothing suspicious.

Yes, she was attracted to him, but that wasn't influencing her judgment. Was it?

The idea was as ludicrous as believing Karen could be responsible.

CHAPTER
FIFTEEN

"Hey man, how are you?"

Jim shook Lucas' outstretched hand. "Not bad, you?"

"Hell, you know me—livin' the dream." Lucas propped his hands on his hips and grinned. "As long as my belly is full, there's a game to watch, and a beer waiting with my name on it at the end of the day, I'm a happy man."

Jim chuckled and stepped out of the doorway. "Come on in. You can see my latest project before we head on over to my neighbor's house."

Lucas followed him down the hallway to the kitchen. "Damn, you've been busy." He peered at the cabinets and opened a couple of drawers. "Are these original?"

"Yeah, they were in decent shape—just needed to be sanded down and stained."

"Nice work. How long you estimate this house is going to take you?"

"Originally, I thought it would run around a year, but it might be earlier. Things are progressing at a good pace."

Jim showed Lucas through the rest of the house before they stepped out the backdoor.

"Looks like you've got another winner here."

"Thanks. The house had great bones. It just needed a little TLC to bring it back to life."

Lucas lifted his chin. "That the neighbor's house you want me to take a look at?"

Jim looked over his shoulder at Allison's house. "Yeah." He checked his watch. It was five after ten o'clock already. "We should probably head on over. I told her we'd be there at ten."

The two strode across his backyard and onto her lawn.

Allison opened the backdoor to the screen porch and stepped down. She must have been watching for them.

He lifted his hand in a wave as she opened the screen door and held it open for them. "Good morning."

"Morning Allison, this is Lucas Jacobs. Lucas—Allison Delaney."

Allison smiled. "Nice to meet you, Mr. Jacobs. Please come in." She stepped back to allow them in.

Lucas stopped in front of her and held out his hand. "Call me Lucas. May I call you Allison? Or how bout Ally?" When she took his hand, he enveloped her hand with both of his.

Jim frowned.

"Um...either's fine, I guess."

"Ally, it is then." He let her hand go with a squeeze and a grin.

Jim folded his arms across his chest.

Allison walked over to the backdoor and stepped up into the kitchen. "Can I offer either of you anything? I made a coffee cake. It's apple streusel."

Lucas rubbed his hands together and followed her. "Count me in. Jim, you didn't tell me your neighbor could cook or that she was so pretty."

Jim glanced at Allison when he entered the kitchen. She stood at the counter, slicing into a cake on a wire rack. Her cheeks were pink.

"Allison is a fabulous cook, but you're here to look at her kitchen and office."

"I can do both." Lucas leaned his elbow and forearm on the counter opposite Allison.

Allison served them each a piece of cake without meeting their gazes. After pouring the lemonade, she wiped down the already clean counter.

"Mmm—this is pure heaven, Ally! Where have you been all my life?"

She blushed once again and smiled at Lucas.

Was she attracted to him? Jim glanced at him shoveling a spoonful of cake into his mouth while still managing to grin at her.

He supposed women would find the blond, blue-eyed guy attractive.

A little on the short side. though. Jim topped him by a few inches.

He took a bite of the moist cake. Apple and cinnamon filled his mouth. "It's delicious as always, Allison."

She murmured, "Thank you."

Jim finished his cake and brought his plate to the sink. She reached out to take it from him, but he set it in the sink and turned to her. His gaze traveled over her features. The blush had faded. There were faint shaded crescents under her eyes.

Was she still not sleeping well?

Lucas joined them at the sink. "I haven't had something this tasty in a while."

"I'm glad you like it. Would you like another piece?"

"Maybe after I look at the work you want done. We can get the business out of the way first."

Lucas walked around the kitchen, briefly inspecting the cabinets and scanning the walls. "Jim said you wanted to add more cabinets?"

Allison glanced at him, probably waiting for him to explain the changes they'd discussed, but he leaned against the counter and folded his arms. He was only here as backup. No point in involving himself any more than he already had. It wasn't like he would be on site when the work was being done.

"Uh...yes, I'd like the cabinets to wrap around to this wall. I'll move the table over to the space by the office. And I'd like a long island."

Lucas took measurements and then stepped back and nodded. "Okay, I don't see any problems with that. You've got plenty of space. What else?"

Warming to the topic, she walked over to the back door and laid her hand against the glass. "I'd like to put French doors here. I also want to update the countertop to granite and get rid of all this white."

"All pretty straightforward. What about the office?"

Allison walked into the office with Lucas close behind her. Jim stepped through the doorway and leaned against the wall.

"I'd like to put a bigger window on this wall and extend the shelves the length of the wall."

Lucas walked over to the wall behind the desk and looked back over his shoulder. "How big of a window do you want?"

"I want it big enough to enjoy the view of the backyard."

Lucas looked at the wall and then walked towards the door. "I just want to take a quick look at the other side of the wall."

"Okay." Allison took a few steps to follow him.

Jim stepped in front of her. "Did you have a nightmare last night?"

She stopped and stared at him. "No, actually, I didn't." She glanced at the doorway and back to him.

"That's good. Any more news?"

"News?"

"Yeah, did you research the fire?"

"Oh..." Allison frowned and nibbled on her lip. "I did a bit—yes."

Lucas returned. "I don't see any problem. You can put a decent size window here. Anything else?"

Allison shook her head. "I don't think so."

"I'll work up an estimate and get back to you. I can probably start in a week or two if it works for you. Sound good?"

"Yes, that sounds great. What about colors and choices like that? Do you need to know those now for your estimate?"

Lucas shook his head and smiled. "Nah, we'll go over the cosmetic stuff later. I'll show you some different choices in the estimate and the price difference."

"Okay, thank you for coming."

"My pleasure. Now, how about another piece of that cake?"

"Oh, of course." Allison turned to Jim. "Would you like another piece?"

Jim shook his head and frowned at Lucas. Lucas either didn't see or ignored him because he grinned at Allison and waved a hand for her to precede him out the door.

She cut another slice of cake for Lucas and handed it to him. He smiled at her and said, "thanks," before taking a bite. Instead of taking his plate to the table, Lucas remained standing in front of Allison as he continued to eat.

Allison settled against the corner of the counter with her hands grasping the edges and glanced over to Jim. "You sure you don't want another piece?"

Jim stood by the back door with his arms crossed across his chest. "I'm sure."

"Would you like to take the rest of the cake with you, Lucas?"

He polished off the last bite and grinned. "That's a very kind offer, Ally. I'd love to. I might have to give you a discount if you're going to supply me with such wonderful food."

Allison smiled. "I'll take it."

Lucas chuckled and stepped closer to her. He leaned over to put the plate in the sink with his gaze on her the entire time.

He put his hands on his hips. "I'll work up the estimate today. How about I come over tonight and go over it with you?"

Jim cleared his throat. "A phone call will suffice, Lucas. Let's go. You have a job to finish if you're going to be available for this one."

Lucas continued to stare at Allison while he smiled. "Good point Jim. The sooner I finish up that job, the sooner I can come back here. I'll be in touch, Ally." He gave her a two-finger salute and walked to the door.

Jim opened the door and waited for him to step out onto the porch. He nodded in Allison's direction and followed Lucas out the door.

Once they had crossed back to Jim's lawn, Lucas glanced over his shoulder with a full smile plastered on his face. "Damn Jim, why didn't you tell me your neighbor was a smokin' hot woman? This job just keeps getting better and better."

"Cool off. She's a widow and not your type."

Lucas reared his head back. "I don't have a type. How recent a widow?"

"I don't know. What does it matter? A year or two, I think. The point is, she's the happily ever after type, not the fool-around-with kind. So dial back the flirtation. She's a job, not a woman for you to pick up."

"There's no reason I can't do both, is there?"

"Yes, she's a widow, damn it."

Lucas chuckled. "Again, I fail to see your point."

Jim gritted his teeth and fisted his hands at his sides. "She's grieving for her husband. She doesn't need you sniffing around, making her uncomfortable. I recommended you to do a job for her. Did I make a mistake?"

Lucas raised his eyebrows. "What exactly is the problem here, Jim?

"Leave her alone. If you can't do the job without making a play for her, don't take the job."

"So it would be okay if I turned down the job but still asked her out?"

Jim gritted his teeth. "No. I told you she's grieving for her husband."

Lucas smiled and put his hands in his pants pockets. "Well, if she's not interested, she can always say no. Maybe going out for a nice dinner is just what she needs."

"How the hell would you know what she needs?"

Lucas grinned. "Jim, if I didn't know you better, I'd say you were jealous. What exactly is your interest in Ally, anyway?"

Jim unclenched his fists and ran a hand through his hair. *Jesus, Lucas was right. He was acting like a jealous idiot.*

He hadn't liked Lucas flirting with Allison one bit. She hadn't been encouraging Lucas with her soft smiles and innocent blushes. She wasn't ready to start dating. Hell, when he'd first seen the open office door, he'd wondered if she was trying to tell him something. But then he realized he was reading too much into it. She was just taking the next step in her grief. She was beginning to let go, but that didn't mean she was ready to date.

"Look, she's not your type, okay."

Lucas snorted. "Unlike you, I don't have a type. She's a classy lady with all the right parts. She's nice to look at and a hell of a good cook. I'd be a fool not to be interested."

Jim frowned and stared at Lucas. Who was he to decide whether or not Lucas could ask her out? Lucas was right. If she wasn't interested, she could just say no.

There was always the chance she might say yes. His fists clenched once again. It wasn't his business. She was just his neighbor, nothing more. "Do what you want. Just don't come on too strong."

They reached Lucas' truck parked in the driveway, and he turned and leaned against the door. "You sure I'm not poaching here? You seem to be taking quite an interest in her. It's not like you to get so involved with your temporary neighbors."

Jim considered telling Lucas Allison was off-limits, but that wouldn't be fair to her. If she was interested in Lucas, it should be her choice. She was a grown woman, and Lucas was a nice guy. He'd had a couple of serious long-term relationships in the past. He wasn't just into casual relationships.

"There's nothing between us. I've just been helping her out a bit is all."

"Okay, I didn't think she was your type."

Lucas opened the door and climbed into the cab. He started the truck and rolled down the window.

"So we're cool? You're okay with me asking Ally out?"

Jim frowned. "Her name's Allison."

Lucas shook his head and reversed down the driveway.

Jim watched him go, frowning the entire time.

CHAPTER

SIXTEEN

The sweet aroma of baking filled the kitchen. Allison pulled the last batch of muffins from the oven and set them on the rack to cool.

Dirty bowls, measuring paraphernalia, and pans overflowed the sink. Dozens of muffins sat cooling on all available counter space. A laugh built from her chest and erupted from her throat. She covered her mouth with one hand and her shaking midsection with the other. Splashes of flour and an assortment of other ingredients covered her blue apron.

Since early morning, she'd been in a baking frenzy. She'd been trying old recipes and making minor changes here and there as she imagined what might tempt Karen's clients.

At first, she'd intended to make just a couple, maybe a blueberry and apple muffin to start. It'd been years since she tried the recipes, after all. However, once she started, she couldn't seem to stop. Ideas kept coming. Apple cinnamon muffins with a caramel glaze, blueberry muffins with a streusel top, pumpkin spice muffins with a sugar glaze, chocolate strawberry muffins dotted with chocolate morsels, and lemon raspberry muffins covered her counters and small table.

Her laughing jag tapered off, and she rested her hands on her hips. Well, when inspiration struck, you had to go with the flow, and she'd certainly done that. Now, what on earth was she going to do with all these muffins?

Of course, she would bring some to Karen to see if she thought her clients would like them. After all, that was the whole point of this venture.

She hummed as she loaded the dishwasher.

There were baskets in the closet she could use to display the muffins. She would fill one with an assortment of the muffins and bring it to Karen. Perhaps she could fill a larger basket and bring it to the senior center in town. It might even generate some buzz for her muffins.

Maybe making some samples to hand out at businesses in town would be a good idea. She could make a little card to go in the baskets so that people would know to go to Guilty Pleasures if they wished to make a purchase. She would run her idea by Karen and see what she thought.

I'm beginning to think like a businesswoman!

A chuckle escaped her as she designed labels and business cards in her head.

Allison let herself in the back door and dropped her car keys on the counter. She was riding high on all the gushing compliments over her muffins. Giving in to the urge to bring the muffins to town proved successful.

Her first stop was Guilty Pleasures. Karen and her employees and clients had all sampled the muffins and raved about them. When she shared her idea of dropping off samples to businesses, Karen liked the idea so much she insisted on going along, much to Allison's surprise. They dropped off samples at local professional offices, the senior center, and a gift shop. At all stops, they encountered nothing but positive responses.

Not every endeavor was likely to be so rewarding or positive, but this was certainly a splendid start.

She checked her voicemail to see if she'd missed any calls since her phone had been silenced while visiting potential customers.

"Hi Ally, it's Lucas Jacobs. I have that estimate for you. I was hoping to reach you so we could go over it. Call me when you get in."

Positive changes abounded today. She absently deleted the message. She'd call him back later.

Her attention rested on the basket of remaining muffins sitting on her table. When she left the basket there this morning, she knew she intended to bring them to Jim. Even if she hadn't quite admitted it to herself.

A small smile lifted the corners of her lips. He'd volunteered to be a taste tester.

She enjoyed Jim's company, and if she enjoyed looking at him too? Well, there was nothing wrong with that either. She enjoyed the view of her backyard too. Of course, her backyard didn't make her insides melt or make her palms grow damp.

Allison popped into the downstairs bathroom to check her appearance. After finger-combing her hair, she reminded herself it was time she picked up some makeup.

She smoothed the front of the sage green blouse and the pleats of her tan shorts before picking up the basket of muffins and heading out the back door.

It took her less than a minute to cross over to his back door and knock. She prepared a quick greeting and explanation of her visit in her head as she waited for him to answer the door.

The door swung open, and her brain shut down.

Her eyes were level with his chest. His wet, sculpted, bare chest.

Her mouth watered as her gaze wandered lower to encounter a pair of swim trunks barely gripping his lean hips.

Allison swallowed hard and quickly shot her gaze to his face. His hair hung thick and wet across his forehead. He obviously just came from the shower.

"Hey Allison, those for me?"

A puff of air was her only response. She cleared her throat and tried again. "I...hmm." She fixed her gaze an inch or two over his left shoulder. "Yes."

He took the basket from her. "Thanks, they look great."

She loved how the corner of his mouth hitched up into a smile, and a small dimple appeared. She blinked rapidly and looked away again. Had the temperature suddenly spiked? Perspiration broke out on the back of her neck.

Allison raised her hand to fan herself but caught herself in time and stuffed her hands into the pockets of her shorts.

Stop acting like a hormonal teenager! Concentrate.

"Oh, and I need Lucas's number."

"What for?"

His sharp reply brought her gaze abruptly back to his face. His eyes narrowed, and he frowned. What was wrong?

"He left a message that he had the estimate. I accidently deleted the voicemail and my recent calls list before I realized I didn't have his number."

The tension left Jim's face, and he nodded. "Come on in." He stepped back, allowing a small space for her to enter. A spicy scent teased her nostrils as she brushed past him.

Allison inhaled sharply and fought the impulse to linger next to him. Instead, she continued past him into the kitchen.

The transformation he made in this kitchen amazed her all over again. She ran a hand along the granite countertop. Now that it was complete, she could appreciate all the little touches beyond the cabinets and flooring, like the copper pulls, farmhouse sink, and pendant lights over the peninsula. The appliances were all new and stainless steel.

"This kitchen is beautiful."

"Thanks." He placed the basket of muffins down. "Can I get you anything?"

Jim walked over to the refrigerator and peeked inside. "I've got beer, milk, coffee, water." He looked over his shoulder and waited for her response.

"Um...water, please."

He nodded and shut the door. Allison watched the play of muscles across his shoulders and back as he turned and reached for a glass and filled it from the built-in water dispenser.

She murmured her thanks and gladly took a generous swallow to ease her dry throat.

"So, what's the story with the muffins?"

Allison tried to grasp the question, but her mind was currently mush. "Uh...muffins?"

His chuckle was rough. It set the butterflies fluttering in her stomach. "Yeah, muffins. Are they for your friend's spa?"

"Oh right, yes, I started with muffins. We also dropped samples off at some businesses in town and got a good response. Hopefully, word of mouth will spread, and people will stop in and buy once I'm up and running."

"Giving out samples is a clever idea. Once people taste what you can do, they'll be itching to buy more. Speaking of which, I've got to try one."

His arm brushed against her shoulder as he reached past and plucked an apple muffin from the basket.

He consumed the muffin in three bites. They weren't quick bites, though. He savored each one thoroughly before taking another.

Allison finished her water and placed the empty glass on the counter next to her. She rubbed her damp palms against her shorts.

"That was fantastic. Any time you want me to sample something, just let me know. I'll be more than happy to help."

Allison laughed, as he meant her to do.

"Careful. I intend to take you up on that offer. You're probably going to be sick of seeing me at your door with a plate or basket full of some sweet concoction."

"Not possible," he whispered.

Her gaze flew to his. His intense stare made her breath catch. She dropped her gaze, only to have her attention snatched by a droplet of water cascading down his still damp chest.

She tracked its path through the sparsely sprinkled hair on his chest and down the ridges of his abs.

The droplet dipped below the waistband of his precariously placed shorts.

He was aroused.

Good lord, she was ogling him as he stood right in front of her!

Her cheeks were on fire. Heat even scalded the tips of her ears.

Allison tensed and gripped the counter behind her for support.

She looked up. His gaze was pinned on her.

He closed the distance between them and caged her in, his palms flat on the counter on either side of her. He stared into her eyes a moment longer before lowering his attention to her lips. She couldn't help but lick them.

A rough sound rumbled from his throat.

His head lowered, and he captured her moistened lips with his own.

Shock, then pleasure spread through her system.

He licked at her lips, and she gasped, giving him the entry he sought. The sweet taste of apple burst in her mouth.

Jim cupped her cheeks in his palms and deepened the kiss.

A moan reverberated in her mouth as she gave in to the temptation she'd had for so long and spread her hands over his chest.

Allison let her hands explore the path her eyes had traversed earlier.

He stiffened briefly, and a harsh groan echoed through his chest. His hands clasped her waist and brought her body into full contact with his. He angled his head and turned his attention to her neck.

She couldn't think, only feel, as every hard edge of his body molded to hers.

His hands began a journey of their own, caressing her touch starved curves.

Allison's breaths came in gasps. Her nerve endings were electrified. Everywhere he touched, she sizzled.

Her body yearned for closer contact. She wrapped her arms around his neck and delved her fingers into the thick hair at his nape. Stretching up onto her tiptoes, she matched their bodies.

His palms pressed against her back, creating a delicious friction.

When was the last time she'd felt so wanted?

So alive?

A shiver went through her, and her breath caught. What was she doing?

Her hands dropped to his shoulders, and she pulled her mouth back.

Jim loosened his hold on her as she stared at his chin.

Why couldn't her mind have stayed numb with pleasure a little while longer?

"Should I apologize?" His voice whispered against her forehead.

Allison shook her head but pulled out of his arms. "I better go."

She saw him nod out of the corner of her eye as she walked out the door.

CHAPTER

SEVENTEEN

A pencil flew across the room, and a metal ruler bounced against the floor, ringing harshly. Jim stalked out of the bathroom and went straight to his bedroom window.

He'd tried measuring the bathroom wall for tile he wanted to install, but his thoughts kept wandering. He'd measured the same area a half a dozen times before he gave up.

With one arm resting high against the wall and the other hand on his hip, he looked out the window towards the source of his frustration. She was home and awake. The lights went on early this morning, and she didn't drive away in her car because he'd been listening.

Jim shook his head and ran a hand over his face. He was becoming obsessed.

He didn't consider himself a vain man, but he'd never had a problem attracting women. They tended to make themselves readily available. Maybe too available.

Was that the attraction to Allison? Was it because she was so different from other women he'd been involved with?

No, he didn't think so. There was just something about her that drew him in, and now that he'd had a taste of the passion simmering inside her, he wanted more. A whole lot more.

It was a bad idea, a colossally stupid one.

The drone of an engine stopping and starting preceded the familiar white box of the mail truck driving down the road. It halted at his decrepit mailbox and deposited a stack of mail. The rusted, dented gray contraption listed to the side, and the post it sat on was probably rotted. It needed to be replaced sooner rather than later, before age and gravity won, and the mailbox ended up in the dirt or the road.

Jim jogged down the stairs and out the front door. Maybe something in the mail would take his mind off Allison.

The lid opened with a screech and a hard tug. He sifted through the assortment of junk and bills, and his hand hesitated when a pale pink envelope slid across the glossy cover of a sports magazine.

It could be another advertisement, but the hard knot forming in his gut said otherwise. The loopy handwriting and Boston postmark confirmed it.

He shoved the lid closed and stalked up the front walk and inside.

Once upon a time, he would have avoided handling the envelope for fear of damaging any potential evidence. He would carefully slide it into a plastic bag and hand it off to his manager to deal with. But those days were in the past. The police never found anything, and he no longer needed a manager or agent.

The messages had tapered off after he had quit football, only to start up again a few years ago. The first time he'd gone to the police again, but it never went anywhere. He'd moved to a new house he intended to flip and hoped that would be enough of a deterrent. Each time he finished a house and moved on, he'd have a few months of reprieve before the envelopes would start arriving.

This one came quicker.

He glanced from the garbage can to the envelope sitting on top of the pile he tossed onto the kitchen counter. It belonged in the trash.

Swiping it off the stack, he carried it over to the garbage. Seconds ticked by while he stood with the envelope clenched in his fist, hovering over the open can.

Shit!

Flowery perfume wafted up when he ripped open the flap. His nose wrinkled, and he shook the envelope over the counter to see what it contained.

A pair of panties had been part of the contents one too many times before.

Only a piece of paper drifted out and landed on the counter this time.

The same loopy handwriting centered the thick paper.

When will you see me?
When will you hear me?
When will you know me?
I breathe for you.
I exist for you.
I will do anything for you.

Jim recoiled. A sour taste coated his tongue, and acid burned his gut. Crazy Cathy had found him.

Her name wasn't really Cathy, or at least he didn't think so. Wouldn't that be a kick in the ass if it were? His manager had begun calling her that when the letters started arriving, and the name stuck. He opened a drawer and swiped the letter and envelope into it.

If they continued or escalated while he lived here, then maybe he'd pass it on to the local police and see if they had better luck.

For now, he needed to burn off some of this anger. He left the kitchen and took the stairs two at a time.

Once in the bedroom, he stripped out of his jeans and T-shirt and pulled on a pair of loose athletic shorts. He went back downstairs into what most would use as the dining room, where a set of weights was set up in the middle of the room.

Running used to be his go-to exercise, but his blown knee ended that. Now lifting weights gave him the burn he sought.

He scrolled through the music library on his phone and put on some Eric Church. The beat of a drum and a twang of a guitar belted out of the Bluetooth speaker sitting on the floor by the door.

After a quick warm-up, he reclined on the padded bench and let the repetitiveness of lifting weights take over his thoughts.

Soon, a sheen of sweat coated his chest and dripped off his forehead.

He knew from experience there was nothing to be done about the envelopes. He might receive a couple more before he finished the renovations on the house and moved on. Luckily, they never progressed beyond the deliveries. It was an annoying nuisance, but one he could live with.

Now, his mind-consuming neighbor was another story.

He never should have touched her.

The bar clattered back in its hold. Jim sat up and grabbed the towel hanging on the side. He wiped the sweat from his chest and face and then looped the towel around his neck and held the ends in his fists.

Allison had made her feelings clear when she'd taken off like a scalded cat after their kiss. He'd known it was a mistake before he ever laid a finger on her. Add it to the list of mistakes littering his life.

Jim stood and did a few stretches to cool down. He didn't want to deal with sore muscles later. Grabbing a glass and filling it with ice water from the fridge, he guzzled it down before heading upstairs to shower and change.

There was only one surefire method to get his thoughts off a woman.

Find another woman.

He'd give his buddy, Brian, a call. The two of them could hit a bar or two. There were bound to be plenty of women to take his mind off his sexy neighbor.

CHAPTER

EIGHTEEN

"What brings you here today, Allison?"

An appointment. She bit back the snarky response.

Dr. King peered at her over his glasses from the armchair opposite her. His wrinkled forehead merged with his bald head.

Allison glanced around his office. A painting of a field and barn hung over his desk, a set of bookshelves filled one wall, and a sofa and chairs took up the rest of the room. She'd sat in one of the chairs when he waved her into his office. No way was she doing the clichéd couch thing.

She shrugged and crossed her legs. "Trouble sleeping, I guess." Hadn't Dr. Thompson filled him in? "I have nightmares."

"Tell me about them."

Drumming her fingers on the arm of the chair, she stared out the window. Cars drove by in an endless stream. His office was in an old brownstone building next to one of the hospitals in the city. Was it for the convenience of submitting patients he thought were insane? Why did a therapist need an office next to a hospital?

This was a mistake. She should have canceled instead of making the almost hour-long drive into Hartford this morning.

"Allison?"

She huffed out a breath. "Didn't Dr. Thompson fill you in?"

"He gave me some background, but I prefer to hear it in your own words. Everyone has their own perspective and their own story to tell. I want to hear yours from your point of view with no one else's opinion or judgments clouding the telling."

Judgments, huh? She was sure Dr. Thompson had plenty of those.

"My parents died in a fire. The nightmares are always about that night."

He nodded and continued to stare at her.

Allison looked away. "The fire was my fault."

Silence filled the room. She glanced out the window and back to the painting on the wall and finally to Dr. King. His gaze remained on her expectantly.

So he knew—no surprise there. He held a pad of paper in his lap and a pen. Both had yet to be used.

"I've had the nightmares for years, since the fire, but they've gotten worse since my husband died."

"Did you have counseling after the fire?"

"No."

"Any counseling after your husband's death?"

"No."

"I see."

Exactly what did he see?

"Grief manifests in many ways. If we don't identify and acknowledge that grief and let ourselves feel the emotions, our brains will seek other outlets."

His voice was low and patient. He most likely spoke that way deliberately—probably thought it was soothing. It made her want to scream.

He'd have a ton of things to say if she gave in to the impulse.

She pressed her lips together until they hurt.

"So you're saying I'm having nightmares because I haven't grieved properly?"

"I'm saying that grief may be one reason."

Who's to say what the proper way to grieve was? Just because she hadn't sought therapy before now to hash out all her feelings didn't mean she hadn't grieved.

She shifted in her chair and wrapped her hands around her knee, lacing her fingers together.

"Allison, when you have these nightmares, how do they make you feel?"

"They're nightmares. By definition, doesn't that tell how they make me feel?" She glanced at the door. "Scared. They make me scared."

"Understandable. What else?"

Her leg swung up and down. She closed her eyes and opened them. "Guilty. They make me feel guilty and ashamed."

He nodded and jotted something down on his pad. Great, now he's taking notes.

Of course, she felt guilty and ashamed. She was responsible for their deaths.

"Dr. Thompson mentioned he prescribed you medicine to help you sleep. Have they helped you rest, or are you still waking up every night?"

Allison frowned. "I haven't taken them. I don't like pills."

He folded his hands on top of the pad. "The pills are a tool. If your body cannot get the rest it needs, then stress is added. More stress plus less sleep equals more nightmares. Do you understand?"

"Yes. I'll think about it."

"Do that."

Dr. King spent the rest of the appointment quizzing her on her relationships. What friends and family she had and whether she confided in them. No family. No friends. Well, there was now Karen. And Jim.

By the time she left, she was exhausted and felt worse than when she had arrived. Not a ringing endorsement for therapy.

During the drive home, she seesawed between never going back and giving it one more chance. He could hardly be expected to cure her in one visit. Some of her father's patients had been in therapy for years.

God help her!

There was a package in front of her front door. Allison frowned as she drove into the driveway. Please don't let it be more black candles. She'd thrown the others away, but maybe she should have made a display of them on her front lawn to thumb her nose at whoever sent them. Too bad it wasn't closer to Halloween. If she set up something like that now, it would only draw more questions she didn't want to answer.

Sighing, she pulled into the garage and grabbed her purse before walking up the walkway to her porch. The box sat in the middle of her welcome mat.

There was no point in delaying. She would only wonder and worry over what was inside.

She smirked. It was probably one of the household items she had on automatic delivery.

The package was the size of a toaster. There was no return label, only a label addressed to her. She glanced around before bending down and picking the box up. It was light.

A quick shake produced no clues. Should she bring it inside to open, or leave it on the porch and open it there?

What if someone was watching?

What if it wasn't something she had ordered, and whoever sent it was watching to see her reaction?

Allison schooled her expression and stole a quick peek from her lowered head. There was no one in sight, but only an idiot would stand in plain view.

What if it was something really horrible?

Damn it! She wouldn't know until she opened it.

Picking up the package, she carried it into the kitchen, grabbed a pair of scissors, and went out onto the back porch. Unless someone was hiding in the woods and had anticipated her going to the back, then...geez, she was losing it.

She opened the scissors and stabbed at the tape from as far away as she could. If whatever was in there got a few holes—so be it.

The tape gave way and the flap lifted. The smell of smoke assaulted her nose. She clapped the back of her hand to block her nostrils and used the scissors to open the top.

Transparent plastic was wrapped around singed fabric. As the top opened wider and pulled on the plastic, the stench of smoke grew stronger.

Allison kicked the box away from her and backed away. She gagged and took several labored breaths as tears wet her eyes.

Damn it! Damn it! Damn it!

Who the hell was doing this to her?

She went inside and wet a dish towel to hold over her nose and mouth to clear away the smell of smoke. After a few minutes, the urge to gag disappeared. The scent, however, lingered.

And it would until she got rid of that box.

Holding the cloth over her nose and mouth, she went back outside. The box was on its side, and the contents hung out onto the floor.

The black and burned cloth had singed holes, and a button remained. Clothes? Someone had sent her burned clothes?

She grabbed the broom next to the door and used the handle to push the fabric back into the box and tip it right side up. After putting the broom back, she went inside and found some tape.

Allison took several deep, cleansing breaths before going back out to the porch. She held her breath as she taped the box shut and then carried it out to the garbage cans by the garage. Her chest burned for oxygen. She lifted the lid.

She slammed the lid down and dropped the box on top. Backing up several steps while dragging clean air into her lungs, she stared at the box. It's evidence. What if she throws it away and then decides to go to the police? She would have no proof.

Her gaze drifted over the garage. She nibbled on her bottom lip and then huffed out a breath. It was better to be safe than sorry later.

Allison marched to the side door of the garage and jabbed in the code to unlock the door. A flick of the light switch and a quick search of the shelves lining the walls produced a frown. It was way past time for her to clean out the garage. Procrastination wasn't one of her more attractive traits.

Plastic bins filled the metal rack closest to her, most of them probably filled with Alan's belongings. The garage had been his domain. She only came in here when she needed the car or the lawn-mower. At least he had been an organized soul. A clear bin in the middle of the shelf was half empty. She pulled it off the shelf and set it on the floor. The lid came off with a pop.

Old towels? Allison squatted and rummaged through the contents. A few towels and sheets, all worn with small tears or stains, occupied the bin. Alan probably intended to use them for work in the garage or something. Not that he had ever worked on the car or did much physical labor. He had hired other people for that.

She carried the bin outside to the garbage cans and dumped the contents in one of them. No time like the present to do some purging. She dropped the box of singed clothes into the bin and held the back of her arm against her nose and mouth for a moment. Dropping her arm, she grimaced. The box of black candles was at the bottom of the can. She should save those too.

Great. Making her dig through the trash—another crime she could blame on the person terrorizing her. At least it was all in garbage bags. She hauled the top bag out and turned her face away. It still stank though.

She dropped the bag on the ground and studied it for a second. *Please don't break open.* Satisfied it remained intact, she gingerly removed the last bag and the box with the candles. Once the bags were back inside the can with the lid on tight, she carried the plastic bin with the gruesome deliveries into the garage, put the lid on, and slid it back onto the shelf. Hopefully, she wouldn't be adding any more deliveries to the bin.

A shower was definitely required. She locked the garage door behind her and went back into the house through the back porch.

What was she going to do about this? If she ignored them, would they get bored and stop? What did they want from her?

It had to be someone connected to the fire and her parents, didn't it? Why else send her these things? And why now?

Allison locked the kitchen door and trudged down the hallway and up the stairs. She turned on the shower before she stripped off her clothes and dropped them into the hamper.

She must have triggered someone by her research into the fire. If she stopped, would they? Or was this only the beginning? And why? Always back to the why.

Someone wanted to hurt her, and they were using her parents' deaths to do it.

CHAPTER
NINETEEN

Light filtered in between the tiny gap of the curtains. Allison threw off the covers and sat up. It's not like she was going to fall back to sleep, anyway. She'd tossed and turned most of the night. The packages and phone call buzzed at her brain like a pesky mosquito—one ready to infect her with some deadly disease.

From what she could gather, only four potential connections could have triggered the harassment. The two people she'd told about the fire, Karen and Jim, and the two people from the past she talked to, Dr. Thompson and the firefighter. Then, of course, anyone they had mentioned it to. Her new therapist needed to be added to the list too.

She wandered downstairs to make a cup of tea. Karen couldn't be responsible. She refused to even consider the possibility. Jim couldn't either. Her instincts couldn't be that horrible. Maybe someone they had innocently told? No, neither was the type to gossip indiscriminately. That left the therapists and possibly their office staff. But they were legally and morally bound to confidentiality. The firefighter could have told his coworkers or a spouse.

Ugh! The list could be endless. He could've told one person who told another and on down the line.

But why? What did anyone have to gain from tormenting her? What purpose did it serve?

She blew lightly over the cup and sipped her tea. She couldn't continue like this. The nightmares, paranoia, and worrying weren't getting better. Dabbling into the past had only made everything worse.

Cupping the mug in her palms, she gazed out the window over the sink. Was it time to go home? Face the consequences of her actions? There probably wasn't much to see. A crumbling foundation and overgrown lot? What remained of her childhood home?

And would it make a difference to see it? Could it trigger a buried memory of that night?

Allison put the half-finished cup of tea in the sink. What was the worst that could happen? She was already a murderer.

She donned a bra and white panties, pulled a pair of black leggings out of the dresser, and yanked them up her legs. Driving all the way to Pennsylvania was a bit like cannonballing into the deep end of the pool after not swimming for a few decades, but what the hell. She'd got around town just fine—slowly, but fine.

A turquoise tunic was on the top of her short-sleeve drawer, so she pulled it over her head. She strode into the bathroom and ran the brush over her shortened locks. The haircut was certainly easy to care for, although the reflection in the mirror still startled her each time. She still hadn't grown accustomed to the fresh look.

Good, another level of anonymity couldn't hurt. It wasn't likely anyone would recognize her in her hometown; it had been too long.

She brushed her teeth a little too overzealously and winced. Resting her hands against the edge of the sink, she took a deep breath. She could do this.

She needed to do this.

Allison rinsed the toothbrush and shook the excess water off. It was time to face her past and move forward. This was the way to do that.

Her purse rested on a chair by the bed. She looped it over her shoulder and looked around the room. A sweater or sweatshirt in case it got chilly. She opened the upper half of the armoire and stared at its contents. The two upper shelves held an assortment of folded sweaters and the bottom shelf sweatshirts. A hood could also add some anonymity. She snatched the navy-blue hoodie from the stack.

Sunglasses. Where were her sunglasses? She opened the top drawer of her dresser and grabbed the closest pair. It might be sunny now, but the sunglasses would add another layer of concealment even if it were overcast. There was no one she wanted to see, and if someone from back home was terrorizing her, they didn't need the added ammunition of her returning to the scene of the crime.

She locked the front door and strode over to the garage before she could change her mind.

"Hey."

Her head shot up. Jim stood next to his truck.

He lifted a hand and walked towards her. "You're up early."

She shrugged.

"Didn't sleep well?"

"Not particularly. What are you doing up so early?"

"I'm a morning person. I was on my way into town to buy a cup of coffee after I realized I was out this morning. You going somewhere?" He tilted his head towards the garage.

Why did he want to know?

Because it was a neighborly question, or something else? No, she wouldn't start suspecting him. It made no sense. It meant nothing that he recently moved in next door, and she told him about the fire right before the packages and phone call. Coincidence at best.

"Allison? You okay? More nightmares?" He propped his hands on his hips and stared at her.

"I'm going to Pennsylvania to see my parents' house. What's left of it, anyway." She studied his expression—nothing but quizzical concern etched his features.

"Why now?"

"Because I'm tired of it all. I want it to end. The nightmares. The guilt..." She raised her arm and dropped it. "I thought if I faced it, it might help."

"Allison, you have nothing to feel guilty about. Please tell me you're not planning on driving out there alone."

Her gaze dropped to the driveway. Right, she never told him the fire was her fault.

"Yes, I do." She raised her gaze to his. "I left a candle burning. The fire was my fault. They ruled it accidental, but I'm responsible for my parents' deaths."

His mouth opened and closed. He stepped forward and wrapped his arms around her. "I'm driving." He released her. "We'll take my truck."

"What?"

"There's no way I'm letting you do this alone."

"You heard me say it's my fault, right?"

"Yes, and I think you've punished yourself long enough. If this is something you need to do to put it behind you, then I'm going with you."

Tears pooled behind her eyes, and she swallowed. He took her free hand and pulled her across the driveway to the passenger door of his truck. Jim opened the door and stood patiently.

Allison looked into the interior of the truck and at Jim. Letting him drive would be one less thing for her to worry about. She wouldn't be alone when she revisited the scene of her nightmares.

"Thank you," she whispered as she climbed into the truck.

Jim gave her a faint smile before he closed her door and walked around to the driver's side. She let out a sigh and put on the seatbelt. Once again, she mentally crossed his name off the list of suspects in her head. This time with a black Sharpie. Unless he was an Oscar-worthy actor, he couldn't be involved.

❧

Jim put the truck in gear and glanced at Allison. No wonder she had nightmares. How the hell had she lived with that burden this long? And she planned to face it all alone. Didn't she have anyone to stand by her?

"Okay if I stop for coffee?"

"Of course. Are you sure you want to do this? I'll understand if you change your mind. You must have had plans for today."

"I'm sure. I was only going to work on the house. It'll keep." He rested his wrist on the top of the steering wheel when he pulled up to the stoplight. "What made you decide today was the day? Nightmare?"

"No, I mean, I had one last night during the brief period of sleep I managed to get, but it was nothing new."

"Then?"

She leaned her head back against the seat. "Have you told anyone about my nightmares?"

He looked over at her and frowned. Her face was pale, with dark circles under her eyes like bruises. She gazed back at him while nibbling on her bottom lip.

"Of course not. I wouldn't do that."

"I didn't mean on purpose. I mean, did it possibly come up in a conversation?"

His hands tightened on the steering wheel. "No. I don't go around talking about my friends behind their backs or sharing their personal information."

"I didn't think you did."

"Then why the question?"

"Someone has been sending me things that I think are about the fire, black candles and burned clothes. There was a crank call too. They called me a murderer."

"Jesus. What did the police say?" He stopped at the stop sign and stared at her.

"I haven't called them."

He gaped. "Why the hell not?"

Allison rubbed her forehead and then clutched her purse tighter to her chest.

Why wouldn't she call the police? Did she have something to hide?

"Because I didn't want to dredge it all up. I doubt there's anything they can do about it. I called the store the candles were sent from. They didn't know anything except a man paid cash for them. There was nothing else identifying on the packages, and the phone number was unknown."

"They might have some other means of tracking them. You should at least report it."

A horn honked. He looked in the rearview mirror. A car waited behind him. He eased off the brake and made the turn.

"You're probably right, and if something else happens, I will. I just didn't want the questions and the looks. No one here knows about it, at least not that I know of. Only you and Karen."

He sighed. It made sense. He wouldn't want people digging into his past or personal business, either.

"You been friends with her a long time?"

"No, just a few weeks, actually."

"But you told her about the fire? What about the packages?"

"Yes, she stopped by after the candles arrived and could see I was upset. She's been a wonderful friend to me."

"You said she and I were the only ones who know about it?"

"In Arlington, you two are the only ones I've told. Then there's my therapist, my father's former partner who recommended him, and the firefighter who rescued me. They're the only ones I've talked to about the fire in years."

"What about relatives? Friends?"

"No." She shrugged and looked out the window. "I don't have any of either."

Jim pulled into the drive-thru. "What would you like?"

"Nothing for me, thanks."

"You sure?"

She nodded, so he pulled up and lowered his window to order his coffee. No family or friends? Why was she so alone? She lost her husband, but why no friends? Once he paid for and received his coffee, he raised the window and glanced at her, still gazing out the passenger window.

"Neither Alan nor I had any other family left, and with his extended illness, friends drifted away."

"I'm sorry."

"For what?"

"Prying."

"We're a bit past that point, aren't we?"

He lifted the corner of his mouth. "I suppose we are."

CHAPTER

TWENTY

The short, paved driveway remained partially intact, but weeds grew through the cracks, zigzagging its length. Potholes and crumbled asphalt appeared every few feet. Jim traversed over or around them until his truck was off the road entirely.

The garage was gone. Only the slab of concrete remained. Why had she thought it would still stand? It had been attached to the house, and Alan had told her the house was a complete loss.

"Do you want to get out?"

"What? Oh, yes." Allison opened the door and slid out. She took a deep breath as she closed the door and faced the lot. The air was clean and fresh, not a trace of smoke. Silly to think there might be after all this time.

The driver's door clicked in place, and Jim walked around the front of the truck to join her.

"How are you holding up?"

"I'm fine." She glanced at him. He watched her somberly. "Really, I am. It's weird and sad to be back, but I'm okay."

"Weird how?"

"I knew there was nothing left, but in my head, I still pictured the house the way it was."

"Understandable if this is the first time you've seen it. Do you want to look around?"

She nodded and walked up the rest of the driveway, stepping over patches of crumbled asphalt and around knee-high clumps of grass and weeds to where the double garage once stood. She wrapped her arms tight around her waist and faced the foundation of the house. Cement stairs at the back still led down. There was debris scattered about, but mostly it was an empty rectangle of cement in the ground. Nothing of her parents' house lingered.

"It must have been a decent size house." Jim walked past her to peer down at the foundation.

"I guess. There were four bedrooms upstairs. Generously sized rooms."

"Colonial, like most of the houses on this street?"

Allison glanced behind her and up and down the street. Only four houses were visible from here, and they were all colonials. There were a couple of contemporary-style homes farther down the street, but most houses were colonial-style. "Yes, it was white with black shutters on the windows. My mother had wanted to add window boxes that year. I remember her telling me about it. She never got the chance."

Weeds poked through the brick walkway that once led to the front door. She walked along it the same way she had thousands of times growing up here. Except for the missing patches of bricks and the weeds, it was the same. Her mother had always kept the yard and house meticulous. The bushes and flowers her mother had planted along the front of the house were all gone. Had they burned too or died from neglect?

The Japanese maple still stood in the front yard, taller than she recalled. Her mother had insisted on taking pictures in front of the tree the first day of school every year. Those pictures were all gone, burned to ash. The row of pine trees in the backyard she played under as a child was the same. A glint of sunshine reflecting off glass caught her gaze. She angled her head.

"What is it?" Jim walked over to stand next to her. "Is there a shed back there?"

"My playhouse. Well, it used to be. My mother turned it into a gardening shed when I outgrew it."

Allison walked around the foundation toward the shed, with Jim trailing behind her. Fallen tree branches and the overgrown yard resembled an obstacle course. A smile twitched her lips as the tiny square building came fully into view. It had been a miniature replica of her parents' house, with white siding and black shutters bordering the two small windows on either side of the door.

"Happy memories?"

She nodded. "Many. I used to pretend it was my fairy house nestled here in the trees."

The door hung askew. She peeked inside. A few old lawn tools were propped in the corner, but mostly leaves and dirt filled the small space.

"There used to be a bright blue rug and a pink bean bag chair inside. I had books and various treasures decorating the shelves in the corner."

The shelves were falling apart. A couple of broken clay pots were on the floor.

"Shortly after I got my driver's license, my mom asked if she could turn it into a garden shed. I said no. Even though I hadn't gone inside in more than a year, I didn't want her to take it away. I was selfish."

"You were a kid."

"She waited until I left for college to change it. I think gardening was what she used to fill the void my growing up and leaving home had left. She no longer had school volunteering or kid activities to fill her time. I doubt I ever fully appreciated all she did for me."

Jim wrapped an arm around her shoulders, and Allison leaned against him. Tears filled her eyes and overflowed in a steady stream.

He pulled her in for a hug and held her while she cried. He rubbed her back while she clutched his waist.

Allison rested her head against his shoulder and sniffled. The crying jag wore her out. Jim's chin rubbed the top of her head. "You okay?"

"I guess so. I'm not sure what I hoped would happen by coming here. I didn't remember anything new or different. It just made me sad. I'm sorry for crying all over you."

Had she thought someone would wave a magic wand and her guilt would disappear? That there was another explanation, and she hadn't been responsible for killing her parents? That they were alive and well, and it was a cruel hoax?

Stupid.

"Don't apologize." He loosened his hold. "Grieving has its own timetable. You've been through a lot in your life. Don't rush it."

"Rush it? It's been ten years."

"Yeah, but like I said, it has its own timetable. Maybe you just needed the closure of coming back here."

She shrugged. "Maybe."

Would this desolate picture replace the memory of her childhood home in flames? Did she even want it to? It was a stark reminder of what she had lost. Of what she had caused. Couldn't she just remember the house the way it had been, a happy home?

She couldn't change the past. Maybe that was the lesson. She needed to see and accept what her carelessness had destroyed.

Jim rubbed her arms. "How about we get out of here and get something to eat? I don't know about you, but I'm starving."

She lifted her head and gave him a wobbly smile. "Okay."

Jim interlaced their fingers. "Watch your step. There's a lot of debris hidden in the overgrown yard. You don't want to twist an ankle."

He led her across the yard to the truck.

There was nothing left here for her. She should probably sell the property. Let someone else build a house and create new memories.

TWENTY-ONE

Darkness shrouded the house. Allison had forgotten to turn any lights on before leaving this morning. She'd been in too much of a hurry. It had been so long since she had been out after dark that it hadn't occurred to her to turn on any lights.

Jim parked in her driveway. "You want me to check the house?"

Allison gazed at him. Would it be cowardly to admit she did?

"Tell you what, give me your keys, and I'll turn some lights on and look around."

She handed over her keys. "I'll go with you." She didn't want to sit in his truck in the dark by herself, either. He waited for her at the front of the truck. "Thanks for doing this. For everything."

"No problem."

They had lingered over lunch. Anxiety had weighed heavily on her walking into the restaurant. Would someone recognize her? Would they dredge up the fire and her parents' deaths? Would they stare at her with accusation?

No one had said a word. She hadn't recognized anyone, either. The tension melted away after Jim had told her amusing stories from his football days. He had probably noticed her anxiety and tried to help her relax.

Trailing behind him as he unlocked her front door, she reached a hand around and flicked on the lights to the hallway and front porch. She stood by the front door as he walked through the downstairs and then jogged up the steps. Lights came on upstairs as he checked each room.

Why was she still standing in front of the door like a child while he essentially checked under the bed for monsters? She lowered her head and rubbed her forehead with the tips of her fingers. The stairs creaked. She jerked her head up.

Jim gave her a tight smile as he walked down the stairs. "Everything looks fine."

"Thank you."

He stopped at the bottom of the stairs and rubbed the back of his neck. "Listen, why don't I crash on your couch for the night?"

"I look that terrified?"

"No."

She raised her eyebrows, and the corner of his mouth kicked up.

"Okay, a little. I don't mind, and anyone would be worried if they were in your shoes. Someone is harassing you, and you've had an emotional day facing your past. I don't want to worry your nightmares are going to send you running out into the night again."

Considering she probably wouldn't be able to sleep a wink, the nightmares shouldn't plague her tonight.

"There's a guest room which is much more comfortable than the couch." Closer too. If he was right down the hall, maybe she would be able to sleep. Then again, maybe not. It had been a long time since anyone else had slept in the house. Having a man she was undeniably attracted to sleeping under her roof, might not be conducive to a good night's sleep.

"Perfect."

Her shoulders lowered as some of the tension drained away. "The sheets are clean, and there are fresh towels in the bathroom."

"I'll be fine."

She walked down the hallway to the kitchen. "Do you want anything to drink or eat? I think I'll have some tea."

"I'm good." His voice rumbled behind her.

She filled the tea kettle and put it on the stove. Jim leaned against the counter with his hands in his front pockets. The mint green T-shirt he wore molded over his shoulders and biceps, accentuating the hard muscle. She swallowed and turned to grab a teacup from the cabinet.

"It might be an old wives' tale, but I've heard warm milk helps people sleep."

"The tea is chamomile. It's a natural sleep aid. I've considered buying stock in the tea company because I use it pretty much every night."

"So, it works?"

"It helps."

"No sleeping pills? My mother swears she can't sleep without them."

"I'm not much of a pill person. The doctor prescribed some, but I haven't taken them."

"You don't think they'll help?"

Allison put the tea bag in the cup and placed it on the stove next to the kettle. She wrapped her arms around her waist and leaned into the corner of the countertop. "I'm more worried they'll work too well, and I'll sleep through an emergency."

Jim lifted his chin. "That makes sense, considering what you've been through. I didn't think of that."

She shrugged. "I guess I prefer to be alert even if it means I'm more prone to nightmares and will be sleep-deprived."

Being unconscious and helpless, unable to sense danger? Her entire body grew rigid. She would never willingly put herself in that situation.

Steam poured from the kettle, and the metal rattled from the boiling water. She turned off the burner and poured the water into her cup. Letting it steep, she glanced back at Jim. "Are you sure I can't get you anything?"

He shook his head.

She picked up the cup and gestured to the table. "Do you want to sit?"

He dragged out a chair and sat. Allison placed her cup on the table, pulled out the chair across from him, and sat with her legs crossed at the knee.

"What's your next step?"

"What do you mean?"

"Are you going to go to the cops about the harassment?"

"If it continues, I guess I'll have to. Right now, I'm just hoping it all goes away. It doesn't make any sense for someone to be doing this after all this time. What's the point?"

"You probably won't know unless they catch them. That's why you should tell the police."

"I hate to dredge it all up."

"What about someone your parents knew? Could they blame you? Hold a grudge?"

"I can't picture any of my parents' friends doing something like this. And why wait until now?"

"Maybe because they heard you were checking into it with the firefighter or therapist that worked with your father. It could have triggered something. Which is why I think you should talk to the police."

"It's all so surreal." After laying the spoon and bag on a paper napkin, she blew over the top and took a sip of the hot brew.

"Will you at least promise to think about going to the cops?"

The warmth of the mug seeped into her chilled hands. The spring nighttime temperature outside hovered in the high sixties. Summer officially started in a few days, yet a chill had settled into her bones and refused to leave. When would this finally be over? Should she suck it up and go to the police? What's the worst that would happen? Brush her off and say there's nothing they could do? No, the worst would be looking at her like she was a criminal who deserved what was happening.

Sighing, she raised the cup and sipped her tea. "I'll think about it."

"Good. What does your therapist say about the deliveries and phone call?"

"I haven't told him."

"Why not?"

"I don't know. I guess I'm not completely comfortable with him yet."

"Isn't the reason for going to a therapist to tell them things you're not comfortable telling anyone else? They're bound by confidentiality."

"I know. My father never spoke about his clients. He took their privacy and doctor confidentiality very seriously."

"My sister married her therapist."

She looked up from her cup.

Jim smirked. "She's only twenty-eight, but she just ended her third marriage. The therapist was number two. My mom is on number five, but it's past the two-year mark, so number six is probably already in the works. She likes to have the next one in line ready."

Wow! What should she say to that?

"I guess my opinion on marriage is pretty negatively skewed. My father left when I was a kid. I barely remember him. He looked me up when I was playing professional ball. He'd been married a few times himself. Told me I probably had a few half brothers and sisters out there somewhere, but he wasn't sure."

"I'm sorry."

He shrugged a shoulder. "I didn't know him, and nothing he said made me want to. My sister came along with Mom's husband number two. Her father wasn't too active in her life either, except to send regular checks. I guess it was a step up from my dad, husband number one. Each husband had deeper pockets than the last."

He rested his forearms on the edge of the table. "Thing is, it sounds like you had a pretty decent childhood with loving parents. Focus on those happy times."

"I do. At least I try to."

"Ready to call it a night?"

She nodded and stood to place her cup in the sink. He waited at the archway to the hallway. He was right. She needed to remember the wonderful memories of her parents more often. But that was also what made their loss so much more painful.

"You going to shut the light off?"

She looked over her shoulder at the light still shining in the kitchen. "Right, I forgot." She walked back and pressed the switch. She hadn't really forgotten. Lights gave the illusion of chasing the shadows away, so she usually left them on at night. Not every light, just those in the kitchen, hallway, stairs—any which left a clear pathway for her. If he looked over her house at night, he probably saw lights always on.

He followed her up the stairs and flicked the switch at the top. Shadows appeared behind him, slipping out of the crevasses and coating the house in night.

She stopped at her door. "Goodnight."

"'Night." He walked down to the door across the hall.

"Would you..."

He stopped and turned around.

"Um...would you mind? That is, would it be too much to ask for you to sleep with me?"

TWENTY-TWO

Bare skin lay beneath her palms—warm, firm skin. Allison's eyes popped open. Her cheek rested on Jim's cloth-covered chest while her hand had somehow delved beneath his shirt. Rigid paralysis shot through her body.

Was he awake? Should she move? Would it wake him up?

"Morning."

She shot up to a sitting position, dragging the sheet up to her chin. Jim cocked an eyebrow up and propped a folded arm beneath his head, his bicep bulging. He rested his other arm across his abdomen. The shirt her hand had apparently lifted in her sleep remained raised, allowing her an eyeful of his impressive ridges of muscle.

"Sleep okay?"

Not trusting her voice just yet, she mutely nodded. The best sleep she could remember in a long time, actually. There were no nightmares, no tossing and turning, just sleep and apparently some cuddling.

She'd blurted out the request for him to sleep with her last night, and her cheeks had promptly burst into flames. She'd rambled a string of words together after that. The exact ones escaped her, but she was quite sure platonic had been repeated a few times.

He had chuckled and taken her hand to pull her into her room. She'd gone into her bathroom to change into a pair of pajamas she'd found stuffed in the bottom of her drawer that covered her from head to toe. She emerged from the bathroom to find him on her bed, and her heart had kicked up its rhythm. She'd told herself she wasn't the least bit disappointed he was still wearing his jeans and shirt. Which, of course, he was since she acted like a skittish virgin.

Somehow, she'd drifted off to sleep lying next to him, and some-time during the night, her body must have sought the comfort her brain was too chicken to seek.

"Not a morning person?"

"Not really." Sighing, she dropped the clutched sheet from her fingers and smoothed it over her lap. "Thank you for last night. I haven't slept that well in a long time."

"Maybe we should make it a regular thing, then."

Her gaze shot up to his. A smile teased his lips. Was he flirting with her?

He propped himself up on an elbow and raised his other hand to cup her cheek. He exerted a slight pressure, and she allowed him to tug her head down. His lips grazed hers while his eyes stared into her own.

He kissed her softly and slowly, watching her closely. The tip of his tongue caressed the seam of her lips. Her eyes drifted shut.

Jim's mouth seduced her own. His hand cupped her jaw while his fingers caressed the spot behind her ear.

She melted against him. He pulled her to his chest without stopping the drugging kisses, his arm wrapped around her back.

Her fingers clutched his shirt, bunching it in her fingers. Her heart pounded in her ears. Heat pooled in her core.

His lips trailed across her cheek. His tongue flicked her earlobe before sucking it between his lips.

"I don't have any protection with me. If this is going to go much farther, I need to run next door."

His whispered words sluggishly penetrated her brain.

"What? Oh!"

Allison pulled out of his arms and sat up. She tucked her hair behind her ear.

Jim pushed up into a sitting position against the headboard and rubbed the back of his neck.

She looked out the window waiting for him to speak because, for the life of her, she didn't know what to say.

"Allison, would you please look at me?"

Allison dragged her eyes over to his face.

"What are you thinking?"

"I'm not sure thinking is involved. I'm too embarrassed to think."

"Why are you embarrassed?"

Her white-knuckle grip on her hands became painful, so she slowly relaxed each finger and rubbed them along her thighs. "I'm not accustomed to this sort of thing. I was married for ten years. It's been a long time since I...well...since I was attracted to a man other than my husband."

"Don't you think I know that?"

She bit her lip and tried to hold his gaze.

"Allison, I realize this is new for you. Believe it or not, this is unfamiliar territory for me too. The women I get involved with...let's just say they know the score."

Jim cracked his neck and sighed. "This isn't coming out quite the way I planned."

"What did you have planned?"

He dropped his hand to his lap and gave her that half-smile she liked so much. "To be honest, I guess I didn't think it through very well because anyway I put it sounds crass."

"You want to have an affair?"

His eyebrows rose to his hairline, and then he laughed. "Yeah, that about sums it up."

Allison pursed her lips and smiled.

"Are you thinking about it?" He grinned. "Because I'm anxiously waiting here for your answer."

A troublesome little tickle was doing somersaults in her stomach. Of course, she was thinking about it. Could she have an affair with Jim? It wasn't a question of whether she wanted to because her body was all for it. It was her mind that had reservations. Was it the right thing to do?

The right thing to do?

She had no one to answer to but herself. If she wanted to have an affair with him, why was she cross-examining every possibility, looking for consequences? He was attracted to her, and she was certainly attracted to him. Why couldn't she just enjoy it while it lasted? Who knew what tomorrow would bring? She, more than most, understood how precarious and fleeting life could be.

"I'm thinking about it," she whispered.

"Okay, any thoughts you might want to share?"

The smile turned into a laugh. "How does one go about having an affair?" Do they negotiate terms or something, or just wing it?

"Is that a yes?" His voice roughened considerably.

Oh God, was it?

Yes. Yes, it was.

Allison took a deep breath and nodded. She would deal with the consequences when they came. And there were always consequences.

"Well, I suppose we could start with dinner and take it from there."

"All right."

"How's tonight sound?"

Tonight? So, not now. Was that relief or disappointment making her muscles turn to jelly? At least tonight would allow her some time to prepare. Prepare what exactly she wasn't sure, but her nerves came to mind. And a shower. And brushing her teeth. And wearing something a lot sexier than her oversized pajamas and plain white cotton underwear.

"I could grill some steaks, or if you prefer, we could go out. I heard there's a decent Italian restaurant in town."

"Um...the grill sounds fine." Going out somewhere would just make her even more nervous. Having dinner next door seemed safer. Her own home would be close if she lost her nerve and needed to escape.

"Six o'clock good?"

Jim stood up, and Allison followed suit, nodding. "That's fine. What can I bring?"

His answering sensual grin kicked her imagination into high gear, and she swallowed hard to ease her suddenly parched throat.

"Do you need to ask? Dessert, of course."

He lifted her chin with a bent knuckle and brushed his lips across hers.

"I'll see you tonight."

Allison managed a smile while he walked out the door. By dessert, he meant food, right?

TWENTY-THREE

Clothes hung from every door and even the curtain rods. Allison stared at them, nibbling on her lips. She fiddled with the sash of her robe, trying to figure out what she was going to wear. What did one wear to a scheduled seduction?

Looking at the large assortment of black and neutral-colored pants and tops, she had to admit that her clothes all looked the same, and none of them could be described as sexy. Apparently, makeup wasn't the only thing she needed to go shopping for.

A few dresses were hanging in her closet, but they leaned toward the matronly side. It was dinner on the grill. She didn't want to be overdressed, anyway.

She pinched the bridge of her nose and sighed. How did she get to this point? Was it too soon? Should she cancel? Was that just being cowardly?

Since Jim left this morning, her thoughts had ping-ponged back and forth all day between canceling and lecturing herself to relax and play it by ear. Baking had produced a kitchen full of baked goods ready to be brought to Guilty Pleasures for sale, but she was still a nervous wreck.

A long, leisurely bath calmed her somewhat. Then when she opened her closet to find something to wear, all the nerves jumped back into play.

The front doorbell rang, making her jump. A glance at the clock confirmed she still had a little over an hour to get ready. Besides, Jim always used the back door. Unless he changed his mind and came over to cancel? No, he would just call, wouldn't he?

Well, standing here thinking about it would not accomplish anything. She cinched the sash of her robe tighter and walked downstairs to see who was at the door. A peek out the side panel spotted Karen on her front porch.

She swung open the door. "Hi, Karen."

Karen smiled until she got a good look at Allison's face. "What's the matter, honey? You look upset."

Allison closed her eyes and frowned. "Is it that obvious?" Of course, it is. She did not possess a poker face. Everything she felt crossed her face, like a neon sign announcing her emotions.

Karen stepped in and stroked Allison's shoulder. "What's wrong?"

"Um...well...I have a...that is." She cleared her throat and tried again. "I'm having dinner with Jim tonight."

Karen grinned, leaned over, and gave Allison a hug. "Oh honey, that's fantastic!"

"It doesn't feel fantastic. It feels like a disaster waiting to happen." A heavy sigh crossed her lips. "I have no idea what I'm doing. I can't even figure out what to wear. I think I'm making a mistake."

Karen grabbed hold of Allison's hands and stopped her from twisting the sash of her robe into a wrinkled mess. "Take a breath."

When Allison complied, Karen nodded and said, "Okay, another one, deeper. Clothes are easily rectified. We'll go up and find something for you to wear. That's not all that's bothering you, though, is it?"

Allison dropped her head into her hands and groaned.

She raised her head and told Karen about the trip yesterday, asking Jim to sleep with her last night for comfort, waking up in his arms, the kiss, and the subsequent conversation.

Karen fanned herself and chuckled. "Good Lord, honey, you've got a gorgeous man after you. What are you worried about?"

She could feel her cheeks heating. "Karen, Alan was the only man I've ever had sex with. To be honest, we didn't even have it that often. And in the last few years, not at all. I'm not what you might call experienced."

"Allison, I promise you, that sexy neighbor of yours knows precisely what to do. I don't think you need to worry about a thing in that regard."

"That doesn't exactly relieve me."

Karen put an arm around Allison's shoulders. "Listen, if it doesn't feel right, then it's not the right time for you, and you say so. Are you worried that he won't stop if you tell him to?"

"No, of course not. I just don't want to make a fool of myself, I guess."

"Did you feel like a fool when he was kissing you?"

Allison smiled. "No, that definitely wasn't what I was feeling."

"Ah hah, there! When the doubts creep in, remember what put that look on your face. You practically glow!"

Karen steered her towards the stairs. "Now come on, let's go see what you've got for clothes."

"Not much, I'm afraid. I've realized that my wardrobe is as sterile as my kitchen and in need of a makeover too."

"Well, now, you're looking at an expert. I'm sure we can come up with something for tonight, and then later this week, you and I will go shopping."

Karen's mouth dropped open as she stared at the contents of Allison's closet displayed all over the room. "Wow. Okay, we've got this." She rubbed her hands together and walked around the room, peering at all the clothes.

Allison stood by the door as Karen snagged one piece hanging from the window and one from the bathroom door before looking in the closet and pulling out something else. She paired a pair of black Capri length pants with a purple blouse and held up a lavender print scarf. "We can use this as a belt. Here, try them on."

"Okay." She disappeared into the bathroom with the garments and emerged a few minutes later. The blouse was bright and bold. It would probably look better if she had gotten some sun beforehand. Her pale skin didn't do the color justice.

Karen unbuttoned several buttons, allowing cleavage to show, and fiddled with the scarf. "There, gorgeous. The pants could be a little tighter, but they still show off your legs."

"You're a miracle worker, Karen."

"Hardly a miracle, but we're not done yet. You need some makeup."

The scrunched nose and guilty frown must have tipped her off. "No makeup?"

"I keep meaning to pick some up."

Karen chuckled and shook her head. "Lucky for you, I always carry a small cache with me."

She grabbed her purse and Allison's arm and directed her into the bathroom. A quick dusting of powder, highlighter, mascara, eyeliner, and a dab of lip gloss were applied. "There, perfect. You don't need much, just a little highlighting here and there."

She turned Allison towards the mirror. "What do you think?"

Allison met her gaze in the mirror and smiled. "I think I'm very glad I have such a good friend."

Karen gave Allison's shoulders a quick squeeze and collected her makeup. "I'm going to put together a kit for you at the shop tomorrow. Now tell me about those delicious aromas I smelled downstairs before I get out of here and let you get to your date."

"Oh, come to the kitchen and see. I made cookies, more muffins, and a cake. I put together a price list and some labels too. I want to see what you think."

Allison told her about the business plan she put together this morning on their way to the kitchen.

"Wow, Allison, you have been busy!"

Allison looked around her overflowing kitchen and laughed. "Well, baking usually relaxes me, and I was really nervous."

Karen's laugh echoed through the kitchen as she inspected all the carefully wrapped goodies displayed in baskets with labels and prices affixed to the front. "This is wonderful, Allison. I stopped by to tell you I've already had a dozen requests for more of those muffins of yours. I didn't know you were this far along."

"Is it too much too soon?"

"No, of course not. I think you're going to be an enormous success! We're going to be expanding before you know it."

"You think so?"

"Absolutely."

"What do you think about packaging? As you can see, I wrapped the muffins and cookies individually, but I thought maybe we could get little boxes to put them in when people make their purchases."

"I think that's a great idea. In fact, I have a few catalogs at the store that have boxes and containers you can look at. You could put your logo on them. I really love the name Confectionary Delights. It's perfect."

"I must admit I'm really excited about this."

"As you should be, I really think this is going to develop into a solid business for you if you want it."

Karen snagged a cookie from the plate of unwrapped goodies Allison planned to bring to Jim's. "Hey, listen, it's time for me to skedaddle. I'm taking this cookie. It's as close to an orgasm as I'm going to get tonight."

A snort of laughter escaped, and Allison clamped a hand over her mouth.

Karen kissed her cheek and whispered, "Just relax and enjoy tonight. The worst that could happen is you decide you're not compatible and go your separate ways. No harm done."

"Thank you, for everything."

Karen waved as she walked to the front door. "Just remember to tell me everything tomorrow!"

Allison closed the door behind her and leaned against it. She rested her palm against her midriff to stem the butterflies. Just because she went over there for dinner didn't mean they were definitely having sex. It was implied, but either of them could change their mind.

Oh God, what if Jim changed his mind?

She squeezed her eyes closed, only to pop them back open. She didn't want to mess up her makeup.

Stop expecting trouble and put your big girl panties on!

The time for deliberations was over. The grandfather clock in the living room chimed the six o'clock hour.

Allison did a final check of her appearance in the entryway mirror. "You can do this," she whispered.

CHAPTER

TWENTY-FOUR

The scent of charcoal permeated the air, and heat bathed his face when he opened the top of the grill. Jim placed the foil-wrapped potatoes on the rack and closed the lid. He wasn't a master chef, but he could use a grill as well as the next guy.

He frowned at the worn railing and glanced over his shoulder at the rest of the small deck off the back of his house. It wasn't much wider than the set of stairs. There was enough room for the grill tucked against the railing, but that was it. The whole thing needed to be replaced. He could sand down the boards and reuse some of them, but he was more inclined to replace all of them and extend the deck across the entire back of the house. Composite decking would last longer but cost more initially. Would it take away from the Victorian style of the house, though? Something he would have to consider another time when he wasn't expecting company.

Allison should wander over soon. Unless she changed her mind and decided she wasn't ready. Had he pushed her too fast? She certainly kissed him like she was ready. Picturing her body beneath his made him burn. He cracked his neck and walked inside.

A quick glance around the kitchen confirmed everything was in place. The salad he'd prepared earlier was in the fridge, with the red wine and steaks he bought for tonight. The table was set for two. He'd put candles in his cart to get as a centerpiece for a romantic setting, but he had put them back. The last thing he wanted to do was remind Allison of her past.

Maybe he should have bought flowers.

He rubbed a hand over his face. It was a date. He'd had plenty. It wasn't like he was preparing for his first date in high school. Hell, he hadn't been this nervous then.

"Get it together, McGregor," he muttered. Allison was probably nervous enough without him adding to it with his own nerves. He was sure she would be looking to him to set the pace.

He didn't want to rush her into anything. That didn't mean he wasn't hoping like hell tonight would end up in his bed. But if she wasn't ready, he wasn't going to push. He could take it slow. It would mean another ice-cold shower or two, but he could handle it. He had them plenty lately. He'd tried hooking up with another woman to take his mind off his sexy neighbor, but he just couldn't drum up enough interest in anyone to make an effort—even for a quick one-nighter.

No, his libido was focused on one woman.

A flash of color turned his head. She crossed her lawn, and he went to meet her at the door.

She was wearing makeup, not much, but enough to make those big, blue eyes of hers even more enticing.

"Hi, here, let me take those." He took the platter of cookies from her and leaned in for a kiss. A quick brush of lips wasn't enough, but he was determined not to scare her off.

His lips twitched as her hands fluttered about for a second before settling around her waist.

"Would you like a glass of wine?"

"Um, yes, please, that sounds lovely."

He poured a glass for her and himself and handed hers over. "You look beautiful."

A pink blush stole across her cheeks. She took a sip of wine and murmured, "Thank you, you too." She rolled her eyes, and her blush deepened. "I mean, you look handsome."

Jim chuckled. He'd dressed in a pair of pants and a white dress shirt. He supposed it was the first time she'd seen him dressed in anything but jeans. Not counting the time he'd just gotten out of the shower and snagged a pair of swim trunks to answer the door.

Remembering her reaction to that had him clearing his throat and reminding himself not to rush anything.

"I better get the steaks on the grill."

"Can I help with anything?"

He pulled the steaks from the refrigerator. "No, thank you. I've got everything under control. It's just steak, potatoes, and salad, nothing fancy."

"Sounds delicious."

"Let's hope so. How do you like your steak?"

"Oh, medium rare."

"Perfect, me too. These will only take a few minutes. I'll be right back."

After tossing the steaks on the grill, he quickly went back inside to set the salad and condiments on the table.

"Are you sure there's nothing I can do?"

A shy smile appeared across her glistening lips, and he tried to resist the urge to kiss her again, but it proved impossible. "Let's just get this out of the way so I can concentrate on dinner."

Jim cupped her cheeks in his palms and kissed her. Her lips were soft and full, and he couldn't get enough of them. He sipped and nibbled at them before taking the kiss deeper.

Allison's arms slowly inched up his chest to loop around his neck. Her fingertips danced along his nape.

Her hesitant but passion-filled response fueled his desire.

He was fast becoming in danger of suggesting they forget about dinner and head upstairs.

Jim eased back, ending the kiss with a lingering connection.

He stared at her kiss-plumped lips for a moment before raising his gaze to her luminous eyes. "I better go check those steaks before they become well-done instead of medium-rare."

A shy nod was her only response as he turned and went outside.

When he returned with the steaks, she was sipping her wine and smiled as he came in. "Were they salvageable?"

"We got lucky. They may be more medium than medium-rare, though."

"I'm sure they're fine."

Allison followed him to the table where he deposited the steaks. "Have a seat. I just need to grab the potatoes."

After they were seated and served, Jim decided light conversation was the only way to cool his painfully aroused body. Short of excusing himself to take a cold shower, that is.

"Tell me what you did today."

She looked up from her plate and daintily dabbed at her lips before replying, "I baked all day, actually."

"For your new business venture?"

Allison nodded and described her plans for Confectionary Delights. "I made a few varieties of cookies and muffins and a cake to start off tomorrow. If they sell well, I'll add a few more products to the list."

Her face grew animated, and she relaxed as she warmed to her subject.

"You've been busy. I'm sure they'll sell very well. Those muffins you brought over were out of this world. I already polished them off."

"Well, now you've got cookies to replace them."

"Mmm Hmm...I'm looking forward to dessert."

Allison paused with her fork in the air and dropped her gaze. She stuffed the bite into her mouth and stared at her plate while pushing bits of baked potato around.

Okay, less than subtle. She might hightail it out of here like she did last time.

"You know I'm not going to push you to do anything if you're not ready, right?"

Her gaze lifted as she set down her fork on the edge of the plate and picked up her napkin to dab at her lips. Her full, glossy lips.

"I'm nervous. I'm sure you can tell."

"So am I."

She rolled her eyes.

"Seriously, I must have checked everything and questioned every decision a half dozen times before you got here. I wasn't this nervous in high school."

She smiled and ducked her head. "Neither was I come to think of it."

He cut another piece of steak. "Tell me about it." He points his fork toward her. "Your first date."

"There's not much to tell. It was a group date, really. We went to the movies together. Mark and I had never done much more than hold hands before, but we called each other boyfriend and girlfriend."

"How old were you?"

"Thirteen. Your turn."

"Not yet. Was he your first?"

"First boyfriend? Yes. First kiss? Yes. It didn't go beyond that, though."

"My first date was a double date with my buddy Tim and his girl and Samantha Covingdale, the object of all my adolescent fantasies."

"And what was she like?"

"Typical beautiful, blonde, cheerleader. As I was the typical football jock, it was my duty to date the cheerleader."

"Of course. Did you date her throughout high school?"

"After a rocky start in middle school and a few others in between, yeah, we dated junior and senior year. She broke up with me after prom and started dating some college guy."

"Ouch."

He shrugged and ate his last bite of steak. "I was devastated for all of five minutes. I was more focused on football and getting ready to play college ball. Who was your high school boyfriend?"

"Mark and I dated my freshman year. He broke up with me when he found a girl willing to go past first base. That story pretty much repeated itself the rest of high school, except the bases might have gotten slightly higher."

"Teenage boys are pretty much horny jerks."

"Oh, and what age does that stop?"

He chuckled. "Some get better at hiding it."

She took a sip of wine. Her blue eyes are luminescent. A guy could drown in those eyes, like a siren luring sailors to ecstasy or death.

"So, what about college? Did you have a steady girl, or did you go the frat boy path, partying and dating a revolving door of co-eds?"

"I was never much of a partier. I wasn't a saint either. I dated a fair amount my freshman and sophomore years, but by my senior year, there was only one. Your turn."

"You can't just end it like that. Who was the girl?"

"Lisa Haden."

"And?"

"We got engaged after college. She dumped me when I got injured and couldn't play pro anymore."

"I guess it's a good thing you found out what she was like before you married her."

He smirked. "Yeah, she married another guy from my team. Last I heard, she was on husband number two, another player."

"I went on a few dates in college, but nothing serious until I met Alan. Not overly exciting, I'm afraid."

Her limited experience wasn't a surprise. Was that why he was nervous? He was used to an entirely different kind of woman. He'd never been anyone's first or second. That probably said a lot more about him and the women he had dated than he cared to think about.

He stood and picked up his plate. She pushed out her chair.

"Sit. I got this."

"You cooked. It's only fair I clean up, or at least help."

She stood and carried her plate over to the sink next to him. He glanced at her profile. He'd never had a date make more than a token resistance to being waited on. Most usually accepted it as their due and would excuse themselves to touch up their makeup or simply arrange themselves in a sexy pose nearby. Allison scraped off her plate and then rinsed it and placed it in the dishwasher. She helped clear the table and pack up the leftovers.

He drew the line when she picked up a sponge. He took it from her.

"I was just going to wipe down the table."

He held her now empty hand and tossed the sponge next to the sink.

"Why do I have the feeling if I let you, it wouldn't stop at the table? You'd move on to cleaning some other part of the house?"

She closed her eyes and frowned. "I clean or bake when I'm nervous."

"We can wait."

"I think I'm more nervous about the waiting than anything else."

"That's easily solved. We can go upstairs right now." He tucked a strand of hair behind her ear. "Only if you're sure it's what you want."

She bit her bottom lip and nodded.

Jim kissed her softly and tugged her hand so she'd follow him out of the kitchen and upstairs.

TWENTY-FIVE

Jim removed her clothing piece by piece with drugging kisses in between. He pulled the bedding back and guided her down before standing. Cool ivory sheets caressed her heated skin. His heated gaze pinned her to the bed while he toed off his shoes and unbuttoned his shirt.

She licked her lips when his sculpted chest was revealed. He leaned down and captured her lips for a searing kiss.

"So beautiful," he whispered before removing his shirt and pants.

She swallowed hard, sat up, and reached for him—no longer able to wait to touch him. Her fingers skimmed over every ridge of his abdomen.

He clasped her shoulders in his warm hands.

Allison gazed up at his handsome face, staring down at her. She leaned forward to press her lips to his skin.

One large palm cupped her cheek. His thumb caressed her cheekbone.

She trailed her lips across his stomach in a series of kisses. Her tongue darted out to taste him.

He groaned and tilted her head back to claim her mouth.

160

The bed sagged beside her when he placed his knee on the mattress. His forward momentum propelled her to lie down. The delicious weight of his body covering hers caused her to gasp.

His work-roughened hand explored her arm and torso, then cupped her breast. His thumb played with her nipple until it hardened, and then his hot mouth replaced his hand.

The sensation washed over her, clouding her thoughts and melting away any lingering hesitation. Allison cradled his head in her hands.

He pressed his thigh between her legs while he ran his palm down the back of her thigh to her calf and back again, lifting and opening her. His fingers teased and coaxed.

Heat and pleasure built like a raging inferno, licking out along her nerves. She panted, desperate to reach the top. Her eyes slid closed, and her back arched as she cried out in bliss.

Jim placed a soft kiss on her lips.

The rustle of plastic and the dip of the mattress as he placed a hand beside her slitted open her eyes. He rose above her, staring down at her with need blazing in his eyes.

She reached for him.

He filled her with an aching slowness that left her gasping. He closed his eyes on a harsh groan as he sank to cover and fill her completely.

Allison wrapped her arms around him. His lips grazed her jaw, and one hand gripped her hip. She lifted her leg and rested it over his backside.

His movements quickened. Hot breath tickled her neck when he gasped and surged against her.

The heat spiraled from her core throughout her body.

She cried out as her orgasm detonated.

Jim clutched her closer as he reached his own completion.

Their sated bodies loosened. Her arms draped over his shoulders while his hurried breaths panted against her ear.

He shifted and raised his head. His gaze traveled over her face before focusing on her mouth. He leaned down and placed a tender kiss on her lips, lingering for a moment.

"Be right back," he whispered before leveraging himself off the bed.

She mourned the loss of his weight and his body heat. Cool air tightened her skin. She pulled the bunched sheet next to her loose and covered herself. Her gaze flitted around the room, taking in the details she'd been too preoccupied to notice before.

The bed was the only piece of furniture in the room. Faded and torn blue floral and striped wallpaper covered two of the walls, and fresh gray sheetrock coated the others. There were no curtains or shades on the windows. The room was clean despite being part of a construction zone.

Jim reappeared from an opening in the wall. There was no door. He'd obviously added the opening recently because she could see exposed lumber and the rough edges of the sheetrock.

His gaze remained on her as he walked naked across the room. She desperately tried to keep her gaze on his, but her eyes disobeyed, and her gaze dropped to catalog the perfection of his form. Toned muscles, not bulging like a bodybuilder, but thick and built like someone who does physical labor for a living. Not that she could remember ever seeing a body like that on any laborer she'd seen. Of course, she wasn't in the habit of checking out men, anyway.

He smiled and lifted the edge of the sheet her arms had clamped to her body. "Penny for your thoughts?" He slid onto the bed next to her and tugged on the sheet until she lifted her arm.

Suddenly self-conscious, she lay stiffly beside him. The perfection of his body made her painfully aware of her nakedness and the fact that she couldn't recall the last time she did any deliberate exercise. She supposed she should be thankful she never struggled with being overweight, but her thin frame lacked the generous curves most men seemed to prefer.

He propped himself on an elbow next to her. She glanced at him and then down to where his fingers toyed with the sheet next to her hip.

"Regrets already?"

Her gaze shot up to his. "What? No!"

How could she have regrets about something so spectacular? She wasn't a prude; she enjoyed sex. Her marriage hadn't been an overly passionate one, but the lovemaking had been pleasant when it had happened.

That didn't sound good.

She couldn't compare the two. It wasn't fair. One was a coming together of a committed married couple, and the other resulted from an overabundance of attraction and hormones.

Wait, did that mean he had regrets?

He lifted a brow. "Then what's the problem?" He touched the spot between her brows. "You have a very adorable little bump here when you're worried about something."

She immediately relaxed her face.

He chuckled.

"I'm just feeling a little self-conscious."

"The afterglow has faded already, huh? I guess I didn't do an exceptionally good job then." He put his hand on her waist. "I'll have to try harder."

Her eyes widened. *If it gets any better. I might die of ecstasy. Was that possible?*

His lips caressed and cajoled hers. Her mouth opened, and his tongue swept in to duel with her own.

She lifted her arms and smoothed her palms over the muscles of his back. Her fingers traced over his shoulder blades and then cupped his sides.

His hand angled her head, and their kiss deepened even more. His leg slid over hers, and she sighed over the feel.

If dying of ecstasy was a thing—sign her up.

TWENTY-SIX

The crunch of glass beneath her feet froze her in her tracks. Allison glanced down and frowned. Shards of glass littered the welcome mat. Jim grabbed her arm and pulled her to the side of her back door. She placed a hand on the siding of the back porch to steady herself.

"Go back to my house and call the police."

His harsh whisper jerked her head up, and she followed the direction of his gaze. The glass panel of her back door was missing.

Someone broke into her house?

She sucked in a deep breath and let it out with a whoosh.

"Allison, go."

He meant to search the house alone? His face tight in anger, he scanned the kitchen and hallway visible from the door. She peeked over his shoulder. More glass littered her kitchen floor in front of the door.

She hugged her arms around her waist. "I'm not leaving without you."

Jim looked back at her and sighed.

"Allison, I'm just going to take a look around and make sure they're gone."

"Isn't that a job for the police? What if someone is still in there? Please come back to your house with me."

She wasn't budging without him.

He stared at her a moment before looking back at the house with a frown. She could see the battle he waged between entering the house and bringing her back to his house to keep her safe. Concern for his safety overrode her appreciation for his concern and valor.

Allison stepped forward and pulled on his hand. "Jim, please."

He sighed and tugged her backward until they were out the screen door and off the porch. The door squeaked, even though he closed it softly. Jim propelled her in front of him and pulled out his cellphone while his gaze tracked over her house.

She searched every window in sight for a sign of an intruder while she listened to Jim report the break-in to the police.

They reached his back porch. Allison huddled by the back door while he stood talking into his phone with a fist planted on his hip. She heard the police dispatcher tell him to wait for the police to arrive.

She rubbed her arms to chase away the ice invading her bones. Who had broken in, and why? Had they taken anything? Was her house destroyed inside?

Jim glanced over and reached out an arm. He wrapped it around her and pulled her into his side.

It was a safe neighborhood. There had never been any reported break-ins as long as she had lived there. It wasn't exactly a high-crime area.

She rested her head on Jim's shoulder. Sirens wailed in the distance. She closed her eyes as a shiver shook her. Would the sound of sirens ever stop sending her into panic mode?

Jim kissed the top of her head and rubbed her back.

"Why don't you go inside? I'll go talk to the police."

The urge to run inside his house and lock the door was overwhelming.

She shook her head.

"No. It's my house. My responsibility. I'm sure they'll have questions for me."

"They can come over here to ask them."

The siren screeched in her head. It sounded like it was coming right through Jim's house to get to her.

"They're here."

Jim jogged down his steps and waved to the officers exiting the two police SUVs parked in her driveway. He called out to them. The words sounded like static in her head. The buzzing grew louder, and the edges of her vision went black.

Allison lunged for the railing for support.

Her chest cramped as her breaths sawed from her lungs.

She closed her eyes and swayed against the railing.

Arms wrapped around her.

"Easy. It's okay. The police are searching your house."

Jim turned her into his chest. She wrapped her arms around his waist and buried her face in his shirt. His unique scent enveloped her, and she burrowed a little closer.

Tension stiffened his posture. She peeked up at his clenched jaw. His arms loosened as he gazed over her head.

She looked over her shoulder. A policeman in uniform approached. He stopped at the bottom of the steps and stared at them for a moment.

"The house is clear. I'd like to get your statements."

Jim kept his arm around her shoulders and turned them both to face the officer fully. "We went over this morning and saw broken glass from the back door. We didn't enter the house. We called and were told to wait over here."

Jim related the events succinctly while the officer jotted down notes. He asked their names and a few questions about where the glass was and if they moved or touched anything. He raised his head and stared at them.

"Whose house is it?"

"Mine." Allison wrapped her arms around her waist and took a deep breath.

"You were together when you went over?"

She nodded.

"All night?" The officer gestured with his notebook to Jim's house. "You said you went over together this morning. Had you spent the night here?"

Was that judgment? In this day and age? Maybe she was being paranoid. He didn't look much older than her or Jim—late thirties at most. He had a receding hairline, but Alan had had one in his twenties.

Jim squeezed her shoulder. "Yes."

"So, you two are in a relationship?"

Jim stiffened. "What does that have to do with her house being broken into?"

"Just trying to get the facts straight. The house was empty all night?"

"Yes, it was." The first time she leaves the house overnight in years, it gets broken into. What are the odds?

"That happen a lot?"

"Excuse me?" Allison raised her chin.

"Ma'am, I'm just trying to ascertain whether anyone watching the house would know it was empty at night a lot."

"Oh...no...that is, this is the first time I haven't been home in quite a while." She winced. Did that make her sound worse?

The officer nodded and scribbled in his notebook. What was he writing? That the hard-up lady was busy having sex with her neighbor while her house was broken into?

The radio on his shoulder crackled to life, and he turned his head to speak into it.

Jim kissed her on the forehead and dropped his arm. "How are you holding up?"

"I'm fine."

"You can go on over now. You'll want to look around and see if anything is missing."

"All right."

Jim took her hand and followed the officer across the lawn.

Another officer stood on the back porch with her hands resting on her belt. She nodded at the officer or them, Allison wasn't sure which, maybe all of them.

They led her into the house, and a numbness seeped into her. Drawers and cabinets hung open. A box of oatmeal was spilled on its side on the counter. Had they been hungry?

The living room and dining room were much the same, cushions all on the floor. Someone had been looking for something. They hadn't touched the few pieces of Alan's family silver in the china cabinet or the money in her wallet now lying on the floor in the foyer. They'd dumped her purse out but hadn't taken anything.

The upstairs revealed more of the same. Her personal papers rifled through, and a mess in every room, but no real damage and nothing stolen as far as she saw.

She answered their questions on autopilot.

Back down in the kitchen, she stared at the dust lingering on the door jamb. They said they hadn't found any usable fingerprints, and any in the house were likely to be hers.

"Is there anyone that holds a grudge against you?"

Allison blinked at the officer. "What?"

"You said nothing appears stolen. Can you think of anyone or any reason someone would break into your house and not take anything?"

"Tell them about the packages and phone call."

The officer looked at Jim and then back at Allison. "Ma'am?"

A sharp ache throbbed behind her eye. She rubbed her palms

together, entwining her fingers. Jim placed his hands on her shoulders.

"Someone sent me a couple of packages. The first one was a bunch of black candles. The second contained burned clothing."

"Any idea who sent them or why?"

"No, not who anyway." She stared at the notebook in his hand. "My parents died in a fire several years ago. I was the only survivor. It was ruled accidental, but I lit the candle the report said caused the fire."

Now the condemnation would begin. The looks. The speculation. The accusation.

The officer was silent, his notebook still clenched in his hand.

The policewoman who had followed them silently from room to room spoke from the corner of the kitchen behind them, "Do you have the packages?"

Allison glanced over her shoulder and nodded. "In the garage."

"Can you show me?"

She led the officer to the garage. Had they broken into the garage as well? Were the contents of the packages what they had been looking for? Why? Would it provide evidence against them?

The garage was locked. When she opened the door, it looked the same. Her car was parked in the middle, undisturbed. She pulled the tote where she stashed the boxes off the shelf and placed it on the floor. The officer squatted next to it and lifted the lid.

The smell of smoke assailed Allison's nostrils. She held her hand up to her nose and stepped back. Jim and the other officer stood in the doorway, staring at the boxes inside the tote. The officer poked through them with her pen, replaced the lid, and stood.

"Okay if we take this?"

"Yes, of course. Do you think you'll be able to find anything?" She explained about calling the store the candles were sent from and the vague description the salesperson gave of the man.

"We won't know until we get it back to the station. You mentioned a phone call as well."

Allison gripped her elbows and pressed her lips together. "They only said one word. I don't know if it was a man or a woman. It sounded electronic—fake."

"What was the word?"

"Murderer."

The officer reached into her pocket and held out a business card. "If you think of anything else, or anything else happens, call me."

Allison took the card and nodded. Jim walked over to stand next to her.

The officers left and Allison wandered back into the kitchen and surveyed the destruction. It would take her at least a week to clean the house.

"Grab what you'll need for the next few days. You can stay with me until a security system is installed."

Allison blinked. She was sure she didn't hear him right.

"I'll rig something up on the door so it's secure until it can be replaced." He examined the doorjamb. "I can take care of the door and have a guy I know come out for an estimate on an alarm."

Although her first inclination was to do just what he said, she hesitated. She was afraid of leaning on him too much. In hindsight, she had depended on Alan for everything. Instead of a true partnership, she'd allowed herself to put her wants and needs after his. It had been easier to follow along. She didn't want to do that again. She was just learning to stand on her own and develop her own interests.

Allison looked around her house. It had been invaded.

Her home didn't feel safe.

Jim walked over and tilted up her chin. "Do you want me to gather things for you?"

His warm brown eyes were filled with tenderness and concern as they gazed down at her. She reached up and softly pressed her lips to his.

"Thank you. For everything. I promise it will only be for a day or two. I'll go pack a bag."

"I'll make some calls while you do and get the ball rolling."

Allison trudged up the stairs. The soft murmur of Jim talking on the phone trailed behind her. She doubted having her for an instant houseguest had ever crossed his mind when he proposed their affair. He really was going above and beyond for someone he barely knew.

She hoped he didn't regret his offer.

Her steps slowed and halted at the top of the stairs. Would whoever was responsible follow her to Jim's? Had they broken in to scare her or for some other purpose?

She couldn't put him in danger. She would only stay the night to get her bearings. If it took longer for the door to be replaced and an alarm system installed, she would go to a hotel.

CHAPTER

TWENTY-SEVEN

The sizzle of butter hitting the pan and the distinctive swish of a whisk scraping against a glass bowl reached her ears before she walked into Jim's kitchen. He stood at the stove dressed in his customary jeans and T-shirt as he turned and glanced over his shoulder at her standing in the opening.

"Morning. I hope you like pancakes."

"I do. Can I help?"

He winked. "I've got this. Pancakes are one of my specialties. There's coffee." He jerked his chin toward the coffeemaker. "Afraid I don't have any tea."

"I'm fine." She leaned against the counter behind him while he poured the batter into the pan.

"I wasn't sure what time you were going to be up, but I heard you stirring upstairs. I recall you like to sleep in."

A reference to the morning they had met, no doubt. It was past eight o'clock already. She'd slept like a log again in his bed. Of course, he had worn her out both nights. Maybe that was the key to finally getting a good night's sleep—sex with Jim.

"Not everyone thinks the crack of dawn is the time to get up and start the day."

"Old habits. I've always been a morning person."

"I hope I didn't hold up any of your work." He'd been concentrating on finishing the suite bathroom. The white marble finishes he'd already installed were beautiful. Whoever bought the house when he finished would have a luxurious bathroom.

"Nothing to worry about. There's always plenty of work to be done. I thought, after breakfast, I'd head over to your place to take some measurements and get that door replaced. Mike said he'd be by this afternoon to see about a security system."

"I need to clean up the mess they left. Do you have any idea how long before they install the system?"

"No. I told him it was urgent, but I imagine he'll have to check out your house first and see what will work best. Probably a couple of days."

He plated the pancakes on square white dishes and carried them over to the table. "Can you grab the syrup on the counter?"

Allison picked up the bottle and followed him to the table. She stared at the pile of pancakes on her plate. "You don't really think I can eat all this, do you?"

"Whatever you don't want, I can finish."

His plate was stacked even higher than hers already. He must burn a ton of calories per day to eat like that. With that body, it really shouldn't be a surprise. She took a bite of the fluffy blueberry pancake.

"This is really good."

"The shock on your face is disappointing. I told you pancakes were one of my specialties."

She smiled and took another bite. "I apologize if I offended you. Alan never cooked a day in his life. Come to think of it, neither did my father. I shouldn't have given into the stereotype, though. The steak and potatoes you made the other night were delicious."

"Don't get your hopes up. My expertise in the kitchen is limited to a handful of items. That pasta dish you whipped up for dinner last night was amazing."

She shrugged. It hadn't been much, just a quick and easy Alfredo sauce with chicken and broccoli. It was the least she could do since he was so helpful and let her spend the night.

"I'm going to check into a hotel after your friend stops by for the alarm system. I'll be out of your hair this afternoon."

Jim set his fork down on his plate and frowned. "Why? I know the house isn't in the best shape. I still have a lot of work to do. I plan on hanging the bathroom door today if you're worried about privacy."

"Oh no, the work you've done on the house is beautiful. I love the bathroom upstairs already. I can only imagine how it will look when you're done."

"Then what is it?"

"I can't keep imposing on you. Besides, has it occurred to you that my trouble might follow me here? I can't put you in that position. I already checked online and made a reservation for a hotel less than a half-hour away."

"That's ridiculous. There's no reason for you to stay in a hotel, and it's safer for you to stay with me instead of alone in a hotel room. Besides, we don't know who broke in or why."

"I have enough guilt on my plate. I can't handle someone else getting hurt because of me."

"I'm not going to get hurt. And I would only worry about you. I'll have to book the room next to yours."

"You can't be serious." Allison gaped at him.

"I'm serious. If you insist on going to a hotel, then I'm going too. Doesn't make sense to waste our time driving back and forth to a hotel when we can just stay here, but if that's what you want...." He shrugged and shoveled another forkful of pancakes drenched in syrup into his mouth as he watched her.

Allison placed her fork on the edge of her plate and pushed it toward the center of the table. Here she was trying to do the right thing, and he was being unreasonable.

"I'm not your responsibility."

Jim stabbed the remaining pancakes on her plate with his fork and transferred them to his plate. "I didn't say you were. Let's say the situation was reversed, and I needed a place to stay for a night or two. Would you want me to go to a hotel?"

She sat back against the chair and frowned. No, she wouldn't.

"Look, let's hear what Mike has to say. It might just be for one more night. There's no point going to a hotel for one night, right?"

"Okay, I'll cancel the reservation for tonight."

"Good, now give me a minute to clean up, and then we can head over to your house. You can grab some tea over there to bring back with you."

ALLISON SNATCHED the phone up on the first ring. Maybe the police had a lead.

"Hello?"

"Ally?"

Allison tried to tell herself she wasn't disappointed. "Hello Lucas, how are you?"

"Great, now that I got a hold of you."

She winced, realizing she never returned his call. "I'm sorry. I meant to get your number from Jim and return your call."

"My fault. I should've left it for you. How about we get together tonight and go over the estimate? I know this great steakhouse."

Was he asking her out on a date? What should she say? She wasn't exactly sure what her relationship with Jim was. Obviously, Jim hadn't said anything to Lucas about their involvement, or he wouldn't be asking her out, would he? Unless Jim told him he didn't care.

Allison chewed on her lip. She needed to know if their affair would be an exclusive one. She wasn't interested in juggling a dating calendar, even when her life wasn't in such turmoil.

Besides, she liked Lucas, but he didn't make her heart race at simply the sound of his voice or an image of him in her head. Jim did.

The affair was casual, hence no commitment. Would Jim be going out with other women—sleeping with other women?

An ache gathered in her chest.

"Ally?"

"Oh, I'm sorry, Lucas. I just have a lot on my mind. I…I, well…I'm kind of seeing someone."

"Kind of?"

"It's complicated," she said with a sigh.

"Strictly business then?" Lucas chuckled.

Allison leaned against the counter and smiled. She went from feeling completely alone to having two men ask her out.

"Yes."

"Okay, I can handle it. How about I drop by and go over the estimate with you tomorrow morning?"

They'd install her new security system tomorrow. Jim had already replaced the door today. "That would be great. Although, I've been thinking of a few other changes I'd like to make to the kitchen."

"All right, what do you have in mind?"

"Well, I'd like to put in a double oven and a larger refrigerator. I'm starting a baking business." It gave her a spurt of pride every time she said it. She was moving forward with plans to carry her baked goods at Guilty Pleasures. Whoever was harassing her would not ruin this opportunity for her. She'd already lost a couple of days because of them.

"Good for you. Now's the time to make the changes. I'll add in some price ranges for you and look over the floor plan to add in the ovens and larger fridge."

"Thank you." She would have to come up with a plan on how to bake during renovations.

"No problem, it's my job. See you in the morning. Around eleven, okay?"

"That sounds fine."

"See you, Ally."

"Bye, Lucas."

She placed her phone down on the counter. She'd talk to Karen and see if they could brainstorm some ideas.

The stairs creaked, and Jim's tread sounded as he came down the stairs and walked into his kitchen. His T-shirt was plastered to his torso. There were beads of sweat on his brow, and particles of dust covered him from head to toe.

She let out her breath with a whoosh of air. Since when did she find sweaty construction workers so appealing?

"Hey." He leaned down and gave her a quick kiss on the lips before drawing back. "Sorry, I'm a mess. I've been cutting tile."

He'd already put the bathroom door in place today, too. At the speed he worked, the entire house would be done in no time.

And then he would leave.

"Jim, this affair we're having...is it an exclusive thing? I'm not trying to push or slap labels on it, but it occurs to me we never established those types of ground rules." She shrugged. "I just need to know one way or another."

The gathering scowl on his face made her regret her impulsive question. Did he think she was being too possessive?

"What kind of question is that?"

"An honest one. I don't know how these things work. I don't know the rules." She threw her hands up in the air.

"It's not about rules. It's about enjoying each other. If one of us gets the urge to enjoy someone else, then it's over. Do you want to date someone else?"

"No," she whispered.

"Then what brought this on?"

Allison shrugged. She wasn't going to mention Lucas had asked her out.

Before she could garner a response, his lips captured hers in a searing kiss.

His hands spanned her waist and lifted her onto the counter. She opened her legs to accommodate his hips and wrapped her arms around his neck.

He tugged on her bottom lip with his teeth before releasing her lips. She opened her eyes to find his brown gaze staring at her. Gold circled his pupils. She'd never noticed that before.

"Now you're almost as dirty as I am. Care to share the shower with me?"

Her lips twitched. "Was that your plan all along?"

He winked. "Maybe."

"I think I can be persuaded."

"Me too."

Jim lifted her off the counter and put her over his shoulder.

She squealed. "Oh my God! What are you doing?" She grabbed hold of the belt loops on his jeans.

He chuckled and patted her on the butt. "Saving time."

It wasn't the most comfortable position, but the view was rather good. She let go of his belt loops and smoothed her palms over his ass as he walked up the stairs.

"Now you're getting the idea." He ran a hand over her thigh and squeezed.

Two could play at that game, and she squeezed his ass cheeks.

He froze. "You keep that up, and we won't make it to the shower."

"Promises. Promises."

Suddenly, she was upright again and against the hallway wall. Jim's mouth latched onto hers. His tongue swept inside and tangled with hers.

He lifted her until they fit perfectly together—core to core. Her gasp met his groan.

Allison clutched his shoulders and wrapped her legs around his hips. Her thin cotton shorts provided little barrier to the feel of him moving against her, but it was still too much. She reached down and unzipped his jeans.

He swelled against her hand. She cupped and stroked him.

Jim groaned and dropped his forehead to her shoulder. "Are you on the pill?"

"Hm...what? Oh, yes."

He lowered her legs and unbuttoned her shorts. They disappeared along with her panties in one smooth move. His shirt went flying over his head, and then he lifted her again, joining them together.

Her head fell back against the wall. His lips grazed her neck.

Allison lost herself. He filled her completely, over and over again.

The rapture washed over her like a wave. She clutched him to her as she rode it out.

Jim reached his pleasure shortly after. He held her tightly and placed kisses up the side of her neck and jaw.

He rested his forehead against hers as their breaths melded and slowed. "How about that shower now?"

CHAPTER

TWENTY-EIGHT

Drills whined in multiple rooms of her house. Jim's friend, Mike, had shown up with a team of four to install her new security system. She would have motion sensors on every door and window in her house when they were done, including a fire alarm that would alert the authorities directly. She'd tried not to blush when Mike had suggested the addition after seeing all the detectors and fire extinguishers in her house.

Lucas had come and gone with her estimate and planned to begin work next week. Jim had finally relented his guard duty when she pointed out she was surrounded by security experts. She'd cleaned up most of the downstairs and waited for the technician to finish in her room before tackling the upstairs. She was determined to sleep in her own bed tonight. Jim might argue, but the longer she waited, the harder it would be.

Or maybe he was ready for her to go home, too. She had invaded his life over the past few days. He was accustomed to living alone, and he hadn't signed up for a roommate. He'd made his intentions clear from the start—a temporary relationship. It implied limited involvement.

She trudged up the stairs to see if her room was free. The doorbell rang when she was halfway up. She wasn't expecting a delivery. Would the police drop by if they had news? She walked back down and opened the door after peeking out the side window.

"Hi. Is this a bad time?" Karen glanced behind her into the house.

"Not if you don't mind the mess or the noise." Allison stepped back to allow her to enter.

"The renovations start on your kitchen already?"

"No, not until next week. They're installing a security system. Someone broke into my house a couple of days ago."

Karen grabbed Allison's arm. "Oh my God! Are you all right?"

"I'm fine. I wasn't home."

"Still, that's awful. What did they steal? Do the cops know who did it?" She gasped and put her hand over her mouth. "Do you think it had something to do with the person harassing you?"

"I don't know. They didn't take anything as far as I could tell. They were either searching for something or just wanted to make a huge mess. I just finished picking up the downstairs this morning and was about to start on the upstairs."

"Oh Allison, what a nightmare. Why didn't you call me? I would've helped you. Wait, have you been staying here all alone? You could've stayed with me. In fact, you still can for as long as you want."

"Thank you, but I'm okay. I haven't been staying here. Now that they're installing the security system, I will."

"Where have you been staying? You didn't go to a hotel, did you? I'm right down the street. I wish you had called me."

"Uh, no, I was going to, but Jim insisted I stay with him."

Karen grinned. "He did, did he? Oh wait, that was the night of your date, wasn't it? I take it the date went well?"

Allison glanced behind to make sure no one was in earshot. "It did."

Karen looped her arm through Allison's. "I can see I'll need to wait for details until we're alone, but I expect to hear every scintillating tidbit. But there is something else I came over to discuss."

"Oh?" Allison waved a hand in the direction of the living room. "Do you want to sit?"

"I only have a couple minutes. The kittens are old enough to be weaned, and I'm ready for them to find some new homes. Charlie insisted you have the first choice. Of course, as I'm saying this, I realize you might not be ready to take on a kitten with everything that's happening."

"Oh no, I still want a kitten." Had it been eight weeks already since she'd first met Karen and Charlie?

"Are you sure?"

"Yes, I even bought food, dishes, and a litter box the last time I was in town."

"We can wait a week or so until you're settled."

"No, that's okay. I'd like to bring the kitten home if it's ready. It would be a pleasant distraction from all the craziness."

"Okay. Charlie wants you to have the mostly white one with the black-shaped heart on its nose and black paws, but let me know if you want a different one."

"That one will be perfect. When do you want me to come get him?"

"Her, actually. I can bring her by in a couple of hours after I pick Charlie up from camp, okay? The little father will probably want to inspect what you've bought for the kitten. I swear he's spent hours online researching how to care for the kittens."

Allison laughed. "I might have fallen into that well myself."

"I better run. So the timing is good for you?"

"Perfect."

She waved Karen off and wandered back inside. What should she name the kitten?

～

PETUNIA BATTED THE TINY, yellow, toy yarn ball across the living room, then chased after it and pounced on her prize. Allison laughed when the kitten repeated the routine.

She finished dusting the room and went to the kitchen to check on the lemon bars in the oven. The citrus confections scented the air with summer and sugar. Karen had asked her what she thought of expanding her offerings and filling an entire refrigerated case by the entrance. Her initial shocked reaction was that it was too much too soon. She'd only been selling goods for a few weeks, and although the response was overwhelmingly positive, she didn't want to move too fast. She wasn't ready to take that step yet, but maybe once her kitchen remodel was done.

Lucas had called and pushed the project back by a few weeks. The changes she requested included adding new custom cabinetry, which took a while to make. There was no point starting any demolition and leaving her without a functioning kitchen for weeks. This way, she could still use a portion of her kitchen for her business throughout the remodel.

She would revisit Karen's proposal when the new kitchen was complete. That would allow her time and provide some hard data on the financial feasibility of expanding. She simply wasn't an impulsive person. She needed to weigh her options and mull over the possibilities.

Petunia followed her into the kitchen and found a new distraction, her tail. Allison chuckled. The kitten had provided endless entertainment and companionship over the past week. Her favorite sleeping spot was smack in the middle of the spare pillow on her bed. The two times Jim had spent the night, the kitten hadn't been ready to relinquish her spot and had curled herself up at the top of his head.

He'd simply picked her up and moved her to the end of the bed. After a disgruntled stare, she'd relented and gone to sleep, but as soon as he left the bed, she went back to her spot.

The timer on the oven chirped, and Allison removed the lemon bars and placed the pans on the racks to cool. She currently made a half dozen options to sell at Guilty Pleasures. If she expanded to a full case, she would probably have to quadruple her offerings, which would mean a lot more hours of work. Something else she had to take into consideration.

The screen door on the back porch squeaked open. Jim's profile was visible in the windowpane of the kitchen door by the time she rounded the peninsula. She punched in the alarm code, deactivating the system and opening the door for him.

"Hi."

Jim brushed her lips with a kiss as he stepped into the kitchen. "Hi yourself. I finished early and wondered if you'd like to go out to dinner tonight?"

"The bathroom is done? I'd love to see it." She hadn't been to his house since they installed her alarm. He'd been coming here. It was easier since the primary bathroom and bedroom were his current projects or had been.

"We can walk over before we go to dinner."

Petunia rubbed herself against his ankles. He bent down, picked the kitten up, and held her against his chest. She fit easily in the palm of one of his hands. Her eyes closed as she purred.

Allison nibbled on her bottom lip. "You think she'll be okay on her own?"

"She's a cat. Of course, she will."

"I guess you're right. I've never had a pet before, so I worry I'll do something wrong."

"Besides spoiling her too much with every cat toy available, I don't think you have anything to worry about."

She wrinkled her nose. Wait until he saw the new cat condo she had ordered online. It was scheduled to arrive at the end of the week.

He leaned forward and kissed her nose. "What do you say?"

"Okay, I'll go change. Where did you have in mind?"

"I was thinking about giving that Japanese grill place a try."

"Oh, the one where they cook everything right in front of you? Karen told me about it. She said it was great."

"Yeah, I've heard good things."

"I'll be back in a few minutes."

"I'll keep Petunia and whatever is on the stove company." He craned his neck to glance at the lemon bars. "They smell amazing. Lemon?"

"Yes. Oh, I have to sprinkle the confectioner's sugar on top before they cool completely. Then I'll go change."

"Should I bother saying you don't have to change? It's not a fancy place. What you're wearing is fine."

She glanced down at her jean capris and yellow T-shirt. A spot of flour was on the hem. She dusted it off before walking over to the stove. The clothes were decent enough for running errands, but she wanted to put a little more effort into a dinner date.

"I've been baking, and I'm wearing the evidence of it on my clothes." She sifted a scoop of sugar over the top of the bars. "Remind me to cover these before we go, please."

Jim frowned. "I don't get to sample them while you're upstairs?"

"They're too warm. You can sample them when we get back from dinner." She pointed to a container on the counter. "There are chocolate chip cookie brownie bars in there. You can have a couple."

His eyes lit up, and he put the kitten down and walked closer. "Only a couple?"

"You don't want to spoil your dinner, do you?"

"I'll start with a couple. But I warn you that the longer you take, the more I'm likely to eat. I'm hungry."

Allison shook her head and dashed to the stairs, calling as she went, "I'll be quick."

She shuffled through the contents of her closet in her head as she jogged up the stairs. Her wardrobe had expanded after a shopping excursion with Karen. But after purging most of her old clothes, she had a lot of empty space. She should call Karen and schedule another trip soon. They had so much fun the last time, making a day of it at a local outlet mall. Karen had mentioned planning a trip to Manhattan and combining shopping with a play on Broadway.

By the time she reached her closet door, she had yanked her T-shirt over her head and sent it sailing towards the bathroom. She shimmied out of her capris while she studied her closet. Nope, nothing had changed. The white summer dress with blue flowers would have to do. It was short-sleeved, so she grabbed a light baby blue sweater in case the restaurant's air conditioning was too cold.

She pulled the dress over her head and let it fall around her as she walked into the bathroom to add a little makeup. Thank God Karen had given her an easy hairstyle and a kit with the makeup basics. She hesitated after putting on lipstick, blush, and mascara. There wasn't time for more.

Snatching a pair of white sandals from her closet, she tucked them under her arm and grabbed her purse. She glanced at the kitchen stove clock when she walked over the threshold. Ten minutes had gone by.

Jim looked up from his phone. His gaze raked her from head to toe. "That was fast. I'm impressed."

She smiled as she slipped on her sandals. "I told you I would only be a few minutes."

"Yeah, but usually when a woman says that, she means an hour at least."

"Maybe you've been hanging around the wrong women." Allison turned her back and covered the lemon bars.

Strong hands gripped her waist. He kissed the side of her neck. "Have to agree with you there."

CHAPTER

TWENTY-NINE

Allison crossed her legs and folded her hands in her lap. Dr. King gazed at her silently from the armchair across from her. He had an annoying habit of leaving his glasses hanging off the tip of his nose. She kept waiting for them to fall. His pen was poised and waiting in his left hand to make notes about her.

She'd canceled their last appointment because she hadn't the time or the inclination to go. This would probably be her last one. She hadn't had any more nightmares in a couple of weeks, at least none she remembered. That was probably due more to Jim and Karen and the fact that there hadn't been any more disturbing incidents or packages since the break-in than to the couple of therapy visits she had.

"Is there anything else you'd like to discuss today?"

"Like what?"

"We haven't talked about your husband or his death."

A frozen stiffness pervaded her limbs as if she were morphing into a petrified wooden statue right in the chair.

"How long since he passed?"

"One year, three months, and five days."

"That's rather specific."

"The day is etched in my brain."

"Tell me about it."

"Why?"

"Isn't his death what triggered your nightmares to return? You lived without them for several years after the death of your parents."

"True, but I haven't had any more nightmares recently. I don't see the point of talking about this."

He folded his arms over the notebook balancing on his knee. "When we bury our emotions, they have a tendency to resurface, often at inopportune times and in unpleasant ways."

Allison unclenched her fingers one by one and rubbed her damp palms on her pants. She wasn't stupid; she understood the connection. She was in a good place now, and she wished to remain there. Confessing her role in the fire had eased none of her guilt. But it had shrunk the boulder of dread and anguish constantly perched over her head poised to crush her.

"It was an unseasonably warm fall day. Alan was always cold, so I couldn't turn the air conditioning on. He'd written blanket on his whiteboard, so I covered him in another blanket as perspiration beaded over my lip and the back of my neck."

"Whiteboard?"

She glanced at him before staring unseeing out the window. "He had esophageal cancer. Towards the end, he'd lost his voice. The whiteboard allowed him to communicate."

"You cared for him at home?"

"It was what he wanted. There was nothing else the doctors could do for him."

It had started with him complaining about trouble swallowing, then he began to lose weight. She'd begged him to go to the doctor, but he'd dismissed her concerns, saying it was nothing. By the time he went to the doctor, his voice was hoarse, and she'd had to have his pants taken in. The diagnosis had been grim, but they'd had hope.

Hope that two years of endless treatments and perpetual decline had eaten away piece by piece.

She stared at the pale pink tips of her flats side by side on the gray carpet. "A nurse came every day to do all the things I couldn't."

"What happened after you covered him with the blanket?"

"I sat in the chair next to his bed and read the paper to him. He dozed off, as he always did. The nurse arrived and left. I gave him his sponge bath late in the afternoon. There was a vivid sunset that night, so I sat on the porch watching it through the trees."

She closed her eyes as a tear slipped down her cheek.

"What happened next, Allison?"

She swiped away the stream of tears and rocked in the chair.

"I killed my husband."

CHAPTER

THIRTY

Thick silence filled every corner of the room as muffled sobs shook her frame. A box of tissues slid onto her lap. Allison plucked one and glanced up.

Dr. King returned to his chair and silently waited for her to regain control.

She wiped her face and blew her nose.

"That's quite a damning statement."

"It was a damning act."

"What was your husband's prognosis?"

"Excuse me?"

"Was he going to recover?"

"No. The doctors said he was terminal. He had anywhere from days to a couple of months left."

"What were his wishes?"

"He begged me to let him go every single day." She held the tissue over her mouth and swallowed back a sob. "He would write the word please repeatedly on the board. When I refused, he would turn his head away and ignore me the rest of the day."

"Why did you refuse?"

Her mouth opened and closed as she stared at him, watching her from the chair. "It's a sin. Not to mention against the law."

"In Connecticut, yes, but it's not in some other states. Under certain circumstances, of course."

She nodded. "I checked into taking him somewhere else, but he was already in so much pain, I didn't want to cause him more."

"And why did you change your mind?"

"I'm not sure I did."

Allison wiped her eyes and sniffled. "I gave him a little extra to help with the pain, but there was no plan for anything more. I didn't think that little bit would kill him. But it did. I went back to check on him before bed, and he was gone."

"What makes you so sure it was because of what you did? You said the doctors told you it could be any day."

"Rather coincidental, don't you think? The day I give him an extra bit to ease the pain is the day he passes?"

"It doesn't matter what I think. It matters what you choose to believe. You've accepted blame for your husband's death similarly to the blame you've accepted for your parents' deaths."

"I was responsible."

"They were both accidental, were they not?"

"It doesn't change the fact that I was the cause."

"Tell me, if your mother or father were the ones to light the candle, would you blame them? You almost died in the same fire. Would you blame one of your parents? Tell them it was their fault? Hold it against them?" He tilted his head for a moment and tapped the shoe resting on his knee. "Would you have blamed your husband if the situation were reversed? Do you think he would blame you?"

Her gaze darted between the floor and his face. "I...I...no, I don't think so."

He nodded and set his foot on the floor. "Something to consider. I'd also like you to think about what your life might be like if you forgave yourself."

He stood and walked over to his desk. "Our time is up. We can talk more about this next time."

Allison absently nodded as she stood and walked to the door.

~

WELL-MAINTAINED, vibrant, green grass stretched over a low hill. The wrought-iron gate at the entrance was open and welcoming. It was a beautiful, sunny day. There were no foreboding shadows or depressing clouds. Allison stared at the headstones visible through the gate and over the stone wall.

Like stone soldiers lined up for battle, they spread across the grass. Blooms of color intermittently dotted stones where loved ones left flowers to commemorate those they lost.

There would be no flowers at Alan's grave. She wasn't even sure if they had put the stone in place. She ordered it when she arranged the funeral, but she'd neglected to follow up on it.

The last time she visited the cemetery was the day of his funeral. It had been a gray, windy day. The leaves had finally changed color. She had stared at the bright yellow leaves of the tree behind the minister delivering the ceremony. A handful of Alan's coworkers and students had stood at the grave with her. She remembered the shapes of them, but not a single face or anything that was said.

Why hadn't she come back? She'd told herself she didn't have the right to be a grieving widow, but maybe it was fear. Fear of facing his grave and her actions. Fear of delving too deep and allowing herself to grieve and possibly move on.

She'd driven straight here from the doctor's office after a quick stop at the nursery. He'd probably call it a breakthrough when she told them at their next appointment. If she went and if she told him.

Allison got out of the car and opened the back door to remove the geraniums and spade she'd bought.

She found the site quickly and easily, and a relieved sigh escaped her. A part of her had worried she wouldn't remember precisely where it was.

His headstone was in place, and it looked so dignified and classic that a small smile graced her lips. Alan would be pleased with it.

It took her only a few moments to plant a geranium on either side of the headstone. She brushed the dirt from her hands and sat down on the grass beside the stone.

"I'm sorry, Alan, for so many things." She placed her hand over his name. The guilt still plagued her. A part of her blamed herself, no matter what Dr. King said, but maybe that was because she wished she had been stronger and gave in to his pleading. Maybe that was where her true guilt stemmed from.

She dropped her hand and her head. She was damn tired of feeling guilty about everything. Wanting to let it all go and cleanse her soul was a dull ache inside her. The hope that she could was a tiny seed waiting for the sun and rain to nourish it and help it grow.

"I don't know if you can hear me. I'd like to believe you can, that maybe you've been watching me. And maybe you can forgive me."

She drew her knees to her chest and wrapped her arms around them. "I've met someone. His name is Jim."

Was it wrong to think or talk about Jim here at Alan's grave? She kept thinking about what the doctor had said about how would she feel if the situation was reversed. She'd want to know Alan was happy.

She might not be ready to call herself happy yet, but she was getting there.

And Jim was a part of that. An important part.

Was she becoming too attached to Jim, too dependent, maybe? Was she moving too quickly and wrapping her world around another man? A man she was destined to lose by his own admission?

Was her life always going to be about loss?

Would it be any less painful to lose someone because they walked away?

The answers remained to be seen.

"Alan, I loved you. Well, I hope. I hope you understand. I hope you forgave me. I hope you're smiling down at me and looking over the top of your glasses like you used to do when you patiently waited for me to come up with an answer to whatever problem I was trying to solve."

Peace descended over her as she sat in silence. Allison turned her face up to the sun. A gentle breeze caressed her cheek, and she smiled.

CHAPTER

THIRTY-ONE

The police officer who questioned her after the break-in stood on her front porch. What was his name? Had he told her? She couldn't recall. She hadn't thought she'd see him again. He'd stopped taking notes and hadn't said another word to her after she confessed to being responsible for the fire.

Officer Loretta Marvin was the one she expected to hear from. The policewoman had returned her call when she'd called to check if they had any more information. They hadn't. No leads beyond the vague description of the man purchasing the candles she'd already gotten.

"What can I do for you, Officer? Do you know who broke into my house?"

"No, I'm here about another matter which involves you." He shifted his stance. "We got a phone call concerning you and the death of your husband."

So much for patient confidentiality. No one else knew. And the doctor had seemed so understanding. Had it been an act?

"Did you confess to killing your husband?"

A calm whispered over her. "I did."

"You have the right to remain silent…" He pulled a set of hand-cuffs from his belt. The rest of her Miranda rights droned on as he put the cuffs on her. The metal was cold and surprisingly heavy.

Who would take care of Petunia?

She gazed up at the house as the officer led her to the back of his vehicle. She hadn't set the alarm or even locked the door. Anyone could walk right in. Not that it probably mattered anymore.

Had she known it would come to this? Had she even considered the possibility? Right after his death she had, but not now. She should have. There was no statute of limitations on murder.

She stared at the houses as he drove down the road. Would Jim come looking for her and find the house unlocked? He would feed Petunia.

What would he think of her when he found out they arrested her for killing her husband?

The scenery outside the vehicle blurred. She stared through the divider at the back of the officer's head. Other than the actual glance in the rearview mirror, he ignored her. The smell of stale coffee battled with the pine air freshener hanging from his dashboard.

The square brick building of the police station loomed ahead. She'd never been in a police station before. Her stomach rolled. What was going to happen to her?

Hours drifted by in a daze after the officer brought her into the station. She'd been fingerprinted and her picture taken. She was officially a criminal with a record now, wasn't she? It would forever be a part of her life. Anytime anyone looked up her name, it would appear. If she ever filled out a job application, would she have to check off the box stating she was a criminal? Or did that only happen once she was convicted?

What did it matter? She wasn't likely to be filling out any applications in the future now, anyway.

The smell of burned coffee and sweat wrinkled her nose. She glanced down at her clothes. It wasn't her. She wasn't even perspiring. Her skin was icy cold.

Allison numbly looked around the room.

Officer Loretta Marvin stared at her from across the room while she spoke quietly with the arresting officer.

She approached with a frown on her round face. She stopped in front of her with her hands on her hips.

"Don't I get a phone call, or is that only on TV? I need to call someone to take care of my cat."

"I don't recall seeing a cat when we were at your house."

"She's new, a kitten. The mother had them under my back porch, so the boy who owned her gave me one. I need to make sure she's taken care of."

"Why did you confess to killing your husband?"

"Because I think I might have accidentally given him too much pain medication. It was only a little more, but he died. Didn't Dr. King tell you all this?"

"Who's Dr. King?"

"My psychiatrist."

She pulled out a notebook and scribbled something down. "Why were you giving your husband pain medication?"

"Because he was terminally ill with cancer and in pain. It was his scheduled dose, just a little more because he was miserable."

Officer Marvin sighed and pulled out her phone. "What number would you like me to dial?"

After Allison rattled off Jim's phone number, the officer dialed it and pressed the speaker button while holding the phone in front of Allison's mouth.

Jim's voicemail immediately picked up. The sound of his voice brought tears to her eyes. She hadn't cried, not once, since she'd been arrested. She wasn't going to start now. If she did, she might never stop.

Allison bit her lip. When the phone beeped, she leaned forward in the chair. "Jim, it's Allison. I've been arrested. Could you please take care of Petunia? And lock up my house? If you can't or won't, maybe Karen would. Thank you."

She leaned back, and Officer Marvin ended the call and put the phone away.

"Do you have a lawyer?"

"Not a criminal one."

"You need to get one."

Allison nodded.

Officer Marvin strode away.

Allison rotated her shoulders with the limited movement the cuffs allowed. Her arms ached, and her eyelids grew heavy as more time passed. How strange would it be if she fell asleep right here in the chair?

How long would it be before they put her in a cell? And how was she going to find a lawyer?

An older man in a uniform with a long face and bushy white mustache stalked down the hallway toward her. Was he in charge? He had a commanding air. Officer Marvin walked behind him.

He flicked a hand in Allison's direction. "Take off her cuffs."

She rubbed her wrists and wiggled her fingers once Officer Marvin complied.

"Do you know Susan Clifford?"

She flinched. "She was my husband's nurse." Were they contacting her and Alan's doctors? Of course, they were. They would probably interview neighbors and Alan's colleagues too. Everyone.

"Did you know she's currently awaiting trial for the assisted deaths of three of her patients?"

The noise in the building was deafening. Phones rang like they were being blasted through a megaphone. Doors slammed shut. People's voices ricocheted like shotguns blasting back and forth at one another.

"Mrs. Delaney?"

Squinting against the roar of sound, she raised her head.

"I...no." Her heartbeat thundered.

"I just got off the phone with the arresting officer. She confessed to giving her patients a lethal dose of pain killer."

"But why wasn't I told? Shouldn't someone have told me?" Wouldn't they have investigated her other patients?

"I'm sure they would have gotten to you before the trial." He planted his hands on his hips. "I had an officer talk to her about your husband. She admitted to giving your husband an unscheduled dose that she knew, combined with your scheduled dose, would, as she put it, end his suffering."

She rubbed the middle of her forehead. "Why would she admit that?"

"Because she paints herself as a martyr or an angel of mercy."

The nurse had killed her husband, not her.

"You're free to go."

Her head rose to meet his gaze. "Just like that?"

"Do you have a problem with that?"

"No." She stood. Her legs wobbled, and she grabbed the back of the chair.

Officer Marvin took her arm. "I'll drive you home."

"Thank you."

She led her down the hall. The pale gray walls appeared to narrow like a tunnel. Allison swallowed and concentrated on placing one foot in front of the other. She wanted out of the building. Once she was safe in her home, she could break down privately.

"You should know it wasn't your doctor who turned you in. It was an anonymous tip from a woman."

Who? And how had they known?

THIRTY-TWO

J im played the voicemail a second time. He couldn't have heard her right, but there it was again. Allison said she had been arrested. For what? Jaywalking?

Cursing, he jogged over to her house to do as she asked. Once he took care of the cat and locked up, he would head to the police station and sort this out.

He should have turned around and gone home as soon as he realized he had left his phone behind, but he'd been halfway to the store already and had thought nothing of important enough to justify the wasted time it would take to drive home and get the phone and then drive all the way back to the store. It would have added a couple of hours to his day.

Petunia was in her favorite spot on Allison's bed. She didn't even open an eyelid when he poked his head in the door. He filled her food and water dishes, then strode down the hallway to set the alarm and lock the front door behind him. He didn't have a key to lock the deadbolt, but at least the door would be locked and the alarm system activated.

A police SUV pulled into the driveway. He lowered his hand from the alarm pad and opened the front door. The officer from the break-in opened the back door of her vehicle, and Allison slid out.

Her face was pale. She kept her head down and wrapped her arms around her waist as she stepped away from the vehicle and mumbled something to the officer.

Jim jogged down the steps. The officer glanced at him, nodded, and got in her car. Allison paused on the walkway when she spotted him. He put his arms around her.

"What the hell happened? Are you okay?"

She rested her forehead against his chest.

"Let's get you inside." He led her to the front porch. "I didn't get your message until a few minutes ago. Petunia is fine."

She nodded as they went into the house.

"Do you want me to make you tea? Or would you like something stronger? You got any whiskey?"

"I'm fine."

"You're not fine. What's going on?"

She rested a hand on the banister and stared at the floor. "They arrested me for killing my husband."

What the fuck?

Jim rubbed a hand over his face. His mind was blank. He didn't know what to say. Obviously, it had to be a mistake.

"Your husband died of cancer, didn't he?"

"Yes...and no. He had terminal cancer. The doctor gave him days —weeks at most."

Allison shook her head and tucked her hair behind her ear. "I gave him a little extra pain medicine that day. Combined with what the nurse gave him, it was probably a fatal dose. But without an autopsy, they probably won't know for sure. I don't even know if it's too late to tell." She glanced at him and then upstairs. "I know you probably have a lot of questions. So do I. I can't process anything right now. My mind is mush. I need a shower and to lie down."

"Of course, we can talk later. Do you need anything?"

She stepped on the first tread and shook her head. "Just rest."

She climbed the stairs and disappeared into her room. Did she just say she might have given her husband a lethal dose of pain medication?

Jim set the alarm, locked the front door before leaving, and walked to his own house. Was she out on bail? Were the police digging up her husband and performing an autopsy? Wouldn't it be manslaughter if she hadn't intentionally overdosed her husband, or were they saying it was premeditated and she planned to kill him? Why? He was dying anyway. What could they say her motive would be?

He grabbed a beer from the fridge and dropped into the kitchen chair. Another accidental death. The bodies were piling up around her. Either she was one of the unluckiest people he'd ever come across, or something sinister was going on.

Two supposedly unrelated and accidental incidents where her family ended up dead. The odds of that happening in one person's lifetime had to be astronomical.

Did he completely misjudge her? Was her innocent demeanor all an act? Could she be hiding the heart of a killer?

CHAPTER

THIRTY-THREE

The parking lot wasn't full of customers, something in her favor today. Allison winced. Karen wasn't likely to feel the same way. Her business relied on customers.

There was an empty parking space at the back of the lot, so she headed there. She had intended to carry the product in the front door, but maybe the back was unlocked. She could peek out front and somehow get Karen's attention without alerting the entire building. A phone call. She'd call Karen from the back or from right outside if necessary. Not that it was likely anyone would recognize her with the scarf she'd wrapped over her hair and tied under her chin or the dark sunglasses she rummaged through her drawers to find. She never dreamed she'd be hiding behind a disguise like a starlet avoiding the paparazzi or a criminal afraid of recognition.

She'd decided not to sit around waiting for Karen to bring the product to Guilty Pleasures because she didn't want to spiral backward and resort to hiding in her house. Karen had been dropping by daily for the last week to pick up the baked goods. She had told Allison to take a break from the business, but baking soothed her and gave her something else to focus on.

203

Once Karen assured her she wanted to stay in business with her despite the latest catastrophe of her life, she'd insisted on picking up and delivering the product to Guilty Pleasures every day. Probably to check on whether or not Allison had had a nervous breakdown since the last time she'd seen her.

Allison carried the box over to the cement stairs at the back door. She juggled the box and then rested it between her hip and the house to free a hand and test the door—unlocked—success.

The door opened unexpectantly. Her hand slid off the handle, and she grabbed for the box with both hands as she stumbled back.

"Allison?"

Resting her butt against the railing and clutching the box in her hands, Allison smiled at Karen standing in the open doorway. "Hi."

"What are you doing here?" She glanced at the box. "Did you bring your product? I was planning to stop by during lunch."

"I needed to get out of the house before I grew roots and planted myself there again. I don't want to regress."

"I get that. Come on in." Karen took the box and turned, bumping the door with her hip until Allison grabbed it and followed her inside.

The backroom doubled as a storage room and office. Karen placed the box down on a table with brushes, combs, and hair accessories lumped in plastic bags. "I was taking inventory, so ignore the mess."

"Sorry for interrupting."

"Don't be. I hate inventory days." She waved her hand at Allison. "What's with the getup?"

"Oh." Allison removed the glasses and scarf. The room lightened considerably. "My ridiculous attempt to go incognito."

"They cleared you of any wrongdoing."

"One part of my brain knows that. It's the rest of me that hasn't quite got the message yet."

"Are you afraid others will judge you or are you judging yourself?"

"Both."

Karen walked over and gave her a hug. "You're too hard on yourself."

"Am I? I still don't know how I feel about Alan's nurse. She confessed to killing my husband, but I can't dredge up any anger towards her. It would be hypocritical of me if I did. She did what Alan begged me endless times to do. Who's to say it wasn't my increased dose that really did it?"

"If we were in Oregon or one of the other states that support death with dignity, then this wouldn't even be an issue."

"I've told myself that too."

Allison twisted the scarf in her hands. "I've been thinking of going to church on Sunday. I haven't been since before Alan's death."

"Understandable. People question their faith at the senseless death of loved ones and you've lost more than most."

"I don't think it was a loss of faith. More like I felt like such a sinner, and I didn't belong there anymore. I didn't have the right to go to church."

"Oh Allison, you have to forgive yourself for being human. You carry too much on your shoulders."

"Mrs. Pannelli across the street used to stop by all the time to convince me to go back to church. She hasn't come by in weeks. I think she may have given up on me."

"All the more reason to go. If you want, Charlie and I can accompany you. I've been neglecting his spiritual education lately. That's my guilty confession."

"I was planning on slipping in the back so no one would notice, but I'd like the company."

"Then it's a date." She propped her hands on her hips. "Speaking of dates, what's going on with you and Jim?"

"Nothing."

"What do you mean?"

"I haven't seen him since the day I got arrested. I can't blame him. My life is a soap opera. I've got way too much baggage for a casual relationship to survive. He was only looking for a temporary hookup."

"Have you called him?"

"No. I picked up my phone several times, but I figured it was up to him. If he'd decided it was all too much, then I had to let him bow out and not try to draw him back in."

"He doesn't deserve you then."

Allison gave her a sad smile. "What about you? Are you dating anyone?"

Karen rolled her eyes and leaned against the table, holding the edges. "You remember that dating app I told you one of my clients recommended?"

"You signed up?"

"Yes, in a weak moment last night—after a little too much wine. Now I have a date on Friday night."

"You sound so thrilled with the prospect."

"He sounds like a nice guy in print anyway, and if the picture is to be believed, he's good-looking."

"Then what's the problem?"

"I'm too jaded. Guys always end up being a disappointment."

"You have to keep trying. What's the alternative?" Eternal loneliness. Endless days and nights.

"Switching sides. What do you say? Want to become a lesbian with me? You and I could be a couple."

Allison threw her head back and laughed. "You think life would be easier?"

"Yes. I've wished more than once I was attracted to women rather than men. We're the more rational gender and definitely more intelligent and emotionally mature."

"I'm so glad we're friends. You provide some much-needed laughter in my life."

"You're laughing, but I'm only half-joking. We become blinded by men's sexy abs and asses, smoldering eyes, and strong shoulders."

"I almost feel sorry for your date on Friday."

"Oh, don't feel sorry for him. Unless he's a complete jackass, he's going to get lucky. I haven't had sex in too long, and my standards are currently at an all-time low."

"Well, be careful. And remember, I'm only a phone call away if you need anything." Allison gave her a one-arm hug.

"Ditto, my friend."

Jim took a long swig from the bottle of beer, then placed it on the counter. He braced his arms on the counter and hung his head. Three boards mismeasured and now useless. A broken saw blade.

Lumber prices were on the rise, and he couldn't afford to keep making mistakes. His head wasn't in the game. Dangerous business when you worked with tools that could slice open an artery or remove a limb in the blink of an eye.

He should call it a day and hope tomorrow he could focus on work instead of Allison.

They had arrested her for murdering her husband. Another accident like her parents? He rubbed his palms over his face.

What the actual fuck.

The odds were not in her favor. Was she some sort of black widow? What did you call someone responsible for the deaths of her parents? Had it really been an accident? Did her sweet and innocent demeanor hide a heart of pure evil? She must be one hell of an actress.

Was he really that big of a fool that he fell for her act hook, line, and sinker?

He admitted the women he'd been involved with had a tendency to screw him over, but they hadn't murdered anyone. Not to his knowledge, anyway.

He was ghosting her. He didn't know what to say. Would she give him some sob story? He only had a couple months left of work on the house, and then he could put it up for sale and move on to the next one. He usually waited until it sold, but he could carry the expense. The way the market was right now, it'd probably sell quick. He could avoid her that long.

Why did he feel like such a dick for even considering it? She was the one arrested for murder. Any normal guy would run for the hills.

The peel of the doorbell echoed through the house, ending in an off-tune crackle. He needed to replace it. The sound was like nails on a chalkboard.

Sighing, he pushed off the counter, walked across the kitchen, and came to a stop. What if it was Allison at the front door?

He rubbed his forehead. He would not hide in his house to avoid her. That would be ridiculous.

Jim cracked his neck, strode to the front door, and swung it open.

Not Allison. Her friend from down the street.

She raised an eyebrow and drummed dark red nails on her folded arms. The scowl on her face straightened his spine. He didn't need to deal with an irate neighbor right now. What the hell was her problem?

Her eyes narrowed, and she pointed her finger in his face. "You're an asshole!"

He reared his head back and planted his hands on his hips. "Excuse me?"

"There is no excuse. Not a single, damned one."

"Look, lady, I don't know what your problem is, but back the hell off."

"I wish I'd poisoned the muffins I brought for you."

Great, she's crazy. "So, what, you're mad I didn't return the container or something? A little overkill on the poison, don't you think?"

"Wow, you are an idiot. Not surprising since most of your gender seems to be infected with that same affliction." She poked him in the chest with that bright red fingernail. "Allison is my friend, asshole."

Shit!

Jim backed up a step.

"You don't get to treat her like garbage. She's going through a nightmare, and you suddenly decide to disappear? She's okay to have sex with, but as soon as one little thing goes wrong, you jump ship?"

He folded his arms over his chest. "Being arrested for murder is hardly one little thing. What's between us is none of your damn business. Now, if you don't mind, I have things to do." He took another step back and grabbed the door.

She slapped her palm against it. "I do mind! If you'd bothered to stick around, you would have known the nurse confessed, and they cleared her. But you wouldn't know that because you found her guilty without asking for the truth. If you knew her at all, you would have had faith in her innocence and known it was all a horrid mistake. But you've made your choice. Now I'm here to tell you to stay the hell away from her. You don't get to go crawling back and hurt her any more than you have, got it?" She raised her chin. "Now I'm done."

She stalked down his stairs and driveway. He closed the door, leaving his hand against it, and hung his head.

Allison was innocent.

Her friend was right. He was an asshole. He'd judged her guilty right off the mark.

His phone rang, and he pulled it out of his pocket. Jackie. He moved his thumb to send his sister straight to voicemail but hesitated.

She could be calling because something was seriously wrong. He'd already screwed up with Allison by making assumptions.

"Hey, Jackie. It's not a good time right now. Everything all right?"

"No! Jack left me! He took off with some anorexic twat who's barely legal!"

Jim leaned forward and banged his head on the door. Who the hell was Jack? Last he knew, she was dating her divorce lawyer. He didn't remember his name, but it was something snooty sounding like Carstairs or Clifton, not Jack.

"Are you listening to me?"

He held the phone away from his ear. Anyone in the immediate vicinity would have a tough time not hearing her. "Yeah, I'm listening."

She sniffled. Both his mother and sister could turn the waterworks on in an instant whenever it suited them. "I'm stuck in Lake Tahoe with no money. Can you wire me some to tide me over?"

He shook his head. Translation—will you support me until I latch on to the next meal ticket?

"Text me the details, and I'll take care of it. I've got to go." He disconnected the phone and threw it across the room.

It landed with a slap against the floor in the corner.

Great! Now he'd have to replace his phone too.

He strode back to the kitchen and polished off the rest of his beer. Since high school, his mother and sister had used him as their own personal ATM. He'd often found his wallet emptied, and his mother even cleared out his bank account once. He'd closed it out and hadn't opened another until he was eighteen, and she couldn't gain access.

He'd tried refusing in the past, but the drama that ensued wasn't worth it. Besides, they were still his family. All he had.

After retrieving his phone and finding it undamaged with just a few more scuff marks, he read his sister's texts and went online to send the money. It's a good thing he'd learned early on to be frugal with his money. His football days had given him a solid nest egg.

Jim leaned a shoulder against the door jamb of the back door. The screen had a few holes. Even the patch someone had done over the years had a hole. Something else he would need to replace unless he wanted to be a meal for the mosquitos.

Allison's yard had been mowed recently, but he hadn't seen or heard her. She must have done it while he was picking up supplies yesterday.

The friend was right. He should stay away from her. He'd known that from the start. This time, he would listen and keep his distance.

Right after he apologized and groveled.

THIRTY-FOUR

Allison spotted Jim walking across his backyard into hers out of the corner of her eye. She gripped the edges of the white wicker chair, prepared to bolt, but then sagged back into the chair. The odds of him not seeing her make a run for the house were slim to none. She sat on her screened porch, directly in his line of vision. In fact, he was staring straight at her.

She turned her gaze away. Hiding in the house was in her past, not her future. He'd decided to talk to her again, and she would hear what he had to say. He probably wanted to tell her they were over in case she hadn't already gotten the message loud and clear.

The tree she gazed at blurred. All her attention focused on his approaching steps. The rustle of grass against his shoes. The whisper of his clothes as he walked.

"Hello Allison, can we talk?"

He stood on the steps outside the screen door. Brown bangs lifted and fell over his forehead in the late afternoon breeze. Milk chocolate-colored eyes gazed solemnly at her. Who invented chocolate? It must have been a man, created as an instrument for women's downfall.

"Of course. Can I get you something to drink?"

Please say no. She wasn't sure her legs would support her.

"No, thanks." He opened the door and stepped inside. Her gaze traveled over his baby blue T-shirt and faded blue jeans and skirted to the side and back to the tree in her yard.

Yup, her heart still reacted to the sight of him. Maybe it was just nerves.

He sat on the wicker couch across from her and rested his elbows on his thighs as he leaned toward her.

Just get it over with!

Jim was obviously gearing up to let her down easy. He'd never been this hesitant with her, like he was searching for the right words or afraid she would make a scene. Was that it? Did he really think she was going to scream at him or beg him not to break up with her?

Maybe that was what he was used to, but he wouldn't get it from her. She'd known it was coming, and she did her breaking down in private. Well, most of the time.

"I'm sorry."

Yeah, me too.

She should let him off the hook and end the misery for both of them.

"I shouldn't have jumped to conclusions."

Wait, what? What kind of breakup speech is this? Conclusions about what? She frowned.

"I judged you guilty without even hearing your side. I have no excuse. I wouldn't have thought I was the type of person to do that, but I did, and I should have known better. I don't expect you to forgive me, but I had to apologize."

"You're talking about me being arrested for Alan's murder?"

His eyebrows pressed together. "Yes."

"Oh." She waved a hand in front of her. "I don't blame you."

The blank look on Jim's face almost brought a smile to hers. Almost.

"Jim, I'm sure anyone would find it difficult not to judge me, considering the circumstances. I judge myself plenty. I was responsible for the fire that killed my parents, and then I was arrested for killing my husband. Only a saint wouldn't doubt my innocence."

"Your friend, Karen, didn't."

"What do you mean?" When had he talked to Karen?

"She stopped by earlier this afternoon and gave me hell. Told me about your innocence, that a nurse had done it."

"She shouldn't have done that."

"I'm glad she did."

Allison sighed and crossed her legs at the knee. Karen shouldn't have gone to Jim, but she appreciated her friend's loyalty. At least she had one friend in the world and wasn't completely alone anymore. Although most of that was her own doing. She'd pushed everyone who remained away long ago. The guilt had been her prison.

"What else did she tell you?"

"That's about it. Called me an asshole a few times. I thought she was going to punch me, but she restrained herself. Quite a firecracker."

Allison winced. "Sorry."

"You don't owe me an apology." He rubbed his palms on his jeans. "Can you tell me what happened, or is it too painful to talk about?"

"There's not much more to tell. I was arrested, and they let me go after finding out the nurse who cared for Alan confessed to giving him a lethal dose of medicine. She's already confessed to doing it to several of her clients."

"That's...I don't know even what to say. At least they caught her. They'll put her away for a long time. You got justice for your husband."

"Did I?"

"What do you mean?"

"You came over and apologized because Karen told you I'm innocent, right?"

"I'd like to think I would have come to my senses eventually, but yeah."

"I'm not."

"Not what?"

"Innocent."

Jim reared back. "What are you saying?"

"The nurse may have given him the fatal dose, but I had increased his medication that day too. He'd been begging me for weeks to help him end the pain. He wanted to die. I think he hated me at the end for not helping him sooner. That will live with me forever."

She pressed her lips together as her eyes filled.

"I stopped going to church not long after Alan got sick. At first, I thought it was because I simply didn't have the time, then I blamed the church for his suffering. Not that he got sick, but that letting him choose his own end was a sin. I blamed religion. I blamed the laws. But deep down, I was really blaming myself for not being strong enough to help him do what he wanted."

She met Jim's gaze. "The nurse did what I couldn't. I don't blame her for Alan's death. I thank her for it."

He stared at her silently. Was he regretting his apology now? Most likely, who wouldn't?

"I can't speak for her other patients, of course. I don't know if they wanted to end their lives like Alan did."

"I don't know if I would be strong enough to help a loved one, either. You can't blame yourself. I've never been in a comparable situation, and I certainly hope I never am. I'm sure your husband didn't hate you. He hated the circumstances probably, not you."

"That's kind of you to say, and I hope you're right."

"I'm confused, though. Why did they arrest you in the first place? Were they investigating your husband's death?"

"No. I thought my therapist reported me since I had just told him about Alan's death and the role I played in our session. But the officer told me a woman had called in an anonymous tip. I have no idea who or why."

"Do you think it's related to your parents' deaths and the person harassing you?"

"I hope not, but the thought has crossed my mind. I don't know how they would know, though. My therapist is the first one I've ever talked to about it. I also thought maybe the nurse had to throw suspicion off herself, but then she confessed to Alan so that doesn't make any sense either."

"The police are following up, right?"

She shrugged. "I didn't think to ask at the time, and the experience wasn't something I wanted to relive. If anything else happens with the calls or packages, I'll call, but otherwise, I'm hoping whoever it was is done."

Jim shook his head. "Whoever is doing this is twisted. Knowing a woman made the call doesn't make anyone come to mind?"

"No. I don't know if they're the same person. According to the store clerk, it was a man who bought the candles."

"More than one person then if they are related."

"It's still a lot of ifs and maybes. Like I said, if something else happens, I'll talk to the police again."

"How about dinner? We could go out, or I've got some chicken I could grill."

Allison blinked. Did he want to continue their relationship?

She'd assumed it was over, had accepted it.

"I don't think so, not tonight." Maybe never. She didn't blame him for thinking her guilty and disappearing, but it had still hurt a lot. How much more would it hurt if they continued to grow close, and it came time for him to move on? Her heart didn't appear to understand what a casual relationship meant.

"Jim, I don't blame you, really, I don't. But I think it's best if our relationship remains platonic from here on. We both know it was temporary from the start."

"Okay, I respect that. Friends can still eat together, can't they?"

A twinge of disappointment spread through her. She hadn't expected him to protest or try to change her mind, but maybe he could have shown a little regret that it was over. Maybe he had already decided it was over and had asked about dinner as a friend. How embarrassing.

Her cheeks heated, and she looked away. "Sure they can, but another time, okay?"

Jim stood. "So, we're good then, right? No hard feelings?"

She forced a smile to her lips. "We're good."

He opened the screen door and glanced over his shoulder. "Call me if you need anything."

"Thanks. Have a good night."

He nodded and walked down the steps. The screen door slammed shut behind him. He walked back to his yard.

For the second time that day, tears filled her eyes. Would that be their final goodbye? He said to call, but she wouldn't. He probably knew that. It was just something people said.

CHAPTER

THIRTY-FIVE

The screech of a smoke alarm woke her. She lurched up and frantically blinked the sleep away. Was she dreaming? Another nightmare?

No, the sharp peal continued, and the unmistakable stench of smoke made her recoil. Allison flung the blanket off her and scrambled out of bed.

She raced down the stairs with her nightgown flowing behind her. The smoke thickened. She stood in the hall, staring in horror at the flames engulfing her kitchen cabinets. Breaths sawed from her lungs as her eyes watered from the smoke stinging her eyes.

She had to get out.

Allison spun to the front door and grasped the knob in her hand. *Wait!*

Petunia! Where was Petunia?

She couldn't be responsible for another death!

Tears poured down her face as she gripped the banister in her hand. She opened her mouth to call for the kitten, but savage coughs erupted from her instead.

Was she still asleep on the bed? No, surely the sound had awoken her. Had she hidden somewhere?

Move, Allison! You'll never find her standing around debating.

She charged up the stairs and back into her bedroom.

The bed was empty.

"Petunia!"

Coughs wracked her. She ran to the bathroom, wet a towel, and held it to her mouth. She dropped to her knees and searched under the bed for the kitten. It was dark, and no eyes peered back at her.

Where could she be?

Allison ran back down the stairs with the towel over her mouth. There wasn't time to search for the kitten.

But she wasn't leaving the cat to die.

She opened the hall closet and yanked out the fire extinguisher. The fire was still contained in the kitchen, wasn't it?

Allison pulled the pin as she ran to the kitchen. Flames ravaged her cabinets and counter, and the curtains over the window had dissolved to ash. Thick smoke filled the room.

She aimed the extinguisher at the lower cabinets and swept it back and forth as she squeezed the lever.

Heat assaulted her face.

The roar of the flames and the whoosh of the fire retardant battled for supremacy in her scalded ears.

Her throat was raw from smoke and coughing. She'd abandoned the wet towel on the floor to hold the extinguisher with both hands.

She aimed the spray higher when the lower cabinets were no longer engulfed in flames.

A pounding reached her ears over the screeching alarms, flames, and extinguisher.

Breaking glass brought her head around.

Oh, God! Was there a fire in the front too? Was she surrounded?

"Allison!"

The extinguisher jerked in her hand. Was that Jim?

"Allison!"

His yells came from the front of the house.

She opened her mouth to respond, but her mouth filled with smoke, and a coughing fit brought her to her knees.

"Allison!" Jim's arms wrapped around her and lifted her into his arms.

She swatted at his arm.

He glanced down at her. "I have to get you out of here!"

"Petunia. I can't find her!" The raw whisper burned her throat.

She pointed to the extinguisher on the floor and pleaded with her eyes to help her put out the fire.

He set her down. "Go! I'll do what I can."

He grabbed the extinguisher and sprayed the cabinets.

Allison ran to the kitchen extinguisher on the wall and joined him.

"No! You have to leave!"

She ignored Jim and continued spraying.

His extinguisher sputtered and died as the last of the flames blackening the cabinets were eliminated.

He dropped his, grabbed hers, and ran to the back door.

What was he doing?

He placed his hand on the door before unlocking and wrenching it open. He disappeared onto the porch.

She stumbled behind him.

Flames licked the entire wall. The screens were gone.

Jim aimed the extinguisher at the fire.

Allison ran back inside. She had two more extinguishers upstairs.

By the time she returned hefting the two canisters, the second extinguisher had sputtered out.

Jim grabbed one from her arms and continued battling the flames, which had been beaten back to the charred corner of her screen porch.

She stepped up next to him and aimed her extinguisher too.

A crash came from the kitchen.

Jim looked at her. "Stay here." He coughed as he ran back inside.

She scanned the porch. The fire was out.

Unless it had been in the walls and reemerged in the kitchen or somewhere else!

She ran back inside with her hand over her mouth and the extinguisher bouncing against her leg.

Her upper cabinets along the back wall had crashed to the floor.

Sirens wailed closer and closer.

"Get outside. The fire is out, and the fire trucks are arriving."

She glanced upstairs.

"I'll find the cat."

She bit her lip. Coughs shook her and scraped her throat.

"You need fresh air. Go."

"What about you?" Her voice croaked like a frog, and she winced in pain.

"You've been exposed longer. I'll be fine." He snatched the wet towel from the floor where she had dropped it and covered his mouth as he jogged down the hall.

Allison turned and went outside. She didn't stop walking until she reached the tree in her backyard.

A shudder went through her, and she sank to the ground, staring at the destruction of her screened-in porch and the kitchen beyond.

The searchlight at the other corner of the house remained and shed light on the charred remains smoking in the night.

The upper story looked intact, but the siding was melted and distorted.

Her hands shook as she wiped her damp cheeks. Soot coated her hands. She scrubbed them on her ruined nightgown.

Jim appeared on the remains of the screen porch while firefighters in full gear assessed the damage.

He carried a towel in his arms.

She planted her hands on the ground to help her stand, but her limbs were shaking too much to support her.

Jim strode down the stairs and crossed the lawn to her.

"I found her in the bathtub."

He held out the towel. Two little eyes peered out. Petunia meowed, and her pink nose appeared in the opening.

Jim squatted in front of her. "How do you feel?"

Allison took the bundle from his arms and cradled her against her chest.

She just shook her head as tears continued to roll down her face.

Jim eased down beside her and wrapped his arms around her and the cat.

THIRTY-SIX

"I've packed you a bag. The last of the crew is packing up. Let's get you settled at my house, and then I'll come back for Petunia's things."

Allison stared at the bag in Jim's hands. Where had he found it? It was Alan's. He'd used the brown leather satchel whenever he'd gone away on business. She hadn't seen it in years.

She sat in one of her front porch rockers under the tree in the backyard next to Petunia, curled up sleeping in her cat carrier. Jim had brought the chair around back about an hour ago and gently insisted she sit.

Firefighters, police, and arson inspectors had traipsed all over her house and asked dozens of questions all day. EMTs had tried to convince her to go to the hospital after poking and prodding at her, but she had refused.

Jim had produced pants and a sweatshirt for her this morning, and she'd stuffed her nightgown into the pants and pulled the sweatshirt over the top.

She reeked of smoke.

He squatted down in front of her and set the bag on the ground.

"Honey, you can't stay here. Not only does the house need to be cleaned top to bottom to get rid of the smell, but it's not safe."

He was right. It wasn't safe. There were holes in the back of her house. The kitchen and porch were destroyed. Good thing she had intended to renovate the kitchen. Now Lucas would have even more work on his hands. She'd have to call him as he was scheduled to start this week.

The lilac bush she'd planted when she moved in was annihilated—gone like it never existed.

"You understand that, right?"

She glanced at him. He had a worried frown on his face. His speech had gotten slower and softer. Did he think she was having a nervous breakdown? The thought had crossed her mind when a fire-fighter mentioned an investigator because they suspected arson.

"It's a crime scene now. You can't go back in there. They only let me get a few things for you while a policewoman followed me around. I put the cat's stuff over there." He pointed to a couple of boxes by the steps. "I've got her food, litter box, and cat bed."

She never used the cat bed, but it was thoughtful of him.

Yellow tape stretched across the back of her house. The term accelerant had been spoken more than once today.

Someone had tried to burn down her house. With her inside.

Who hated her so much to want her dead?

This went far beyond harassment.

"Allison?"

She tilted her head back and looked up at the branches of the tree and the hundreds of green leaves with glimpses of the blue sky beyond.

So much for keeping her distance from Jim. Where else could she go? A hotel? Karen would let her stay on the couch for a few days, but how long would the investigation take? Could she impose that long?

No, she couldn't bring this danger to Karen and Charlie.

"Are you sure you want me in your house?" Her voice sounded foreign to her ears. Her throat was still sore.

"What kind of question is that?"

"An honest one. Someone set fire to my house with me in it. What's stopping them from doing the same to yours?"

"I'll stock up on fire extinguishers." A smile twitched his lips. "I've got to admit when I first saw the number of extinguishers you kept in your house, I thought it was overkill, but now I understand. If you hadn't had so many, you probably would have lost the house completely."

"A silver lining?"

"Too soon?"

"It's never too soon."

"Okay, you're alive and well, Petunia's fine, and your house can be repaired."

All excellent points.

"The police are going to patrol the street. Whoever is doing this has escalated to attempted murder now. It's sad to say, but that bumps you up the priority list."

"Lucky me."

"What do you say? I'll draw you a bath in my newly renovated bathroom. You'll be the first to use it. I'll defrost some steaks and throw them on the grill. Sound like a plan?"

"Thank you. Have I said that yet? Without your help, I don't know what would have happened."

"You have a few dozen times. You were actually handling it quite well on your own. Scared the hell out of me, though. Most people would have just gotten out and not tried to put it out themselves."

"I couldn't find Petunia, and I couldn't let her burn in the house. It was the only option I could see."

Jim stood and tugged on her hand. "Come on, let's get cleaned up and comfortable. Neither one of us has eaten all day. I'm starved."

She let him pull her upright and then slipped her hand out of his to pick up Petunia's carrier. He picked up the bag and tilted his head towards his house.

∼

Jim lay in bed with his arms crossed beneath his head. He hadn't begun any renovations in this room, so the guest room remained firmly stuck in the last century with faded, torn gold striped wallpaper and ugly shag carpet. At least he had a bed to sleep in. He missed his bed.

He missed sleeping in it next to Allison.

At least she had agreed to come to his house. How long she agreed to stay was another matter entirely.

He was an idiot for thinking she could murder her husband. How could he have doubted her?

Because he'd lumped her in the same category as all the other women in his life. Allison wasn't like them. He'd known it from the first. Why hadn't he remembered that when it counted?

If he hadn't judged her, she probably wouldn't have been alone and vulnerable. He would have been there, or she would have been here.

Maybe he could convince her to get away, take a vacation or something until the son of a bitch was caught. He'd go with her if she agreed, but he doubted she would. She made it clear they were only friends now.

Friends went on vacation together.

A cry sounded from the other bedroom.

He was out of bed and down the hall in seconds, knocking on the door. "Allison?"

Without giving her a chance to answer, he opened the door. What if the bastard had followed them and got inside without setting off the alarm or alerting him?

Allison sat up in bed with the bedding pooled around her. Her blonde hair hid her features with her head lowered. Petunia blinked at him from the end of the bed. At least she wasn't sleeping on his pillow.

"Are you okay? I thought I heard you cry out."

She tucked her hair behind her ear and frowned. "Nightmare. Sorry."

He let go of the doorknob and walked across to the bed. "Nothing to be sorry about."

She gave him a wobbly smile. He sat next to her and put his arm around her. She didn't pull away, just rested her head on his shoulder.

"How about I stay here with you? Strictly platonic, I promise. I wasn't getting any sleep in the guest room, anyway. It's been a hell of a day."

She nodded.

He glanced at the cat before he got up, walked around to the other side of the bed, and climbed in. Allison lay down and pulled the covers up to her chin. Her big blue eyes watched him slide under the covers. He lifted his arm, and after a few seconds of hesitation, she scooted over and snuggled against his chest.

"Do you want to talk about the nightmare?"

Her hair tickled his chin as she shook her head. The faintest scent of smoke drifted up his nose. They'd both showered and bathed for a long time to wash away the stench of smoke, but it lingered.

He kissed the top of her head. "Go to sleep. I won't let anything happen to you."

She tilted her head back and gazed up at him. "Would it be so wrong if I asked you to make me forget?"

Her hand slid to the center of his chest, and her gaze dropped to his lips.

His body responded instantly. He lifted his hand and cupped her cheek.

"I'm probably shooting myself in the foot here, but are you sure? I don't want you to have any regrets. You're vulnerable right now, and I don't want to take advantage."

"I think I'm the one taking advantage." She lifted herself up on her elbow and kissed him.

It wasn't a friendly sort of kiss. It was a deep dueling of tongues that made every part of him tingle and stand up for attention.

She straddled him.

Her heat settled over his erection, and he groaned. Even through their underwear, her heat engulfed him. He put his hands on her hips and pressed against her.

She leaned over him and captured his lips again.

He slid his hands under her nightgown and pulled it up and over her head, sending the cloth flying and baring her to his hungry gaze. He was becoming partial to her old-fashioned nightgowns. They were sexy as hell on her.

Their lips and tongues tangled as he massaged her breasts.

She rocked against him.

He palmed her ass and surged against her. She gasped and rocked faster.

Holy. Shit.

He would finish in his underwear if they kept going like this. A definite first for him.

He tugged at the back of her panties with one hand and reached for his nightstand with the other. *Please let there be condoms inside.* He'd already broken his own rule about always using a condom once with Allison because he couldn't wait. He'd never done that with any other woman—never trusted them enough.

"Baby, help me get these off."

She lifted slightly and yanked down her panties while he removed his boxers and fumbled with the package of condoms.

Bliss raced down his spine like lightning when she enclosed him in her liquid heat. He arched his head back and gazed at her through slitted eyes as she rode him.

She was a goddess.

A beautiful, perfect goddess.

Her eyes closed, and her teeth bit into her bottom lip as she braced her hands on his chest. He ground his back teeth together, trying to make it last so she could find her pleasure before he lost control.

Her mouth opened, and a low keening moan escaped her just as she tightened around him and sent him flying over the edge.

CHAPTER

THIRTY-SEVEN

Allison snuck glances at Jim across the kitchen table. He'd made them French toast for breakfast after making love to her again this morning.

There'd been no words or conversation. She'd opened her eyes to find him watching her. He'd kissed her, and all thoughts had vacated her brain.

Until now.

Should they have a conversation? Had this morning just been a continuation of last night—which she had initiated and didn't regret one bit.

"Do you have any plans today? I was going to go to the store to replace some equipment and wood, but I can put that off if you don't feel like going with me. We could hang out here."

"You know you don't have to babysit me, don't you?"

He paused with his fork hovering over his plate. "I'm not leaving you alone."

"Who knows how long it will be before the police catch this person, if they even will. You can't glue yourself to my side forever."

"Sure I can."

"Jim, be realistic. I'm perfectly fine on my own. You have a security system."

"So did you. No."

He took a bite of his breakfast, like a T-Rex chomping on its prey. Several more pieces disappeared the same way.

She sighed. He was angry. On her behalf, yes, but still...she wasn't his responsibility. They were supposed to be putting distance between them, not attached to each other at the hip. She was living with him again. How was she supposed to get over him if she lived in his house and in his bed?

"I'll go to the store with you today."

He glanced at her, and the corner of his mouth ticked up. "You sure? We can go another day."

"I'm sure." She rose and carried her plate over to the sink. "I need to shower and get dressed first. When do you want to leave?"

She walked back to the table and paused next to him. He took her hand and pulled her onto his lap.

"We could save time by showering together."

His lips captured hers. The sweet taste of maple syrup coated his tongue.

Oh yes, she was definitely in trouble.

"Who are you? Why are you answering his door? Is that his shirt?"

The woman's belligerent tone put Allison's back up. Who was she? The woman had short dark hair with a streak of pink at the top. Heavy, smudged eye makeup ringed a pair of ice-blue eyes. She would be pretty without the scowl on her face.

Allison had found the shirt hanging in Jim's closet. All her clothes reeked of smoke, so Jim told her to wear whatever she wanted of his while she washed and dried hers.

The woman grabbed a fist full of the football jersey.

"Hey!" Allison knocked the woman's hand away.

"What's going on?" Jim charged through the house. He had been out back measuring wood. It had taken her over an hour to convince him it was safe to go outside. He'd never leave her side after this. She shouldn't have answered the door.

He shouldered past her and tucked Allison behind his back. "Who are you?"

Allison peeked around Jim's shoulder. The woman widened her eyes, opened her mouth, and snapped it shut before whirling around and running down the steps across the yard. She hopped into a red compact parked on the street and took off.

Jim stepped out on the stoop and snapped several pictures of the car as it drove away. He turned back to Allison. "What happened?"

"I don't know. I opened the door, and she demanded to know what I was doing here and why I was wearing your shirt. She grabbed the shirt like she wanted to tear it off me. You don't know her?"

Jim swore and dialed his phone. "I'm calling the police."

Allison closed and locked the door while he talked on the phone. He paced back and forth across the living room while he recanted the events. She wrapped her arms around her waist and looked out the window to her house. Who was the woman? She couldn't be the one responsible for terrorizing her and setting fire to her house, could she? Why? She'd never even seen her before. And why would she knock on Jim's door? She had looked surprised to see anyone but Jim there, especially a woman wearing his shirt. She really hadn't liked that.

"I'm sending the pictures now." Jim punched something into his phone and raised it back to his ear. "Did you get them? Good, yeah, you too."

He disconnected and stared at her. "The police are searching for her. I got her license plate, so hopefully, if the car belongs to her, they'll catch her."

"You have no idea who she is? She seemed surprised to find me here and wearing your shirt. I don't think she could be the one harassing me."

"I think she's my stalker. She very well may be the one harassing you if she knows we're together."

"You have a stalker?"

Jim rubbed both hands through his hair and dropped his arms with a sigh. "Back when I was playing football, I would get all sorts of fan mail and strange things. Most of it stopped after I quit the team, except for these pink envelopes. At first, they talked about my performance at a game, but then they got weirder. The notes were scented with perfume and talked about how much she loved me and wanted to be together. Sometimes she would send intimate articles of clothing. My manager and the police got nowhere with them. Every time I move into another house, they eventually show up. She's never knocked on my door before or terrorized anyone I was involved with. Although she did send an angry letter once when I was still playing. Some pictures of me with a woman I went on a couple of dates with were posted on social media. She ranted about betrayal and how I was cheating on her."

He threw his hands up in the air. "It never occurred to me she could be behind all the stuff happening to you. I'm so sorry." He walked over and wrapped her in his arms.

Allison leaned her head against his shoulder. "We don't know for sure she's even your stalker, let alone if she's mine. Let's wait until we hear what the police have to say. Regardless, it's not your fault some crazy woman latched on to you."

"Still, I should have thought of it and mentioned it to you and the police earlier."

She rubbed his back.

"Why did you answer the door?"

She lifted her head. "What?"

"The door. Why didn't you get me? You shouldn't be opening the door. Did you even look before you did?"

"No, I thought it was Karen. She called and asked if she could drop by. I haven't seen her since before the fire. We've only talked by phone."

"Please, next time, look. Better yet, don't open it all. I will. Okay?"

"You're right. It was stupid."

"Not stupid, but dangerous." He kissed her forehead. "Should I dig out my old helmet and pads for your friend's visit?"

Allison smiled. "Afraid?"

"A little."

"I promise to protect you."

/

CHAPTER

THIRTY-EIGHT

The muscles in her shoulders tensed. She was being watched. She could feel it. Allison glanced over her shoulder from left to right. There was no one in sight, but the feeling continued.

Her grip on the platter of brownies tightened. She regretted deciding to walk to Karen's. Then she immediately chastised herself for being paranoid. It was a simple walk down the road, less than a mile. It would be silly to drive on such a pleasant day.

The police had arrested Jim's crazy stalker. They charged her with arson when she ranted about burning Allison's house to the ground with her in it if she went near Jim again. The woman needed help. Luckily, she was getting a psych evaluation. She would probably end up in a treatment facility rather than prison.

Allison shook her head at her own foolishness. It was a beautiful day, and her troubles were over—mostly. She breathed deeply and smiled. The smell of cut grass and barbecue wafted the air.

Karen had invited her to dinner when she had to call and cancel her visit the other day. Jim hadn't been thrilled with the idea. He was still worried. But they locked the woman up. She didn't need a babysitter anymore. In fact, she should probably make plans to move back to her house. Lucas had started work on the house once the police had given the okay.

It would be weeks, if not months before her kitchen was functional and the screened-in porch replaced. She couldn't live with Jim that long.

Her baking business was on hold indefinitely. She couldn't bake without a kitchen.

An engine revved behind her.

She turned her head.

A shiny black exterior and the sun's glare reflected off the windshield.

She braced her body for impact.

The platter slipped from her hands, and she lunged to the right, trying to escape.

Pain exploded in her left leg.

The impact lifted her off the ground. She felt weightless for an instant before her elbow and back slammed into the car.

A scream lodged in her throat. The breath disappeared from her lungs.

Her body plummeted to the hot pavement.

The stench of exhaust battled with the sweet smell of grass. A new, cloying scent danced at the edges of her perception—blood.

A cacophony of sounds assaulted her ears. A sharp yell, the crackle and snap of something running in the woods, the squeal of tires, and the sound of running feet seemed to echo in different directions.

The sounds all faded away as she blinked to clear the clouds descending around her. Darkness claimed her. She welcomed the respite from the agony ripping through her battered body.

JIM FOLDED his arms across his chest and stood at his living room window, watching Allison walk down the road.

She wore a pair of white shorts that ended a couple of inches above her knees. He smiled slightly, remembering how sensitive the spot behind her knee was.

A light blue polo shirt skimmed her assets nicely but not too tight to be blatant. She always dressed so that some mystery remained. Jim discovered he found that infinitely more appealing than women who dressed in clothing so tight or revealing that their bodies had nothing left to hide.

He frowned when she disappeared around the corner and out of his view. He got a tense feeling at the back of his neck lately anytime she was out of his sight.

A black Mercedes drifted into view. It pulled into the Pannelli's driveway and turned around.

It wasn't uncommon for a car to make a wrong turn and realize this road led them nowhere they wanted to go. Still, Jim didn't like the feeling churning in his gut. He would follow Allison at a safe distance to make sure she arrived at Karen's okay. He would call her later and insist on picking her up when she finished.

He'd already offered to drive her, but she refused. He hadn't pushed the point then, and he already regretted it. Her safety was more important than sensitive feelings. Yeah, Crazy Cathy or whatever her actual name was behind bars, but until the police had solid evidence linking her to the fire and all the harassment, he would be on guard.

Jim jogged down his front porch stairs and down the street. He slowed to a fast walk when he reached the corner. If she caught him following her, she wouldn't be happy. No point in having a confrontation now. It would probably make her more adamant later about not accepting the ride home.

A series of thuds and the squeal of tires rent the air.

Jim broke into a run.

The Mercedes sped off down the road, and he searched frantically for a sign of Allison. Had someone abducted her?

His attention turned back to the car. He squinted, trying to read the license plate, but the distance was too great.

A flash of blue leaped into his vision. A boy erupted from the woods.

He tracked the boy's path.

Allison was crumpled on the ground by the side of the road.

His heart stuttered in his chest, and a loud roar reverberated in his head. Blood soaked her white shorts.

The boy dropped to the ground beside her and reached out a hand towards her.

"Don't touch her," Jim yelled. He didn't want the boy to accidentally do further harm.

He wrenched his cell phone out of his pocket and dialed nine-one-one as he skidded to a stop next to her.

Allison wasn't moving.

The boy cried and stared at her. "The car....it...it hit her."

Jim didn't respond. He was too busy frantically searching for a pulse and giving the dispatcher all the information he could. "A hit and run. Wigmore Lane. She's hurt bad. There's a lot of blood. She's unconscious."

There, he found it. A soft thump on her slender neck.

He held his fingers there a few seconds longer, reassuring himself it was there and steady.

"She has a pulse." His voice caught, and he swallowed back the hard lump in his throat.

He gently brushed her hair away from her face. She was so pale. Her face looked untouched. He quickly scanned the rest of her, relaying any injuries he could see to the dispatcher.

"Her leg is bleeding. There's a deep cut on her upper thigh."

Jim yanked off his shirt and applied it to her wound, trying to stem the blood.

"Charlie!"

Karen ran down the street toward them. The boy jumped up and ran to meet her. She enfolded him in her arms before pulling away sharply and searching him for injury. "Are you okay?"

Jim focused on Allison, willing her to wake up and tell him where she was hurt.

His heartbeat thundered in his ears. What if she was bleeding internally and there was nothing he could do to help her?

He scrubbed his free hand over his face and then touched the underside of her wrist so he could continue to feel her pulse. *Think, damn it!* What could he do to help her?

She was so damn pale, and she still hadn't moved.

"Where the hell are they?"

The dispatcher assured him they were on their way.

"Oh my God! Allison!"

Karen dropped to the ground beside him. She kept a firm grip on her son's hand. He hovered behind her, still sniffling.

The wail of sirens approached. Jim jumped to his feet. He disconnected the nine-one-one call and stuffed his phone in the back pocket of his jeans.

The police and the ambulance arrived simultaneously.

Jim, Karen, and Charlie moved out of the way while the EMTs quickly assessed Allison before moving her to the gurney.

"Did anyone see anything?"

Jim looked between the ambulance and the police officer. He clenched his fists at his side.

"It was a black Mercedes, recent year. I didn't see the driver or the license plate."

The policeman scribbled his notes. Jim turned as they loaded Allison into the ambulance. He told him about the fire, the stalker, and the detective in charge of the case.

The ambulance pulled away with the lights flashing.

He'd done all he could here. He needed to get to the hospital and find out how Allison was. Her pulse had been strong and steady. She had to be okay.

Jim ran home and got into his truck. Sweat poured off him, and his knee throbbed.

When he drove past the accident site, more policemen had arrived and were measuring and taking pictures of the scene. He passed Karen and Charlie in their driveway. He imagined she would arrive at the hospital soon after him.

He clenched the steering wheel so hard his knuckles turned white. Allison had to be all right. The alternative just wasn't acceptable.

THIRTY-NINE

Allison peered over the steering wheel, searching the mailboxes and down the driveways as she drove past.

She was probably making the biggest mistake of her life, but she had to know why.

She'd seen the driver of the car that struck her, but she hadn't told the police or Jim when she'd woken up in the hospital. At least she'd left detailed voicemails for the detective and Jim when she checked herself out of the hospital and taken a car service home to get her own car. Jim had finally left to go home to shower and change after she convinced him she was fine. He hadn't left her bedside in two days.

There, that was the house. She recognized it. She'd been here a few times with her parents for parties.

Allison glanced at her phone on the passenger seat. She'd turned it off after leaving the voicemails so no one would distract her from her goal or sway her to change her mind.

No, she had to do this.

Allison climbed out of the car and shut the door. The contemporary house loomed over the landscape. The manicured yard and house all looked the same.

She started up the paver walkway and rang the bell like she was on a social call instead of confronting the person responsible for trying to kill her at least once—probably multiple times.

The door opened to reveal the bell-shaped blonde hairdo she'd worn since Allison was a child. Ms. Thompson would reprimand her anytime she got too close to the breakables, as she had called them. She'd always been standoffish, but Allison had never suspected she was a murderer behind her polished facade.

"You should know the police are on their way, but I wanted to see your face for myself and hear your reason why."

Her bosom heaved as her black gaze darted behind Allison.

She tried to slam the door in her face, but Allison slapped her hand on the door and placed her foot in the way. Pain shot up her already injured arm and leg.

The woman turned and ran into the house.

Allison stepped in and left the door open, hoping the police were close but not too close. She wanted answers first.

The suspicions churning in her mind were growing blacker by the minute. The rage grew too, so much her body shook.

Ms. Thompson reappeared with a gun in her hands pointed at Allison. "You're a stupid fool to come here alone."

Allison paused with her hand against the gray wall. She sucked in a breath. Was this how her life would end?

She dropped her hand and raised her chin. "Maybe, but you won't get away with it. I was telling the truth about the police. I told them everything. I wanted to see your face when you confessed."

Allison stared at the woman her parents had let into their home on so many occasions. The woman they had trusted. Was her husband involved?

The threats didn't start until she talked to Dr. Thompson about the fire. Was he the man who bought the candles? Was his wife the anonymous caller to the police, which led to Allison's arrest? She was the one who had tried to run her over with her car.

"Where's your husband?"

Ms. Thompson blinked and waved the gun. "At work, of course. You think he'll save you? Albert's a blind old fool. He believes anything I tell him. I'll tell him you went crazy, and I had to defend myself."

"So he hasn't been helping you this entire time? He doesn't know you tried to kill me with your car? Or burn me alive in my house?" Allison stared hard at the woman's expression, ignoring the gun pointed at her entirely. "Send me threatening packages and phone calls? *Kill my parents?*"

"You should have died that night too!"

Allison lunged at her, grabbing the gun and wrenching it towards her.

The murdering psychopath shrieked at her and pulled the trigger. The shot whizzed by and hit the wall somewhere behind her.

Pain lashed at her back and arm while they wrestled over the gun. Her recent injuries weakened her, but anger coursed through her veins. This woman had killed her parents!

Allison kicked at her knee, and Ms. Thompson dropped to the floor, dragging Allison with her.

The gun went off again.

Blood bloomed on the woman's shoulder over her heart.

Horror etched her face.

Allison scrambled to a stand with the gun clutched in her clammy hands. She pointed it at Ms. Thompson, bleeding on the floor. Sweat soaked her skin, making her grasp slick. She tightened her hold and widened her stance. Her chest heaved with panicked breaths.

"Help me!" The murderer clamped her hands over her wound and sobbed.

"Tell me why!"

She shook her head as her gaze darted around the room. Gasps and sobs mixed as tears tracked rivers through her makeup. She stared at Allison with a trembling chin.

"Your father found out I was stealing. Forging prescriptions and embezzling funds from the practice. He was going to tell Albert and turn me in! I didn't mean to kill him! I panicked and grabbed a bookend from the shelf and hit him on the back of his head when he turned to pick up the phone. He slumped forward and hit his head on the edge of the desk. I checked his pulse, but he was dead. What was I to do? I couldn't be arrested for murder!"

"So instead of being arrested for one murder, you went for three and burned the house down?"

"I couldn't go to prison! I saw the candle, so I lit it and set the curtains on fire." She raised a hand towards her. "Please call an ambulance!"

Allison stood with her finger on the trigger. It would be so easy to pull it. No one would question her.

Blood drenched the woman's white blouse. She would probably bleed out if Allison didn't call nine-one-one.

She could watch the life fade from her eyes, knowing that her parents' murderer was dead.

"Who was the man who bought the candles?" Did she have an accomplice? Was she lying to protect Dr. Thompson?

Ms. Thompson whimpered. "I don't know. Just a beggar on the street. I paid him a hundred dollars to go in the store and have them sent to you."

"How did you know about my husband?"

She sneered. "You act all innocent, but you're guilty too." Her face turned white, and she closed her eyes and moaned. "I bought a listening device online and sat in the bathroom next door during your appointment. I heard every word. It would have been the answer to everything. You wouldn't be digging into the past if you were in prison. But, of course, you slipped out of that too." Ms. Thompson coughed and sobbed into the carpet.

Blood stained the beige carpet.

Allison pulled her phone from her back pocket where she had stuffed it while getting out of the car. She glanced at it. It was still recording.

She'd planned to have evidence of her attacker's guilt for the police.

Now she supposed her own guilt was being recorded. The guilt of wanting the woman who ruined her life dead.

Allison stopped the recording. She could delete it. No one would know.

Instead, she dialed nine-one-one and reported the shooting.

She grabbed a blanket from the sofa and tossed it to her. "Hold it over the wound."

Ms. Thompson sobbed and begged for her life.

Allison raised her chin and dropped the gun to her side. She walked over and placed it on a table next to the sofa.

She was done living with guilt.

CHAPTER

FORTY

They loaded Ms. Thompson into an ambulance with a police escort. The detective handling her case had called the local police and informed them of the circumstances. They'd arrived intending to rescue Allison.

Instead, she'd rescued herself.

"Allison! Thank God!"

Allison turned. Jim ran down the driveway, past all the police cars and police milling about. Two tried to stop him but waved him on after a brief conversation.

He yanked Allison into his arms and then pulled away to scan her from head to toe. He pulled her into his arms again.

Allison returned his hug with a wince over her aching body. The adrenaline had worn off, and her injuries were protesting her actions.

"Are you okay? You had me so terrified! Why did you take off like that?"

"I'm fine. I'm sorry. I went a little crazy when I recognized her as the driver and realized she was probably responsible for everything, including my parents."

She told him about the confession and the gun going off. The police had taken her phone for evidence, so she couldn't play the recording for him. She hadn't deleted anything. She'd told the police everything. If they felt the need to arrest her for not providing immediate aid, so be it. They'd only glanced at her and continued taking notes. Before leaving with the ambulance, the officer in charge had told her she was free to go. So, she guessed they weren't going to arrest her.

Jim squeezed her tighter. "I probably would've pulled the trigger."

"No more guilt hanging over me. I'm done letting it rule my life."

"Let's get out of here." He kissed her on the forehead and led her down the driveway with his arm around her.

She paused as they neared her car. "I drove, remember?"

"I'll make arrangements to have it picked up."

"Okay." There was no reason to argue.

When they reached his truck, he opened the passenger door and helped her inside. He gripped the edge of the door and started closing it but stopped.

"Just so you know, I'm not going to be able to let you out of my sight for a solid month, at least. Probably a lot longer."

She smiled. "I understand."

He nodded and closed the door halfway again, then halted and opened it again.

"And this is probably not the time, but with all the attempts on your life, I don't want to waste any time." He rested his hand on the top of the door and stared at her. "I had a lot of time to think on the drive here. You should know I'm in love with you and have every intention of making you my wife."

Allison grinned. "Okay."

"Okay?"

"I love you too. I'd like nothing more than to be your wife."

He grinned and stepped into the doorway to kiss her until she gasped for air.

"We can live in my house or yours once it's repaired if that's what you want. It's up to you. I'm fine either way. As long as you're mine, I don't care where we live."

"I don't know. I kind of like the idea of a fresh start. Moving somewhere new and helping you renovate a house and bring it back to life like you brought me back to life sounds pretty appealing."

"You want to sell both houses? What about your new baking venture?"

"I like to bake, but I don't need to sell anything. I'm glad I tried it and proved to myself I could make it a success if I wanted. My house is part of my past. I want to make new memories with the man I love."

Jim pulled her out of the truck and into his arms. He twirled her around in a circle as she laughed and then winced over her injuries.

"How big of a wedding do you want? Can we keep it small and make it soon? I don't want to wait."

"I'll fly to Vegas with you right now if you want."

Jim threw his head back and laughed. "Let's do it!"

They climbed into the truck, and Jim turned it around. "Any idea how to get to the closest airport?"

EPILOGUE

Jim lifted Allison's hand and kissed the back of it. Her ring shone in the light.

They were married!

The pilot came on and announced the final approach to Connecticut. Jim had arranged for both vehicles to be delivered home from Pennsylvania so they wouldn't have to make the long drive after the flight.

"Could you have ever guessed you'd end up marrying your crazy neighbor who screamed at you like a shrew in her old nightgown for waking her up?"

Jim grinned and squeezed her hand. "I never thought I'd get married, period, but if anyone could tempt me, it was you in those sexy old-fashioned nightgowns of yours. I'm going to buy you another dozen or so. I've developed a fetish."

"No sexy lingerie for you, hmm?"

"We can give those a try too. The fact is, I'd find you the sexiest woman alive no matter what you wore."

She leaned her head on his shoulder.

He kissed the top of her head and rested his head against hers.

Joy bubbled over and filled her completely. She'd never dreamed she could be this happy. She'd never believed she deserved happiness. All the guilt shrouding her life had lifted. She was a new person.

Ms. Thompson's evil couldn't touch her anymore. The woman had lived, but she would spend the rest of her life in jail. Jim's stalker was in a psychiatric ward getting the help she needed. Alan's nurse was going to trial for murder on multiple counts. The press was calling her an angel of mercy, but some of the families weren't so forgiving. Allison wouldn't take part. She and Alan's story was their own and in the past.

Karen had squealed in surprise and delight when she'd called from Las Vegas and broke the news of their marriage. She'd insisted on talking to Jim and threatening him with bodily harm if he ever broke Allison's heart. Then she'd squealed again and said they'd restored her faith in love.

"What are you thinking about?"

"How happy I am."

"In that case, please proceed."

She chuckled. "What's the first thing you want to do when we get home?"

"Carry my bride over the threshold and then take her upstairs and show her just how much I love her."

"I concur. Please proceed."

And he did—most thoroughly!

About the Author

Denise Carbo writes Contemporary Romance, Paranormal Romance, and Romantic Suspense. She is a voracious reader, loves to travel, is fascinated by the supernatural, and enjoys solving mysteries.

She lives in a small, picturesque New England town with her high school sweetheart and their three amazing sons. Find out more at https://www.DeniseCarbo.com and sign up for her newsletter to be the first to hear about sales, giveaways, contests, and exclusive content. https://eepurl.com/dt5N7M

ALSO BY DENISE CARBO

My First My Last My Only

Covet thy Neighbor

No Choice At All

www.ingramcontent.com/pod-product-compliance
Lightning Source LLC
Chambersburg PA
CBHW061154210726
48294CB00006B/1667